The
SWORD
that
SAVES

a Sam Stone novel

Ambrose Merrell

Hornet Books

First published 2016 by Hornet Books
Text © Ambrose Merrell
This work © Hornet Books Ltd
Paperback ISBN 978 0 9934 3538 6

Editors: Ahna Weisser and David Roberts
Cover illustration © Colin Turner

Hornet Books
Ground Floor, 2B Vantage Park, Washingley Road,
Huntingdon, PE29 6SR

www.hornetbooks.com

info@hornetbooks.com

Printed and bound by CPI Group (UK) Ltd, Croydon, CR0 4YY

For Sam, Isabelle and Gabbi,
who are my light
and Reverend Kensho Furuya,
who was my friend

CHAPTER 1

Uchiyama Wakes Up

Moonlight filtered through the trees, glinting off the sword's curved blade. In the wooded glade there were two swordsmen, one old and one young. The old man was standing silent and still, his sword undrawn. The young man, with sword drawn, was breathing hard as he circled him.

"Fight me, you coward!" cried the young man as he lunged to drive his sword deep into the old man's chest. The old man easily anticipated the attack and no sooner had it begun than he was standing behind the young man, his posture relaxed, his expression grave. The young man whirled around, his muscles taut, his breathing becoming ever more laboured.

"As I have told you many times, Uchiyama, I will not fight you," said the old man. "I wish you no harm."

"Wish me no harm?" said Uchiyama, his grip tightening on the sword handle as his face darkened with fury. "You brought dishonour to my family. There is no greater harm. Tell me your name so I might know whose life I shall end. Or shall you forever be known simply as the 'Coward'?"

As he spat out the last word, Uchiyama brought the sword in an arcing cut from high on his right down to his left, aiming to slice the old man in half. Once again the old man moved quickly and easily so that Uchiyama's sword cut nothing but air. Uchiyama's exhaustion was now complete and he stumbled and fell. As he hit the ground, his grip on the sword failed, and it rolled across the forest floor.

Moonlight glinted off the curved blade once more, as the old man picked it up and came to stand over Uchiyama, who lay on his back gasping for air. Fear filled Uchiyama's face as he awaited the final cut. Instead, the old man smiled warmly and said once again, "I wish you no harm, Uchiyama."

Then, after carefully laying the sword down on the ground beside Uchiyama, he vanished into the forest making no sound as he left.

Uchiyama lay exhausted on the ground. He was too tired to move and too tired to think. He simply lay there listening to his breathing. His gaze fell upon the moon high above him. For the first time in his life he noticed how incredibly beautiful it was, and tears welled up in his eyes.

CHAPTER 2

A Leap of Faith

As Sam stood in his bedroom in the darkness, all he could hear was his rapid heartbeat. He was nervous and excited. The house was silent except for the occasional hum of the old refrigerator in the kitchen below. It was a warm late-May night, and he had his bedroom window wide open. The moon was bright and filtered through the Douglas fir tree in the back garden. The sky was lit by city lights, but there were still some stars struggling to be seen.

In his mind, Sam ran through the things he needed. He had just enough money for the bus; he had the address his friend Jake had given him; he had some chalk, the keys and the letter; and he had a pocket knife and a little torch. He was ready.

He heard a car coming up the street. Taking a deep breath, he climbed onto his desk standing in front of the window. He had practised his window escape a few times when his foster parents were out during daytime. This was the first time he'd attempted this risky manoeuvre in the dark. As quietly as he could, he climbed out of the window and slowly lowered his body until he was hanging from the window ledge. His plan was to use the noise of the passing car to mask the sound of his landing. He pushed his feet against the outside of the house and waited for the car to go by. It seemed to take an age and, as he waited, he could feel his grip slipping. Finally the car rolled by and he jumped. The air briefly rushed by sounding very loud in his ears. He just made it over the concrete path and landed on the soft grass. He rolled and immediately leapt up and hid behind the large trunk of the fir tree.

His heart was pounding as he waited to see if a light would go on in his foster parents' bedroom. They too had their windows wide open in an attempt to draw in the cooler night air from outside. Sam crouched silently for a minute or two just to be certain no one looked out and then sneaked over to the shed. He unlocked the padlock, and began to slowly open the door. Grimacing as the rusty old hinges screeched and groaned, he paused once more to check for signs that his foster parents waking up, before slipping inside the shed. He turned the torch on, unlocked his foster father's mountain bike and then used the quick release to lower the saddle to his height. Sam didn't have a bike as his foster parents wouldn't get him one, so he had to take this one or else walk. Taking it didn't sit well with Sam even if he didn't like his foster parents. But he knew he'd return it, so in the long run no harm would be done.

He wheeled the bike out, relocked the shed and headed out to the street. It was around 3 a.m., and unsurprisingly the street was deserted. He estimated it would take him an hour, maybe two, to get to the house Jake had told him about. It was the house where Zoe and Sophie, Sam's younger sisters, were being fostered.

He wanted to avoid being seen, especially by the police. He was fourteen, nearly fifteen years old, and quite big for his age, but he knew there was a chance of being stopped and questioned if he were to be seen at this time of night. If that happened, he would almost certainly be driven back to his foster parents, and all hell would break loose. He jumped on the bike and cycled across the street to the alley that ran behind the houses opposite. East Vancouver was laid out in a grid with all the houses facing the street and back alleys behind them providing access to garages. Although taking the rough back alley would slow Sam down, he knew it would keep him out of sight and be the best route for him for as long as he could ride it.

The moon lit his way down the dark alleys, and at first his journey was mostly uneventful. He had a couple of encounters with skunks that were rather too close for comfort. If he was sprayed, his plan would be blown as he'd have to head home, wash his clothes and scrub the foul smell off. He also saw a coyote that appeared to size him up, perhaps considering an attack, before slinking off into the darkness.

Timing, however, was not on his side when he came to cross Highway 1. There weren't many bridges and most of them were at busy intersections. Sam's plan was to cross the highway on a quieter street called Adanac, despite the fact that it provided no cover and no escape from a possible encounter with the police. But at that time of night on a quiet street off the main routes, he felt sure there would be no one else around. He was wrong.

Sam was halfway across the bridge when he saw headlights turn off Boundary Road heading towards him. He couldn't tell if it was a police car but he didn't want to take the risk. The car was still maybe 600 metres away and coming slowly as it negotiated the speed bumps on the street. Sam decided to ride across the last part of the bridge as fast as he could and try to head off to the right when he got to the end, hoping he wouldn't be spotted. Peddling for all he was worth, Sam dashed to cover the remaining metres. The street was very well lit, so as Sam dived off to his right and then cut across to a garden for cover, he wasn't sure if he'd been seen or not.

Sam laid the bike on the ground beside him and looked through the laurel hedge he was hiding behind. Sure enough, he saw a police car cruise slowly by. It seemed to slow down, though maybe that was just Sam's imagination, before continuing on its way. Sam stayed where he was for a while catching his breath and letting his heart calm down. Once he was sure the police weren't coming back, he got back on the bike and headed out onto the pavement. Sam had used Google Maps to plan his route. He knew that for the next few blocks he couldn't use back alleys because none ran in the direction he needed to go. Now, he had to ride along the street and just be ready to hide if he saw headlights approaching.

Having crossed Boundary Road his next challenge was to cycle up a steep hill, at the top of which he hoped he would find the girls. It was approaching 4 a.m., and the cloudless sky ahead was beginning to lighten with the first signs of dawn. He was still in a dense residential area. Unfortunately it would be like that, he guessed, for the remainder of his journey. Sam was determined to get to the address Jake had given him and see his sisters, despite the risk of being caught.

CHAPTER 3

The Compost Heap Note

S am had tried to run away with Zoe and Sophie twice before and been caught both times. After that, his foster parents and the foster care people refused to tell him where the girls had been moved. They had had their email accounts shut down and didn't seem to be online anywhere. The foster care people said they were doing their best to have all three of them fostered in the same house, but Sam didn't believe them because nothing was happening. It had been a month now since he had last seen his sisters. When he had finally found out through Jake where they were, he knew he had to find them and let them know he hadn't given up.

Sam realised he had to push on, so he stood on the pedals and powered his way up the hill. His legs were burning with the effort and, despite the fact he was wearing shorts, he was beginning to sweat. Getting close to 4:30 a.m., he only had maybe another 45 minutes to find the girls' house. As he pressed on he went over his plan for what he would do first when arriving at his destination. He wanted to check the area out and get himself into a good position to watch the back of the house before anyone was up. It was soon going to be quite light and his chances of being spotted would obviously be much greater.

So it was with some relief when he finally arrived in the street where their house was supposed to be. Although it had taken him a little longer than expected he was still okay for time. He was hoping the girls' bedroom was at the back of the house. Then, if he was sure which window was theirs, he'd try to catch their attention and indicate where his letter to them was hidden. If that didn't work he'd use the chalk he'd tucked inside his pocket to leave a sign they'd recognise, to let them know he'd found them. That was his back-up plan.

After cycling past the front of the house to see what it looked like, Sam headed along the back alley behind it. As he drew near to their house he began to smile broadly. Compared to all the alleys he had just cycled along, this one resembled a zoo. There was a family of raccoons, squirrels by the dozen and pigeons lining the telephone wires. The dawn chorus of little song birds was more cacophony than chorus, their cheerful singing filling the air with joy and excitement at the new day dawning. Sam knew without a doubt he had found the right house. "Oh, Zo, you special girl!" he thought as he pushed his bike quietly along. No one had an explanation for it, but wherever Zoe went, wildlife gathered. It was uncanny.

It was hard to get into the garden of their house as the double garage blocked the whole rear. He would have to go through a neighbour's garden, and then try to get into the girls' garden from there. He locked his bike alongside the garage. Looking down the alley Sam could see the distant mountains behind which the sun was quickly rising. He stood for a moment transfixed by the wonder of the scene. The sun was now only hidden by a tall peak shaped liked a shark's tooth. All around the edge of the peak the sun's rays shone out and the edges of the peak seemed to be aflame. It reminded Sam of the solar eclipses he had seen on TV just at the moment when the sun was about to re-emerge from behind the moon. In an instant the tiniest edge of the sun appeared from behind the peak and Sam's eyes blinked shut against the fierce brightness.

As full daylight approached Sam was all too aware that he might be seen by some early risers, so he had to be very cautious. He looked around carefully, saw no one and opened the gate into the garden next door to the girls' house. He scanned the neighbour's windows for signs of movement, but all the blinds were firmly closed and he saw none. He quickly walked along the edge of the garden and hopped over the low wooden fence into the garden of the house where he was now sure the girls lived. Their house was silent and there was no sign of anyone being awake. The windows in the upstairs rooms were open, but all the blinds were down.

Sam sat down behind a compost heap up against the fence, knowing he was well- hidden. He guessed he had at least an hour to wait before his sisters would get up. He didn't have a cell phone, but, much to his friends' amusement, he had a watch. He set the alarm for 6:30 a.m just in case he fell asleep and closed his eyes.

Sam dozed for maybe half an hour before he was stirred by strange sounds in the garden opposite. At first, he thought it was someone doing something in the far neighbour's garden, but the reality was far more surprising. As he looked across at the fence, he saw two paws suddenly appearing atop. They were shortly followed by the face of a black bear cub. Sam's heart skipped a beat. He knew that where there was a cub, there was always a mother, and mother bears are very protective. This could turn out very badly, he thought. He waved his arms and hissed, trying to sound scary. Apparently wavy, hissy things are irresistible to bear cubs as this one immediately jumped the fence and slowly walked toward Sam. Oh god, Zo, he thought, I know you love animals, but really, a bear?

No, actually. Not a bear. It turned out to be three bear cubs all of whom seemed to find Sam fascinating. After all three had climbed over the fence, they slowly approached him, sniffing the air and taking hesitant steps.

"Go away! Shoo! Go away, bears!" Sam motioned as quietly yet forcibly as he could, but all to no avail. Eventually, the bravest cub stood mere inches from him. It began to sniff his leg and then to lick it. Maybe it likes the salt from my sweat, thought Sam. He shifted his leg suddenly, and the cub stepped back briefly before moving in to resume licking him. Then it lifted its head and began coming still closer to sniff Sam's face.

Sam was torn between feeling pleased and excited to be so close to this lovely cub and terrified of what would happen if its mother appeared. The cub's nose got closer and closer to his face and its sniffing was sounding loud. It reminded Sam of the puppy his parents had brought home when he was little. He had laid down on the kitchen floor and the puppy had sniffed right in his ear before licking him and nipping his ear with its sharp little teeth. Oh how his parents had laughed. It was one of Sam's happiest memories, the sound of his parents' laughter. Like the puppy, the cub had decided Sam was a friend and it too began to lick his face. Sam, while raising his hands up and trying to push it away, laughed uncontrollably and quietly yelled, "Stop it, you silly bear", but the cub just kept pushing in for more.

Then Sam heard the mother bear, or rather he heard and felt the thud as she clambered over the fence and landed in the garden. He froze and held his breath. The mother made a quiet lowing kind of a sound, and the cubs ran back to her. Sam was left sitting behind the compost heap facing a mother bear with her three cubs gathered around her. She was stretching her head out and sniffing the air while looking at Sam. This is it, thought Sam. She will smell my scent on the cubs, and she'll maul me. He knew his best bet was to stay absolutely still, look nonthreatening and, should she attack, just play dead. Her instinct was to protect her cubs, just as Sam's was to protect his sisters. If she felt Sam was no threat she might leave him alone.

The mother bear seemed to be unsure what to do, and for an age, it seemed, she sniffed the air and looked at Sam. Her decision-making process was suddenly interrupted by a loud noise from the house. Sam and the bears all turned to see what it was, and there, noisily pulling up the venetian blind, Zoe appeared at her bedroom window. Sam saw her spot the bears. Her face lit up, as she brought her hands together in front of her chest in sheer delight.

Fortunately for Sam, the noise was enough to convince the mother bear that it was time to go. She turned and leapt the fence heading back the way she had just come. The cubs followed suit, their back legs scrabbling comically as they tried to get their little bodies over the last rickety piece of wood panelling.

Sam heard Zoe quietly call out, "Oh, don't go, little bears! I'm sorry I frightened you!" and decided he'd better show himself now in case Zoe went to wake anyone else up in the house to see the bears. He raised himself up a little and waved from behind the compost heap. Zoe's face was a picture. One minute she had the gift of a bear family in her garden and the next, her big brother was there. Sam brought his finger to his lips, and Zoe nodded before disappearing. For a moment, Sam feared she was going to come running out into the garden to see him. But instead she reappeared at the window with Sophie who bounced up and down, her red hair falling into her face, and waved. Sam cautiously waved back. He was smiling too now, wanting to go to his sisters so very much. But knowing he couldn't do so right now, he took the letter out of his pocket, held it up for them to see and then hid it behind the compost heap.

It was so hard to leave them, but it would be a disaster if he got caught there. He waved at them again and pointed that he was going. They waved back and kept blowing him kisses. Then Sam once more checked all the windows to see if anyone was watching before leaping the fence back into the neighbour's garden. He ran out of the gate, unlocked the bike and quickly headed back down the alley. Once he was beyond the double garage, he could see the window, where the girls stood, waving wildly at him and blowing kisses. He waved back but kept walking with the bike, though his heart was breaking to leave them. He had to avoid being caught or else he risked the girls being moved yet again to another family where he wouldn't be able to find them. As he reached the end of the alley, he turned and gave a last wave, before jumping on his bike and heading back downtown.

CHAPTER 4

The Secret Message

Zoe and Sophie craned their necks to look out of the window as far as they could to watch Sam leave. Zoe had her arm protectively around Sophie, making sure her excited little sister didn't fall out. Finally, he disappeared from view leaving just the two of them together feeling immensely relieved. Their big brother had found them again! Although neither of them mentioned it much, both girls felt safe and secure when Sam was with them, but sad and lonely when parted from him. Now for a moment they just hugged and then began to dance around the room, holding each other ever more tightly and feeling so, so happy!

Zoe who was twelve and nine-year-old Sophie were unusual children. Zoe had her strong connection to nature. It wasn't just animals that were drawn to her: she also had a magic touch with plants. Her bedroom was full of potted plants that grew incredibly healthy and large. Sophie didn't talk or behave like a nine-year-old. She spoke like a wonderfully innocent adult. She was very kind, gentle and uncannily perceptive. This made life a little difficult for her. Finally, they stopped their impromptu dance, and Zoe held Sophie's hands as she said, "You were right as ever, Soph. You just know, don't you?"

Sophie nodded and said, "I feel him. I feel everyone, Zo. I just sense what they want, what they're feeling. It's getting worse. Or maybe better; I don't know. It's so confusing. But yes, I felt Sam would soon be here. I know his love and determination, as well as his anger, confusion and sadness."

Sophie's eyes began to well up, and Zoe hugged her saying, "It'll be alright Soph. It'll be alright."

"I know. I know you believe that. I feel that too," said Sophie, sniffling.

Sophie pulled back. "What about the bears?" she asked? "What was Sam doing with the bears? Where did they go?"

Zoe and Sophie turned and rushed back to the window, looked out but couldn't see the mother or cubs anywhere.

"When I looked out, the bears were standing only a few metres away from Sam. I wonder what happened!" said Zoe.

Zoe stood for a moment looking puzzled before suddenly turning to Sophie, her eyes wide and cried out, "The letter! We need to get the letter! No one will be up yet, Soph. I'll run down and get it now. I can empty the compost bin so no one will wonder why I'm down there."

Once Zoe had retrieved Sam's letter, the girls prepared to read it. They pulled the duvet off the bed and arranged cushions placing them against the wall. Zoe sat on the bed with Sophie close beside her and then they pulled the duvet back over their legs.

"Ready?" asked Zoe.

Sophie nodded enthusiastically. Zoe nodded enthusiastically back and said, "Then I shall begin."

With that Zoe began to quietly read Sam's letter aloud.

Dear Zo and Soph

I found you! I told you I would and I did! I'll always find you no matter how far apart we seem. Remember that! I love you!

First things first. Don't let anyone find this letter! If they know I've found you they might move you again.

Second – I've set up an email address dianajones379@gmail.com that you can email me on. I don't get online at home much so don't worry if you don't hear from me straight away.

I'm still working on a plan for the 3 of us to be back together again. I don't know how but I will make it happen, ok?

If the email thing doesn't work for some reason then I'll leave another letter at the compost heap in 7 days. You could leave me a letter there too.

Send me an email now – I'll check as soon as I get online!
Love
Sam
XOXOXO

"But how will he get us all together again, Zo?" asked Sophie looking at Zoe.

Zoe looked back at Sophie. She wanted to say something comforting and reassuring, but she knew Sophie would sense she wasn't speaking the truth, so she simply said,

"I don't know. But I do know that Sam won't stop until he does."

Just then a hawk landed on the window sill. It stood there looking at the girls as the girls sat still and looked back. It was motionless – just its head shifting - for perhaps a minute before turning and flying off again.

"Why do you think the hawk comes to see us wherever we are?" asked Sophie, turning to Zoe.

"I don't know, Soph. But I think she is looking out for us. That's what I feel. How about you?"

"Yes. She is looking out for us," repeated Sophie, feeling reassured.

After they had read Sam's letter several times, Zoe and Sophie headed downstairs for breakfast. Their foster parents, called Susie and Neil, were actually pretty nice. They themselves had two daughters aged four and six, who both liked Zoe and Sophie very much. Zoe knew that neither Sophie nor she would be able to contain their excitement at seeing Sam so she pretended the excitement was about the bear family and told Susie, who was preparing breakfast, about their encounter with the mother bear and her cubs. Susie looked shocked and called up to Neil, telling him she wanted him to check that the bears were gone and then call the conservation officers to let them know.

"I know they look cute," Susie explained to Zoe and Sophie, "but bears, particularly mother bears with cubs, can be very, very dangerous. Promise me you'll never go out into the garden if you see them again."

The girls promised, and then Zoe said, "Can we use the computer, please? We want to look up information about black bears."

"Of course," said Susie, and they both hurried off along the hallway.

Zoe wasn't really looking up bear information. She was hoping to send Sam an email. First, she created a secret new email account that no one else would know about. Then, with Sophie keeping an eye out, she wrote a message to their brother telling him that they were fine, and their foster parents were great. They had arranged to meet a friend at the mall that Saturday and Zoe thought they would be unsupervised for an hour or so and was hoping to sneak in a visit with Sam if he could get there.

CHAPTER 5

Being Real

Sam was making his way to a bus stop to get the bus back into town. On the way, he found a park and cycled in. Leaning the bike against a bench he sat down. Suddenly, the emotional reunion with Zoe and Sophie caught up with him and he began to cry. He cried for his sisters. He cried for his parents. He cried for the way his life had gone so terribly, terribly wrong. He cried for the injustice of a world that would keep his sisters and him apart.

Sam had his face in his hands as he sobbed so didn't see the large scruffy dog approaching. The first he knew of its presence was when it bashed its cold, wet nose into his hands and then began nudging Sam's legs. As Sam lifted his head out of his hands he heard a girl's voice saying,

"Suki! Stop it! Suki! Come!"

Sam looked in the direction of the voice to see a teenage girl running towards him. The dog was still trying to nuzzle into Sam so he held its face and said, "I think you're in trouble."

The girl grabbed the dog's collar and started to apologise. However, when she caught sight of Sam's tear-filled and red-rimmed eyes she looked enquiringly at him.

"Oh hey, are you okay? What's the matter? Can I help?"

Sam caught his breath when he looked up and saw the beautiful brown eyes that met his gaze. As the girl sat down on the bench beside him, and put her arm over his shoulder, Sam tried to stop his tears. He felt vulnerable and weak to be crying in front of her. He quickly rubbed his face with his hands, wiping the tears away as he ran his fingers under his eyes.

"It's okay, it's okay. Whatever it is, it'll be okay," said the girl.

Once again the dog began to nuzzle into Sam's face licking his ears and neck.

"Suki!" said the girl, "Stop it! Go on! Off you go."

"Your dog's name is Suki?" asked Sam.

"Yes," said the girl with a broad smile, "that's right, and I'm Grace. What's your name?"

For a brief moment Sam hesitated. He was concerned he might jeopardise future plans to see Sophie and Zoe now he had found them again. But looking into Grace's stunning eyes he knew he couldn't lie.

"I'm Sam," he said, "and the dog my parents gave me for Christmas when I was ten was called Suki."

With that Sam burst into tears again. Once more he buried his face in his hands and grabbed his hair in fists, pulling tightly. Overwhelmed by his feelings as rage, loneliness, fear, abandonment, frustration, inadequacy, and self-loathing all boiled away within him, he also felt embarrassment. He was crying like a baby in front of Grace.

"Well," he thought, "she must think I'm pathetic and will get out of here as fast as she can." He gripped his hair even tighter and gently rocked back and forth as the emotions flooded out of him.

But Grace didn't leave. Instead, with her arm still over his shoulder, she pulled him closer saying, "That's it. Let it all out, let it all out. It does you no good bottled up inside. Let it all out, let it all out. It's okay, I'm not letting go."

As she said that she hugged him tighter and, with all attempts to hold it back now gone, Sam cried from the very depths of his heart.

Sam didn't know for how long he cried but for however long it was Grace never did let go. She held him tight, occasionally saying reassuring words. Finally the crying began to ease. Sam sat upright, rubbing his face vigorously once more before wiping the tears on the sleeve of his shirt. "Wow," he said quietly, not looking at Grace, "you must think I'm pathetic." He shook his head and looked down at his shoes.

"Look at me," said Grace, as she pulled him upright.

Sam reluctantly turned to meet her gaze. Grace paused for a moment before saying,

"There is no greater courage a man can have than to show his vulnerability. All men are vulnerable. All women are vulnerable. It's crazy that some men pretend they aren't and bottle it all up. It's not strong or manly, it's stupid. Strong is revealing the vulnerability. Strong is saying, 'I have these vulnerabilities and still I embrace life with all my being.' Strong is to be authentic, to be real."

Sam was trying to listen but he was still reeling from Grace calling him a 'man'. No one had ever called him a man before, least of all a beautiful girl.

Grace looked long into his eyes then pushed back her dark brown hair before saying, "Sam you are strong. Much stronger than you realise. You're also pretty cute," she added as a broad smile appeared on her face.

Sam's struggle to find something impressive to say back to Grace was broken by his watch alarm.

"What's the time!" asked Grace.

"It's 6:30," said Sam.

"I'm late! I'll be in trouble with my dad. I've got to go Sam," said Grace as she leapt up.

Sam stood up and Grace stepped in and gave him a tight hug. She then turned to Suki who had been patiently sitting beside the bench and picked up the dog's lead.

"It'll be okay Sam. It is okay right now, you just don't realise it."

With that she was off running down the path toward the park gate with Suki bounding alongside her. As she reached the gate she turned, waved and shouted,

"Stay strong!" before disappearing out of sight.

Sam sat for a long while on that park bench, the sun rising and warming the morning air, as joggers and dog walkers filled the park.

"What a morning", he thought and shook his head.

Suddenly a thought popped into his head. Actually more than a thought, it was a kind of 'knowing' that rose from deep within him. It said calmly and clearly, "I just met my wife."

Sam wasn't attuned to this deep, inner voice yet though. He just laughed to himself and, picking up his bike, he walked back out to find a bus stop.

CHAPTER 6

A Sudden Appearance

Though it was a school day Sam had no intention of going. Any minute now his foster parents would realise he had run away, so he was in deep trouble anyway. His foster father would go to the shed to get his bike and no doubt tell the police that Sam had stolen it. So he decided that he might as well make the most of his temporary freedom before the police picked him up and took him back.

He loaded his bike onto the rack at the front of a bus heading downtown and squeezed in amongst the commuters. He stood by the doors, watching the shops and houses go past. He was tired not only from the lack of sleep, but also from the release of emotions that were pent up inside him. Suddenly he laughed out loud as he remembered the incredible encounter with the bears. It had been quite magical being so close to a bear cub. What a tale he had to tell the girls! His mood became more serious as he reflected on how he might bring what remained of his family together again. His sisters trusted him and he could not let them down.

As the bus swayed and clattered along Hastings Street he wondered where he should go now. For no other reason than he'd never been to that part of town before, he decided to get off at Dunlevy Street. This was a part of Vancouver called the Downtown Eastside, and it was rough. All the homeless, the drug users, the mentally ill, the flotsam and jetsam of society washed up here. It seemed appropriate to Sam that he should find himself here too. He felt like he was on the periphery of life, with no place to belong to and no roots.

He began to cycle down towards the harbour. He didn't know it, but it used to be called Japantown and was once the home of a large Japanese community. That was before World War II. When war broke out with Japan, the Canadian government had forcibly removed all the Japanese people to 'internment camps' that were little more than prisons. While they were in the camps the government also sold their homes and businesses, leaving them with nothing when they were finally released after the war ended. It was a dark period of Canadian history, and the Japanese never returned to Japantown in any numbers. Had Sam known the history, he would have understood how the Japanese must have felt. The lack of control, the sense of injustice and the deep anger were feelings that Sam would have shared with them.

Sam cycled through a park and saw a homeless man slumped on a bench, an old shopping trolley holding his few possessions parked alongside him. He wore a thick, blue coat that was dirty and torn. Sam couldn't see his face but he saw that he had a long, bushy brown-grey beard. Sam also noticed the big bottle he clasped in his right hand. He wondered if that was going to be his fate. Would he too end up lost and living on the streets? A drunk just like his father had become. As he pondered that possibility he thought of Zoe and Sophie alone, abandoned even by their brother. The thought fanned the flame that burnt within him. It was a flame fed by rage and frustration. He grimaced and he crushed the bike's handlebar to release the rush of energy that coursed through his body. No way will I end up living like that, thought Sam, with grim determination.

Heading back out of the park he ended up on an old street. Cruising slowly downhill, still in the direction of the harbour, he noticed an alley to his right. He suddenly found himself sliding the bike in a big wide skid and doubling back to go down the alley. Something powerful drew him there, and his sudden change of direction happened quite without any conscious thought.

The alley was deserted. It was narrow, and on either side the old red brick walls of the buildings towered above him. The sound of the busy streets seemed muffled and very distant. Had he been aware, he would have noticed a distinct shift in the energy around him.

About halfway down the alley, he brought his bike to a halt. He scrambled off the bike, leaned it up against the brick wall and took his drink bottle out of its cage. He was thirsty and took a couple of deep swigs before the water ran out. He squatted down, leaning against the cool wall. Still the rage bubbled away inside him. He felt so helpless in the face of everything he had to deal with. He and his sisters were caught in a system over which they had no control. No one seemed to care about them: not the people working in the system, nor the foster parents who seemed only interested in the money they got for taking care of them. His foster parents certainly spent little of that money on him. His meals were small, his clothes second-hand and he had very few possessions. He woke up to the same question day after day: Why did this happen to me?

He leant his head back against the wall and, for the first time, noticed the wooden fence in front of him. It seemed very odd and out of place in this run-down alley. Everywhere else was dirty and dishevelled, and yet here was a wooden fence in pristine condition. For the first time, he also became aware of the tinkle of water that seemed to be coming from behind the fence and the tops of bamboo gently rustling in the light, warm breeze.

He looked quizzically at the building against which this little narrow garden lay. It looked much as the other buildings, though obviously far better taken care of. Sam noticed that its windows were spotlessly clean.

At that moment the rage he felt inside him welled up stronger than ever. For reasons he didn't understand, he felt an incredibly powerful urge to smash those windows. He looked down and saw a broken brick lying beside the wall he leant against, with a dandelion flower growing over it. He snatched the flower, tossed it aside and then picked up the broken brick. He looked up and down the alley. It was empty and still completely silent. He looked left and right again. No one. He scanned the windows that overlooked the alley. No one. He weighed the brick in his hand. The brick felt heavy and satisfying. This will do the job nicely, he thought.

Sam did one more scan of the alley from left to right and one more careful glance at the windows to see if anyone was watching. No one was in sight, and still the silence held. He stepped away from the wall and drew his arm back as his grip tried to crush the brick with rage.

He was just about to launch the brick with all his might when suddenly there was a cry of "Hi!" beside him. Astonished and filled with fear, he wheeled to his left to see an old Asian man standing right by his side beaming a radiant smile at him!

Sam was stunned. For a moment he stood there looking a fool with his mouth agape and brick now loosely held in his right hand.

"Is this your bike?" said the old man, looking at the bike leaning against the wall.

Before Sam could reply, he continued, "Oh it looks like a great bike. You must be quite the mountain biker. Here! Your water bottle is empty. It's a hot day, and you've been cycling hard, I can see. You must have a drink with me. I have this most delicious green tea, which I bring from Japan myself, and it tastes wonderful. All my friends say so. They say, 'Kensho, your tea is delicious!'"

Kensho let out a deep belly laugh and looked Sam deep in the eyes.

"Sam," he said, "Come in. Come in and see my humble abode."

With that, Kensho turned and began to walk over towards the wooden fence.

Sam's face was a picture. He was beyond stunned now. Where had this old man called Kensho come from? He'd been so careful to check up and down the alley. There had been no one. He knew that for certain. How had this old man appeared beside him in that instant? How did he know that his name was Sam? Why was he being so friendly when he must have seen what he was about to do?

Kensho was opening a small gate in the fence now.

"Sam! Come and join me!" he said in a loud yet friendly voice, and disappeared through the gate.

Sam didn't know what to do.

"Run, you fool!" yelled one part of him.

"You don't know this man. Don't be crazy!" yelled another.

But a quieter, yet far more powerful voice, was reassuring him.

"Go in, Sam. You are meant to go in. Trust. Go in," it whispered.

Sam hesitated a few more seconds before finding himself walking over to the gate. He wasn't actually sure who was making his legs walk. It almost seemed he was watching someone else walking. As he approached the gate a very odd thought popped into his mind bright and clear. This is how adventures begin.

CHAPTER 7

A Humble Dojo

As Sam approached the gate, he noticed above it an old wooden sign written in what he thought was Chinese writing. He went to pull the gate open and realised he still had the brick in his hand. Feeling foolish, he rolled the brick against a nearby wall. Then he pulled the gate open and peered into the little garden that lay before him. It was very narrow with a path made of large pieces of flat stone. Moss grew between the stones. On the right hand side was a line of tall bamboo and at the end of the garden, perhaps two metres away, was the source of the tinkling water sound Sam had heard. As he walked through the gate, Sam felt no fear. In fact, he felt quite the opposite: he felt a great peace and softness fill him. He paused to look at the water flowing down a piece of bamboo that had been cut in half along its length. At its end, the water poured into a little pool carved into the top of narrow, moss-covered rock that stood tall. The melodious sound of the water as it gently fell into the shallow pool had a very soothing effect.

Sam turned to look at the entrance to the building. The open door was inviting. From somewhere inside came the far off sounds of Kensho clinking glasses and talking loudly to himself. Sam stepped over the threshold, but he had to wait for a moment for his eyes to adjust from the bright light outside before he could clearly see what lay before him. It was a very large square room unlike anything he had ever seen before. The ceiling was high, and apart from around the edges where it was wood, most of the floor was covered with something different. It wasn't carpeted nor was it wood or concrete. Sam wasn't quite sure what it was. He was about to step onto it when a voice called from upstairs.

"Sam," called Kensho, "please take your shoes off when you come in! I'll be down shortly."

Sam sat down on the wooden floor of the entrance to hurriedly pull his shoes off. He tossed them to one side before jumping back up and stepping onto the strange floor. It was soft under his feet! It was a bit like the mats they had in the school gym, he thought, only a little firmer maybe. Sam looked around him. A staircase ran up the left wall, and it was from up there that the sounds of Kensho came. Unusually the walls of the room were covered in large white panels with thin strips of dark wood separating each panel. In fact, everywhere he looked there was wood.

Many long narrow pieces of thick-looking paper, decorated with calligraphy and pictures of old Asian men, hung from the walls. One picture was very big, and the man in it looked very old indeed. There was also a rack that held lots of wooden sticks stacked horizontally to the ground. Some of the sticks were the length of a baseball bat but thinner, while others were much longer. Sam guessed it was some sort of training room, maybe for something like judo.

Just then Kensho appeared. He was coming down the stairs carrying a tray with a tea pot and two cups. The contents of the tray appeared to be very old and a bit battered but Sam liked how they looked.

"Well, Sam," Kensho said. "Do you like my dojo?"

Sam nodded cautiously, not really knowing what a dojo was but trying to be agreeable. Once again Kensho laughed his deep belly laugh.

"Oh, Sam, I am sorry. You've probably never heard of a dojo before. A dojo", continued Kensho as he placed the tray on a very low little table in the corner and beckoned Sam over, "is a sacred place where people come to train in the martial arts."

Sam walked over to the table.

"Here. Sit on a cushion. In Japan people do not traditionally sit on chairs. They kneel in what is called 'seiza'. But if you are not used to it then it can be quite uncomfortable. So you may sit cross-legged if you like," said Kensho.

Sam watched Kensho kneel in seiza and then copied him, kneeling so that he sat on his ankles.

Then Kensho filled a cup from the tea pot and handed it to Sam saying, "Now try my tea and tell me what you think."

"Thank you very much," said Sam as he took the cup.

"Very good!" said Kensho, his smile broader than ever. "I see you have learnt excellent manners. Very good. Very good. Etiquette, which is just another word for manners", explained Kensho, "is very important. We have lots of etiquette that must be followed in the dojo. Like taking your shoes off when you enter. It ensures everyone is safe and comfortable, and that there are no misunderstandings. But I hear your English accent. The English are well known for their manners. Your parents must have brought you up well."

Sam was holding his cup, listening politely and nodding.

"Drink!" said Kensho.

Sam took a few sips of the tea. His first impression? It was very hot. Then he noticed the taste - which he didn't recognise but nevertheless felt was so wonderfully pure and clean and remarkably refreshing.

"Delicious!" announced Sam happily, echoing Kensho's enthusiasm.

Kensho laughed his laugh and said, "I told you! That's what all my friends and guests say! They ask me 'Kensho how is your tea so good?' 'It's magic', I tell them!" said Kensho with a twinkle in his eye.

"So, Sam. What do you think of my humble dojo?" began Kensho for a second time, spreading his left arm as if presenting the dojo to Sam. Sam looked around again for a few moments and replied,

"Well, I think it's incredible. It's simple and old. I like simple and old."

Kensho laughed.

"Well, I am very glad to hear that you like it. It looks old, but actually it isn't that old. I built it with the help of some dear friends from Japan about 20 years ago. It is just like a samurai warrior's home would have been in Kyoto, the old capital of Japan, back in the 16th century. So, that is why it looks old. It is very traditional and very authentic."

"Oh! So, all the writing is Japanese? I saw a wooden sign when I came in, and I thought it was Chinese."

"Oh, that old sign. No, that is Japanese and it says 'Home of the Untalented Teacher.'"

Sam looked disappointed. As he had listened to Kensho talk, he thought he had bumped into some amazing martial arts master who would teach him some cool techniques so he could take out anyone who attacked him. But all those hopes fell away when he heard that Kensho was an "untalented teacher".

"Oh, I see," said Sam trying but quite failing to disguise his disappointment. "Are you the untalented teacher?" he asked rather hoping that maybe the sign was talking about someone else. "Yes, I am Sam! Yes, I am!" said Kensho as he let out his biggest, deepest belly laugh yet.

Suddenly Sam remembered the bike. He had left it in the alley unlocked! In all the drama of meeting Kensho, he had totally forgotten it. In this part of town, it would surely be stolen.

"My bike!" exclaimed Sam as he jumped up and began to run to the door. But he was stopped dead in his tracks by the powerful voice of Kensho.

"Sam!" called Kensho sternly.

Sam turned to see Kensho walking slowly towards him.

"Sam", he said more gently, "Do not worry. Your bike is quite safe. It will come to no harm here. But let us go and bring it in so that you may relax."

Together they walked outside. Kensho held the gate open, and Sam ran out not for one moment expecting to see his bike still there. But there it was, exactly as he had left it. He did as Kensho suggested and wheeled it into the little garden. Despite Kensho's assurances, Sam locked the bike before returning with Kensho to the table. This time Sam sat cross-legged as his knees were hurting from sitting in seiza.

"Now, Sam," said Kensho. "In a little while, I will be teaching the morning class. I teach aikido, which is a wonderful Japanese martial art. Would you like to stay and watch? You would be most welcome."

Sam thought for a moment. He had never even heard of aikido and was very intrigued to see it. But then he thought it might not be very good given that Kensho himself said that he was untalented. Sam thought that anyone who admitted they were untalented must really be pretty hopeless. All the top sportsmen he so admired were pretty consistent in claiming they were the best. In the end, Sam's curiosity got the better of him.

"I can stay for a little while, but I might have to go quite soon if that's okay."

Kensho's face lit up.

"Of course, Sam! Of course. Stay for as long as you like. All that I ask is that when you do leave, please do so very quietly. That is the etiquette of the dojo. Sit here for now, but when you leave, walk around the edge of the mat and look out for flying people!"

CHAPTER 8

On The Way

Flying people? thought Sam. What was Kensho talking about? He was about to ask but at that moment a man appeared at the entrance, and, much to Sam's surprise, the man paused and bowed. He was also an Asian man but much younger than Kensho. To Sam, it looked a bit as if the man was wearing white pyjamas though he knew it was really a martial arts uniform. He was also much thinner. In fact, now that Sam thought about it, Kensho was actually quite a big man. Sam's foster mother used the word 'big' to describe people who "could do with losing a few pounds" as she put it. Sam seriously doubted that Kensho would be any good, but he felt it was too late to leave now. He ought to be polite and stay for at least a little bit of the class.

The man who had appeared at the entrance slipped off his sandals and he stepped onto the mat. Next he sat briefly in seiza before bowing once more. This time, as he bowed, he pressed his hands to the mat and brought his face to his hands. He stayed there for a few seconds before returning to sit in seiza. Finally he stood up.

"Welcome, Jonathan!" said Kensho joyfully.

"Morning, Sensei!" said Jonathan, before tilting forward a little in a bow.

Then Jonathan began to do all sorts of stretches and warm up exercises, some Sam recognised but many he did not.

Over the next ten minutes another 15 people arrived. They were a wide mixture of ages and ethnicities, but perhaps most were Asian. Most were men but there were six women as well. Every one of them wore identical uniforms. Some also put what Sam thought at first was a black skirt on, even the men. But when he looked carefully, he saw they were actually more like very baggy black trousers. They all followed the same routine that Jonathan had used, pausing and bowing at the entrance and then sitting in seiza and bowing when they stepped onto the mat before commencing warm-ups.

Then, without saying a word to each other, they all lined up in seiza along the edge of the mat, facing the big picture of the old man Sam had seen when he walked in. Sam hadn't noticed, but Kensho had disappeared upstairs. He now came back down, and he too was wearing the uniform with the black baggy trousers. He smiled at Sam as he walked past before stepping onto the mat and walking to the front, right before the old man's picture. Sam noticed a shift in Kensho as he stepped onto the mat. He couldn't quite put his finger on what it was, but it seemed almost as if Kensho sharpened. First he sat in seiza, facing the picture. After a little while, he bowed, and all the students followed suit. Then, he raised his body back up, and the students once again followed. Next, he turned and bowed to the students, who all bowed again before arising once more to sit in seiza after Kensho did.

Kensho stood up. Surprisingly sprightly, thought Sam.

He addressed the students, "It's so good to see you all here. Remember: most of your training is simply turning up to training. You've done the hard bit. As Lao Tzu said in the Tao Te Ching, 'The journey of a thousand miles begins with the first step.' Each class is one more step on your journey and before you know it you will have travelled a thousand miles. Now let's have a wonderful class full of energy, please!"

Then Kensho turned, looked at Sam and introduced him."This is our guest Sam. He has kindly agreed to stay with us for a while and see what aikido is all about. So I'd like to give him a short demonstration."

So it was that Sam's life changed forever, though he had no idea quite how great this adventure would become. Kensho pointed to one of his students. The student shouted,"Hai!" and bowed quickly to Kensho. Then, much to Sam's amazement, he jumped up, came straight at Kensho, and out of nowhere he launched a powerful punch straight at Kensho's face. Even more amazing to Sam was Kensho's response. In a flash he was behind the attacker, and the attacker was flying through the air.

Now Sam understood Kensho's 'flying people' warning. But the flying attacker didn't land in a crumpled heap as Sam expected. Far from it. Instead, he rolled almost silently on the mat. In a seamless flow, he was back up and this time aiming a blow to the side of Kensho's head with his hand. Once again Kensho moved so quickly, so effortlessly and with such grace that the attacker was drawn into a spiral before he was sent flying through the air. It seemed to Sam that Kensho was at the centre of an invisible tornado and his attacker was caught in its tremendous winds before being flung out. Again, the attacker rolled softly and, in an instant, was back up and attacking Kensho with total commitment.

Kensho was attacked by many of his students. Sometimes they were armed with the wooden sticks, and other times with what looked like wooden replicas of daggers. At one stage, four of them were attacking Kensho at once. Yet, the whole time Kensho moved with astonishing grace and speed. Often, he seemed to do nothing, and still the attackers went flying.

All this from the 'Untalented Teacher'? Sam thought to himself. It was the most amazing thing Sam had ever seen, and it lit a passion in him that would burn fierce and bright for the rest of his life. With every fibre in his body he knew he had to learn to do what Kensho did. The adventure had begun.

CHAPTER 9

The Student Finds the Teacher

Once the demonstration was over, Sam stayed for the entire class. He watched and listened as Kensho showed the students one technique at a time. Each technique had what Sam presumed to be a Japanese name, which he didn't understand, but he was still mesmerised by it all. Kensho was quite stern as he taught. If he saw students doing something incorrectly, he would say, "No, no, no," and clap his hands.

This intervention would prompt the students to line up in seiza. Then he would show where many were going wrong with the technique before asking them to try again.

Once the class came to an end, Kensho came over to Sam.

"Well Sam I do hope that you enjoyed the demonstration and class."

Sam jumped up and nodded enthusiastically.

"It was awesome! Incredible! Mind blowing! The way you threw them, and the way they just rolled and bounced back up! And when all four attacked you and you threw them into each other. Wow! It was just....awesome!"

"I think I can take from what you said that you liked it," said Kensho laughing.

The students began wiping the mat down with cloths. Kensho looked at Sam intently and his face became more serious.

"Why aren't you at school, Sam?"

Sam looked down and began to shuffle his feet nervously. He thought about lying, but he sensed that Kensho would see straight through him. So he decided to just be completely honest with Kensho.

"I've run away from my foster home. I have two sisters. Zoe is

twelve and Sophie is nine. The foster people say they can't find a
family to have all three of us, so the girls are with one family and I
am with another. Our mum died in a car crash three years ago. My
dad was driving. He killed himself almost two years ago."

Kensho shook his head slightly and reached out to grasp Sam's
shoulder reassuringly.

"I've tried to run away with the girls twice before," Sam continued.
"After the second time, they moved the girls to another family and
wouldn't tell me where they were or let me contact them. I found
out from a friend - he's being fostered too - where they are. So this
morning I went to their house and saw them. I was hiding in the
garden and I left them a letter to tell them of a new secret email
address I've made, and I told them that I will get us back together
again. I will!"

As Sam said that, he looked at Kensho with a fierceness burning
in his eyes.

"But I don't know how," said Sam, looking down. "I don't know
how."

Sam felt the tears beginning to well up again, but he held them
back. Despite what Grace had said to him, he still believed that
Kensho would see his tears as a weakness.

As Kensho listened to Sam's story he was very aware of the pain,
the incandescent rage, the confusion that filled him.

"I won't presume to know how you feel, Sam, but I lost my parents
when I was a child. I have no brothers or sisters, no cousins, aunts
or uncles. My grandparents had already passed away. I felt so lost
and so lonely, so perhaps, in a small way, I can begin to understand a
little of what you are going through. I have poured my life into aikido
and this dojo. My students and my master are my family. I've never
had the time to get married and have a family of my own. My life is
this dojo and constant training in the martial arts."

Sam had no doubt that Kensho knew exactly how he felt. Indeed,
hearing Kensho's story, he realised just how lucky he was to still

have his sisters, even if he was separated from them. He could not imagine the loneliness Kensho must have felt as a child with no family at all.

"My mum was Canadian, and my dad was English," said Sam, wanting to share more of his story with Kensho. "We all grew up in England until I was twelve, and then we moved here. My dad drank too much in England, and he wanted a fresh start. He had been out at a party or something with my mum. On the way home they were hit by a car that was driving down the wrong side of the highway. Everyone said it wasn't my dad's fault. But he had had a couple of drinks, and even though he wasn't over the legal limit, he still felt that if he hadn't had any, he might have reacted faster and my mum would have still been alive.

"Slowly, he started to drink more and more. He cried all the time and kept saying sorry to us. I tried to help him, but what could I do?" Tears were starting to run down Sam's cheeks now, and he wiped them away angrily.

"Anyway," he continued, "Eventually, my dad killed himself. He jumped off the Lions Gate Bridge into the ocean. They never found his body. Only his shoes left on the bridge with a note in them. So we couldn't even bury him beside mum. I don't understand why he killed himself. How he could do that to Zoe and Sophie? How could he do that to me? We had nobody!"

Sam began crying uncontrollably, just as he had done with Grace. Kensho put his right arm around Sam's shoulder and hugged him tight, just as Grace had done. Kensho didn't say anything, but Sam felt soothed by his presence.

Sam's crying subsided quite quickly. Perhaps because he had cried a little earlier or perhaps because of Kensho's presence, he wasn't sure.

"How are your foster parents? Is everything okay with them?"

"Oh, they're okay. They don't give me much food or any stuff, really. Their own children have bikes, an Xbox and a load of games and a Mac so they can get online. Sometimes, I get to play on the Xbox, but mostly I'm left on my own. But it's okay. The girls looked okay too, but I don't know what their new foster family is like. I hope they'll email me soon, and I'll hear how they are."

Kensho nodded, before saying, "Sam, would you like to learn aikido? You would be welcome to train with us. You are young, but you look strong and tall enough. In the beginner's class we train gently and with great respect."

"Of course! I'd love that! That would be awesome," said Sam, with a huge grin on his face.

"Okay. Well, I will need to get the permission of your foster parents."

"I doubt they will," said Sam, looking disappointed. "They won't want to spend the money."

"Let me work that out, Sam. Give me your address and their phone number, and let me see what I can do, okay?"

"Of course! Thank you!"

"However, if you are to train here, you need to do something for me."

"Okay."

"It is very important that you do not run away from home again and that you do not miss any school, okay? I understand the challenges you face Sam; really, I do. But I will only teach you if you make and stick to the commitment to not run away and not skip school. Can you make that commitment to me?"

Sam hesitated. He needed to be able to see the girls although now, if the email worked, they would be able to arrange secret meetings. Anyway, if the worst came to the worst, he would just stop his aikido training and run away with them again.

"Okay. I will not run away, and I will go to school."

"Right! Let's get your address and phone number, check your email on my computer and then get you home, okay?"

"Wow! You have a computer!" Sam said with a cheeky smile.

"Yes, and I even have a TV as well!" said Kensho, laughing.

"What did your students call you?"

"They called me Sensei. It is a Japanese word for teacher. If you begin to study aikido here, then you will call me Sensei too. It is traditional in Japan to put the name first though, so I would be called Iwata Sensei rather than Sensei Iwata."

Then Sam paused before hesitantly asking, "And how do you know my name?"

"It's on your name tag," said Kensho laughing and pointing at Sam's chest.

Sam looked down and realised with embarrassment and frustration that he still had his damned name tag on. He worked for a few hours after school a couple of times a week in a coffee shop, and the owners made him wear a name badge. He'd got dressed in the dark that morning and hadn't noticed he still had it on his shirt. He always felt such a loser when he forgot to take it off.

Kensho lead the way upstairs to the computer. Above the dojo was Kensho's small and simple living quarters. The ceiling was much lower, though the rooms were built in the same style as the dojo downstairs with wood surrounding white panels. At the top of the stairs was a large room to the right, which was a changing room with showers for the students to use if they so wished. To continue past the entrance to the changing room, it was necessary to slide open a very thin door. Sam had never seen a door quite like it and asked Kensho about it.

"This is called a shoji," Kensho explained. "It is a traditional Japanese sliding door that is still popular in Japan today. The little white panels are actually made of paper."

Beyond the shoji was a small kitchen on the right and then a small bathroom, followed by a small bedroom and finally an office that was overflowing with books. That was the extent of Kensho's megre living quarters. Kensho lived what many would think was a very spartan existence.

Kensho allowed Sam to check his email on the computer in his office. Sam was delighted to see he already had a message from the girls. Kensho let him send a reply. In his reply, Sam told his sisters the crazy bear story and said he thought he'd be able to meet the girls at the mall. When Sam had finished, he and Kensho went downstairs and outside where Sam unlocked his bike. Then Kensho lead the way to his car, which was parked further down the alley. Sam didn't recognise the make but it was small and old, its red paint dusty and faded. Despite its diminutive size they managed to squeeze the bike into the boot.

As they drove back to East Vancouver Sam looked out of his open window at the city passing by. He looked at the faces of the people they passed and wondered what battles they fought in their lives. He was young, but Sam was wise enough to know that everyone was struggling with something. Everyone had some pain and sadness that they hid from the world.

CHAPTER 10

Permission is Given

As Sam had predicted, his foster mother was furious when he returned home and immediately sent Sam to his room. As he went upstairs, he heard her thanking Kensho for his help.

Sam walked across his bedroom and looked out of the window. Above the trees, he could just see the very tops of the North Shore Mountains with the last of the winter's snow still shining in the sun. He dreamed of living out there in the mountains. He had a vision of a small old cabin by a lake. He'd grow his own food, catch fish from the lake and build mountain bike trails on the mountain. He'd have a beautiful girlfriend, perhaps even Grace, he thought.

He sat down on the edge of his bed and reflected on his encounter with Kensho. He lay back and clasped his hands behind his head, looking up at the ceiling. He replayed the whole scene in his mind. Where had Kensho come from? The alley was empty; of that he was utterly certain. There had been no doorways near him that he could recall. Kensho certainly hadn't come out of the dojo as Sam had been facing it as he was about to throw the brick. Why hadn't Kensho shouted at him about that? It was blindingly obvious what he was about to do, and there was no way a man like Kensho would have missed his intentions.

Then he recalled how Kensho had called him by his name. Sam lifted his head and looked at his chest and groaned. He still had the name tag on. He went to take it off and held it for a second. He turned it over to look at the side with his name on it. His heart stopped. The name tag didn't say 'Sam'. It said 'Ray'. He had picked up Ray's tag by accident at the start of his shift yesterday. He hadn't realised as the tag hangs down so unless he tilted it up he couldn't read it, looking down. So, there was no way Kensho got his name from the tag. How had Kensho known his name then? Surely, Kensho would have known that he'd later see that the badge said 'Ray' and know that Kensho hadn't got his name from the name tag.

"Wow," thought Sam. "This is really messing with my head."

Sam was just thinking maybe he should run downstairs to chase after Kensho and talk to him about it when his bedroom door opened and his foster mother walked in. He sat up ready for her to yell at him. But she wasn't anywhere near as furious as he had expected.

"Well, you were incredibly lucky to bump into such a wonderful man," she said. "He told me about what you did this morning."

Sam's heart skipped a beat, but then she continued, "Why you wandered the streets near the Downtown Eastside is beyond me, but I am glad you didn't try to run off with your sisters again. That was what I thought this was all about."

Sam was elated that Kensho had not revealed his secret, but he hid his elation and said, "I know I was stupid. Again, I am sorry to cause you so much hassle."

Sam was genuine in his apology. He really didn't want to cause these people grief. They weren't great, but they weren't bad either, and they did give him a home to live in.

His foster mother stood in the doorway looking at him for a few moments and then said,

"Well, I have decided to give you permission to study aikido at Kensho's dojo. He thinks the training will do you good and will give you something positive to focus on. He also very kindly agreed to waive the fees. He will even drive you home after class. So, you just have to get there by yourself after school. Sam, I know you are angry, and I do understand. But please don't mess this opportunity up, okay?" Then she left, closing the door.

Sam flopped back on the bed and just lay there trying to comprehend what had happened to him today. It was a lot to take in. He had been licked by a bear cub, stared the mother bear in the face, found his sisters, agreed to a rendezvous with them, met a beautiful girl, met an aikido master, and had gained permission to learn aikido.

On the whole, he thought, it hadn't been a bad day so far. He laughed out loud and punched the air with both fists in excitement.

CHAPTER 11

A Sudden Disappearance

When Kensho returned to the dojo, he went straight upstairs. To the very keenly aware, there was something odd about the upstairs. The area of the rooms didn't quite match the area of downstairs. Those who were even more keenly aware would notice that the height of the dojo, plus the height of the upstairs, did not match the height of the building. Kensho went into his office, slid the door shut and walked over to the left-hand side wall. Though the wall looked solid Kensho easily slid it to the left revealing a secret staircase.

Kensho stepped into the small space at the foot of the staircase and slid the hidden door silently closed behind him. He lightly but quickly climbed the steep staircase and, at the top, pushed open a trap door and climbed through. He emerged into a large room with a ceiling so low he had to kneel. Light filtered in through dusty skylights set in the flat roof of the building. A simple, wide wooden cabinet and an altar on a low wooden table were the only objects in the room. Closing the trap door behind him, Kensho then 'walked' on his knees toward the cabinet in the centre of the room. In Japanese tradition this knee walking was called 'shikko'. Kensho could move as easily and quickly in shikko as a normal person could walk standing up.

Reaching the cabinet he pulled out a small key that was attached to a thin chain around his neck. He slid the key into a lock and turned it clockwise. Then he opened a door that covered the entire front of the cabinet to reveal a set of drawers which were as wide as the cabinet but not very high. The cabinet was made with such fine craftsmanship that when Kensho pulled the top drawer out it opened almost effortlessly. The drawer was lined with a soft fabric upon which lay a long, narrow object wrapped in more soft cloth. Kensho took the object out of the drawer and carefully unwrapped the fabric. He now held in his hand a Samurai sword in its sheath. The sheath, which was black, smooth and quite plain, protected the entire blade of the sword. Only the handle of the sword was visible. He slid the sword, still in its sheath, through his belt on his left side so that the handle was pointing forward.

Kensho then carefully folded the cloth the sword had been wrapped in and neatly placed it back in the drawer. He shut the drawer and then closed and locked the cabinet. Still in shikko he went over to the altar that was at the end of the room farthest from the staircase. The altar consisted of two tall white vases each containing a few small branches with dark green leaves, some fruit in a wooden bowl, a smooth stone with Japanese writing engraved upon it, and a small white jar with a lid. Positioning himself before the altar, Kensho sat still and began to meditate. The room was absolutely silent. After a few moments, a barely audible hum began, though it did not disturb Kensho who continued to meditate. The hum grew steadily until, at its loudest, it was as loud as a bumblebee on the wing. Then, it abruptly stopped, and silence once again returned to the room. But other than the simple wooden cabinet and the altar, the room was now empty. Kensho and the sword were gone.

CHAPTER 12

The Soul of the Samurai

S am spent the rest of the afternoon in his room keeping out of the way of his foster mother. After dinner, he chanced his luck and asked if he could look up 'aikido' on the web. To his relief his foster mother agreed.

He discovered that aikido was created by a man called Morihei Ueshiba in Japan in the early 1900s. Ueshiba was known as 'O'Sensei', which means 'Great Teacher'. Sam saw a picture of O'Sensei and realised it was the same man that Kensho had a big portrait of in his dojo. In most of the pictures O'Sensei was very old. He had little hair on his head, but he did have a long, wispy white beard and very bushy white eyebrows. In all the pictures he was wearing traditional Japanese clothes. But what struck Sam most was how incredibly tiny O'Sensei was. Sam read that O'Sensei failed to get into the military because he was less than five feet tall!

He was barely 1.5 metres tall, thought Sam, and he was a great martial arts master? No way.

But reading on, Sam learnt that O'Sensei was widely regarded throughout Japan as one of the greatest martial artists ever to have lived. He was highly skilled with the sword, the spear and the wooden staff as well as jujutsu. It was from the sword and jujutsu in particular that O'Sensei created aikido.

As Sam read more, he began to understand how Kensho had thrown his attackers with such apparent ease. aikido techniques used the attackers' energy against them. As the attack came in, Kensho had been 'blending' with the attack and redirecting the attackers' energy. The harder the attacker came, the harder the attacker was thrown. The attacker was basically throwing themselves following some redirection by Kensho. Whoa! thought Sam. That is just way too cool.

He loved the simplicity and efficiency of it. Just take the attacker's energy and redirect it. It looked so easy. He didn't understand why all martial arts weren't doing it. In time, he would realise how looks can be deceiving and just how far from easy Aikido actually was.

Sam read that the black baggy trousers were actually called 'hakama'. They were another traditional piece of clothing that were originally worn by samurai warriors in Japan a long time ago. Of course, Sam had heard of the samurai, but he didn't know that much about them so he researched them too.

The samurai had first emerged as warriors in Japan well over a thousand years ago. They were renowned for their courage, honour and bravery though not all were like that. They were well educated, and they were amazingly skilled with the samurai sword as well as other weapons such as the bow and the spear. The samurai faded away about 150 years ago when Japan formed a proper army and the samurai were banned from wearing a sword in public.

Their swords were amazing pieces of craftsmanship that involved many different highly skilled craftsmen to make them. They were perhaps the finest weapons ever created and were described as 'the soul of the samurai'. They were incredibly strong and could easily cut through bone undamaged. They could even cut a man in half. Such was the sharpness of the blade that a piece of silk laid upon it would be sliced in half.

Sam was completely absorbed. This all seemed to bring together everything that he so loved, except maybe cutting a man in half. These incredible swords crafted with such skill, the history of the samurai warriors, the discipline of their training and the power of aikido, all filled him with excitement. He wanted to know everything about it all and to practise, not just aikido, but also the handling of a samurai sword.

He would have liked to read more, but his foster father said he needed the computer so Sam had to stop. He went up to his room and stood looking out of the window, feeling he actually had something exciting to look forward to. For the first time since his father had died, he began to feel positive.

CHAPTER 13

A Coming Storm

Zoe was lying in her bed trying to get to sleep. She had been thinking about Sam all day and was worried about him. Zoe's intuition was strong. His anger had been growing, and that concerned her. But her intuition told her that Sam was facing danger. She didn't know what the danger was, but she had a sense of growing foreboding. It was like on a hot summer day, when the black clouds of a massive thunder storm threaten. As it approaches the air begins to stir, as if agitated by the oncoming storm it seeks to flee. But it cannot. As the storm that Zoe sensed approached, Sam too would be unable to flee. He would have to stand and face this danger. Zoe resolved to stand beside her brother, no matter how violent the storm became.

As she lay quietly under her duvet with these thoughts going through her mind, she heard Sophie beginning to cry in her bed on the other side of the room. She switched on her little bedside lamp and quietly went over to comfort Sophie. She could see that Sophie was crying in a dream. Zoe knew that as keen as her own intuition was, Sophie's was many times keener. Such sensitivity to that which is unseen was an amazing gift, but Zoe knew it also made Sophie's life very difficult. Sophie was forever sensing the contradictions in people. People often say one thing yet feel and mean quite the opposite. Sophie didn't hear the words anywhere nearly as clearly as she sensed the truth the people carried in their hearts. The contradiction left Sophie very confused and unable to trust people. Zoe knew that Sophie too was sensing the approaching storm, but far, far more vividly and with a far deeper sense of foreboding than Zoe would.

Zoe caressed Sophie's forehead gently. She knew not to speak out loud, so she spoke soothing words in her mind to Sophie. She imagined love pouring from her heart and wrapping Sophie in a soft violet blanket of protection. Sophie began to settle, and her whimpering cries stopped. Zoe asked all the animals and the trees to protect her sister, her brother and herself. An owl began to hoot in the tree outside her window. Many would call it a coincidence but Zoe knew better than to believe in coincidences. Others doubted, but Zoe simply trusted. She lightly kissed her sister's forehead and went back to her bed. Before long she was sleeping a deep and restful sleep, unaware that as she slept the storm clouds were beginning to appear over the horizon.

CHAPTER 14

Trust

Kensho, his sword still sheathed by his side, sat in seiza on the slopes of a steep wooded mountain beside a waterfall. The air was cool, and every now and then a gentle breeze would carry the mist from the waterfall over to where he meditated. As it caressed his face, he noticed the cooling water droplets but he did not move. He continued to just sit, eyes closed and breathing slowly. In time, Kensho stood up. He was relaxed but his awareness of what was going on around him, as well as inside him, was absolute. He knew he was being watched. He stretched out his legs and back before returning down the steep and rocky path that wound through trees and groves of tall bamboo.

Eventually he emerged from under the canopy of the wood and into bright sunshine. The path now wound through a vegetable garden. Because the slope was steep the garden was arranged in terraces so that the vegetable patches were flat and easy to work. Some way below was an old wooden farmhouse with a roof that came almost down to the ground. Kensho was high enough above it that he looked along the length of the peak of the roof. He could see down into the valley and across an enormous blue lake far below. Smoke gently rose from a hole in the top of the thick thatched roof. There were no windows in the sides of the house because the roof came down so low. But at either end, doors and small windows had been placed in the wooden walls.

Close by, to the left of the house, stood another small wooden building not much bigger than a shed. To the right side, stood a large single storey wooden building with a roof covered in grey tiles, shaped such that it looked as if little waves were washing over it.

Kensho picked his way through the terraces abundant with vegetables until he arrived at the back door of the farmhouse. It was a shoji, much like the one in his dojo. Kensho slipped off his shoes, placed them neatly against the wall, then quietly slid the door open. As Kensho stepped into the poorly lit room, its air heavy with the smell of smoke, he took a moment, allowing his eyes to adjust. He slid the door closed behind him and walked over the smooth wooden floor to the fire that burned low in a fireplace in the floor. The fireplace was made from stone, and above it, hung a kettle. Thin mats surrounded the fireplace. Kensho sat on one of them, before removing his sword and laying it by his side. Apart from the occasional crackle from the fire, the house was still and quiet.

Kensho sat there for a while looking into the embers of the fire. Then the shoji to one of the rooms off to the side of the main room silently slid open, and an old man emerged. Sam would have said he looked a bit like O'Sensei, but this man was a little different. His name was Hiroshi Nagato, and, like O'Sensei, he was Japanese, only around five feet tall and very slightly built. Unlike O'Sensei, he had more white hair on his head, and his white beard was thicker. He certainly was an old man, yet he moved gracefully and easily. An unmistakable sense of power and light emanated from him.

"Hello Sensei," said Kensho, bowing as he spoke.

"Hello Kensho," replied Hiroshi as he walked over to the fire and sat beside Kensho. Kensho also sat down once more.

"Well, Kensho", said Hiroshi, "I am sure you feel his heart as much as I do."

"Hai, Sensei."

"He has much anger and frustration, but he also has much light, courage and a deep sense of honour", continued Hiroshi.

Kensho nodded again.

They sat in silence for a few minutes before Hiroshi announced, "The water is boiling. Let us have some tea!"

Kensho stood up and fetched two simple wooden cups and a little tea pot from a small kitchen area next to the large room. He scooped some green tea from a pot on a shelf and dropped it into the tea pot.

Then he took a thick cloth, grasped the kettle's handle and lifted it off the hook that held it just above the fire. He poured the hot water into the tea pot, put the tea pot and cup onto a tray and brought them over to where Hiroshi sat.

They sat in silence as they waited for the tea to steep. Then Kensho poured the tea into a cup and handed it to Hiroshi.

"Thank you, Kensho," he said and took the cup.

Kensho then poured his own tea, and the two men sat once more on the mat in front of the fire. Before they began drinking, they both bowed their heads and silently gave thanks for the tea.

"Ah, Kensho, as ever you have made a fine cup of tea. So, you have found your disciple," said Hiroshi after he took his first sip.

Kensho nodded.

"But your heart seems heavy, Kensho. Why is this?"

Kensho was quiet for a few moments before answering,

"We both know what this means, Sensei."

"Indeed we do!" said Hiroshi, laughing. "I shall soon be dead! As the 'Old Master' said:

> Being natural is to be one with the Tao
> you will be one with all that arises in your life
> And though your body dies, you are eternal.

"I have been one with the Tao for over one hundred years, Kensho. I have embraced all that life has brought. I embrace all that death will bring. Life and death are one, as night and day are one."

Kensho looked deep into the embers of the fire before saying,

"But am I ready to become the Master to Sam?"

"When the student is ready, the teacher appears," replied Hiroshi. "Kensho, I remember when I found you. I too knew what that meant. I had this very same conversation with my Sensei. I too was full of fears, full of doubts. But remind me what a Sensei is for, Kensho. Tell me you have not forgotten?"

There was a playfulness in Hiroshi's voice as he spoke.

Kensho sighed and then repeated one of the first things he had learnt from Hiroshi when he was first his student,

"You are only a disciple because your eyes are closed. The day you open them, you will see there is nothing you can learn from me or anyone."

"What then is a Master for?" asked Hiroshi.

"To make you see the uselessness of having one," replied Kensho.

Hiroshi laughed a deep, roaring belly laugh that filled the room. "I am useless! I am useless!" he bellowed before laughing once more.

Then Hiroshi's demeanour became more grave.

"The signs are clear, Kensho. Never have we been in more serious danger. Perhaps my death will not be a peaceful one as past Masters have enjoyed. Ah, but if it is our lot to face Darkness, then face it we will. Darkness is as much an illusion as fear, Kensho. If we can see through our fears, then we can see through Darkness. Remember, Kensho, you are unlike any previous apprentice, and you will be unlike any previous Master. O'Sensei gave us an incredible gift. His light transcended Darkness, and that which was designed to kill and maim became that which would love and protect."

Kensho shifted uneasily on his mat and then mindfully drank the last mouthful of his tea. Hiroshi looked at him compassionately.

"Kensho, look at me," he said gently. Kensho slowly drew his eyes away from the embers and looked into the eyes of his teacher. In those eyes he saw a light burning far brighter than the embers.

"Kensho, I know the weight of responsibility that you carry for I too have carried that weight. We cannot fail, or we condemn the world to Darkness. We may be able to see through Darkness, but ordinary folk cannot. They see their fears as real and not the illusions that they are. But, Kensho, please trust. Even when all seems lost, please trust. Because with trust, Darkness can never prevail. It is only through the loss of trust that Darkness can prevail. Trust to the universe; trust to the Tao; and trust to yourself."

Hiroshi put out a hand and held Kensho's shoulder.

"Kensho you are as a son to me. I love you as a son. Trust me when I say that I know that you will prevail, especially now that you have found your disciple."

Kensho nodded and smiled at Hiroshi.

"Thank you Sensei," he said. "And now, if you will excuse me, I must return. I judge I have been gone for four hours. I know that is only half an hour back at the dojo, but nonetheless my students may begin to wonder why I have not come back down."

Hiroshi smiled and said,

"Bring a watch next time! The 16th century may have its perks, but a good time piece would be most welcome!"

Kensho laughed. Then he bowed deeply to his master and walked over to the altar that was set out on a low table against one of the walls of the room.

Suddenly he turned and said,

"Sensei! What am I thinking? I have forgotten to clean up after our tea! I am so sorry for my oversight!"

He bowed deeply again and began to return.

"Kensho!" said Hiroshi waving his hand dismissively. "I am old, but I am quite capable of cleaning up for myself. Go now!"

Kensho bowed once more, turned and went to the altar. He sat before the altar and began to meditate. The low hum became audible and grew louder before suddenly ending once more.

Hiroshi sat for a very long time alone in front of the fire, watching it burn down. He knew that it was not his destiny to face the full might of Darkness. He knew that it would fall to Kensho and Sam. Doubts kept rising in him. Had he taught Kensho well enough? Would Kensho be able to teach Sam enough before Darkness launched its assault? Had the Masters over the many centuries passed down the secret transmission perfectly? Finally, Hiroshi heard his own words to Kensho echo back to him,

"It is only through the loss of trust that Darkness can prevail," he began. "Trust to the universe, trust to the Tao and trust to yourself."

"Hai!" announced Hiroshi to the silence, and stood up to tend to the fire.

CHAPTER 15

A Wrong Turn

Sam was to begin learning aikido two days after his first encounter with Kensho. In order for Sam to get from school to the dojo, his foster parents had finally agreed to give Sam a bike. It was second hand and very far from the pro mountain bike Sam dreamed of. But it worked and Sam was still delighted as he peddled hard along Vancouver's streets.

As he hadn't made his way from school to the dojo before he'd looked up his route online, but he must have made a wrong turn and soon realised he was lost. He was determined not to be late for his first aikido class, so he tried to take what he thought would be a short cut down an alley. He was back in the Downtown Eastside and as soon as he entered the alley his intuition began yelling for him to turn around. Sam, not being attuned to his intuition, only faintly heard the yell and ignored it anyway. He was focused on not being late, so he cycled on. It was a narrow, dark alley with wooden power poles running down the sides. It was filthy with lots of large metal dumpsters pushed up against the walls, many with their lids open and rubbish strewn about them. Between some of the dumpsters, Sam could see dirty blankets and cardboard boxes, the beds of the homeless.

As he continued down the alley, he heard a scream, and a thin woman with long black hair, wearing a very small tight black dress suddenly appeared from behind one of the dumpsters and ran wildly towards Sam. He slammed on his brakes and tried to avoid her, but they collided and Sam tumbled off his bike and slid into a wall.

Sam picked himself up and turned to help the woman, but she was already off and running down the alley. As Sam bent over to pick up his bike he noticed three men approaching him. The men were looking at him in a way that he knew meant trouble. Sam realised that he had to act fast, so he grabbed his bike, jumped on and tried to cycle back the way he had come. But before he could get going, a hand grabbed his shoulder and he was dragged off the bike.

Sam hit the ground hard, and the air was knocked out of him. A boot smashed into his side and he let out a scream of pain. Then another kick hit him in the lower back, and he screamed again.

One of the men leant down and grabbed the front of Sam's jacket, pulling him up and said, "We want your cell phone and your wallet." Sam could smell the alcohol on the man's breath. He could see his broken and yellowed teeth, and he could also see the cold, detached look in his eyes. Through the pain and shock Sam managed to say, "I don't have a cell phone."

The man sneered at him and said, "Don't lie to us, you little punk", and then he punched Sam hard in the solar plexus. Sam collapsed to the ground writhing in pain. He gasped for air, but none would come. I can't breathe! I'm going to die, he thought, blinded by panic. Then the man kicked Sam hard in the head and everything went black.

CHAPTER 16

Intuition

At the same time Sam was being attacked in the Downtown Eastside, Zoe and Sophie were in the garden of a friend called Jemima. They had known Jemima for a few years, and all three of them had become close. Jemima had two other friends there, and Jemima's mum, Kate, was sitting on a lounger reading a book in the afternoon sun. The girls were standing in a group by a trampoline giggling uncontrollably when the attack on Sam started. Zoe and Sophie's giggles were cut in an instant. Zoe gasped, and all the colour drained from her face. Sophie cried out and fell down to the grass.

At first, the other girls thought Sophie was messing around, but they very quickly sensed something serious was happening.

"Mum! Mum!" called Jemima.

Kate picked up the fear in her daughter's voice and leapt up from the lounger. Meanwhile, Zoe crouched down to hold Sophie.

"Sophie, Sophie, I felt it! I felt it! But I don't know what it was that I felt. Tell me! Tell me!"

Sophie's eyes were wide with fear. She started to mouth something but was unable to form any words. Then she suddenly drew a deep breath and said loudly, "It's Sam! He's dying!"

Kate reached them at that moment. She had always known that these two unusual girls had a special gift. She had seen so many unusual things occur around them. That the garden was filled with wildlife when they arrived was one thing. Sophie's incredible intuition was another. Kate was also 'gifted' and, though she had long since stopped being aware of it, she knew such powers to be real. That was why when she heard what Sophie said, she acted immediately.

"John! John!" she yelled as she helped Sophie up.

Her husband was home today, watching a golf tournament on TV.

"What?" came the irritable reply from inside the house.

"Watch the girls! I am taking Zoe and Sophie home!" she called as she guided them to the car.

"Jemima, you and the girls go in and see your father. Tell him I don't know when I will be back" she said gently to Jemima.

"What's wrong?" asked Jemima, tears welling up in her eyes, "What's happening to Sam?"

"I don't know, Jemima, my love," Kate said. "But I do know we need to get Zoe and Sophie home. Okay? Everything will be fine. Now go and see your father."

CHAPTER 17

The Rescue

Kensho was sitting in his office as Sam was being attacked. Kensho, like Sophie, keenly felt Sam's pain. But Kensho's perceptions were far better tuned than Sophie's, so he felt that Sam was close by. He knew by the time of day that Sam must be on his way to the dojo from the school. He leapt up and ran down the stairs, passed some of his students who were already arriving and ran out of the dojo. He paused for a minute, sensing where Sam was, before jumping into his old car and speeding off in search of Sam.

He didn't have to drive far. Only a few blocks away, he turned up a narrow alley and saw Sam lying motionless beside his bike. Kensho stopped the car, jumped out and ran up to kneel beside Sam.

Kensho could see that Sam's face was bloody from a big cut on his temple. Kensho could perceive the flow of ki through a person's body. Ki is what the Japanese call the life-force energy that flows through all living things. When someone becomes ill or badly injured, the flow of ki is hindered or blocked altogether. Kensho slowly passed his hands a few centimetres above the entire length of Sam's body. Kensho could sense that life was draining from Sam.

He knew that many of Sam's ribs had been broken. He also sensed some internal bleeding and damage to Sam's kidneys. But it was an injury to Sam's brain that was killing him. His brain was bleeding and swelling. Kensho's hands hovered just above Sam's head, as if holding it like a ball. The same hum that accompanied Kensho's sudden disappearance from the dojo began to fill the alley. After a minute or so Sam groaned and began to stir.

"Lie still", said Kensho softly as he held his hands motionless above Sam's head for another few minutes.

Once Kensho was certain that he had healed the worst of Sam's brain injury he then worked on the injuries to his ribs and kidneys.

"How do you feel Sam?" he asked, carefully helping Sam up.

Sam paused for a moment before replying, "I feel sore all over."

Then Sam paused as he took a few deep breaths.

"It doesn't hurt when I breathe. When I was lying on the ground I felt like I was being stabbed in the chest with every breath. But not now."

"It must have been the position you were in. Let's get you into the car and off to hospital." Kensho made no mention of the healing he had done.

He helped Sam to stand up and then opened the passenger door of the car. He carefully guided Sam into the seat, put Sam's bike into the boot of the car, and then set off for a nearby hospital. When they arrived, Sam was immediately taken into emergency for treatment. Kensho phoned Sam's foster mother to tell her what had happened and where Sam was.

When Kate and the girls arrived at their foster home, Kate spoke to Susie. She tried to explain what had happened with Sophie and that she was convinced that Sophie had felt something happen to Sam. Susie was obviously sceptical and hesitant to call Sam's foster mother but eventually agreed to do so. She spoke to Sam's foster mother, Ruth, shortly after Kensho had called. Ruth confirmed that Sam had been in some sort of an accident and that she was going to see him at St Paul's.

Susie hung up the phone and turned to Sophie.

"How could you know? I don't understand."

"Is he alright? What has happened?" asked Zoe.

"He has been in some sort of accident, and he is at St Paul's hospital. I don't know how he is. His foster mother is going there now," replied Susie.

"We have to go too!" said Zoe as she jumped up.

"Oh, no ... no, I don't think that is a good idea at all," said Susie.

"Susie, I think it really is best if the girls go to the hospital," said Kate. "Though I am sure all will work out well, they should be with

Sam or at least close to hand. I will take them if you like."

Susie thought for a moment and then nodded.

"Kate, if you are okay to take them and think it is for the best, then by all means go."

Zoe and Sophie immediately ran to the front door, and Kate quickly followed. They got into Kate's car once again and headed into Vancouver. As they drove, Zoe turned to Kate and said,

"Thank you very much, Mrs. Cowan."

"It's okay Zoe, and I am sure Sam will be fine. But hopefully this way you'll get a chance to see him. I didn't want you to miss that opportunity."

Kensho met Ruth in the waiting room of Emergency. He explained that Sam had been taken to be x-rayed and to be treated for the large gash on his head.

Not long after Ruth's arrival, Kate walked into the Emergency waiting room with the girls. Ruth was not impressed to see them. Kate sat the girls down on a bench, before taking Ruth to one side and explaining, in no uncertain terms, that this was an exceptional circumstance.

As the ladies spoke, Kensho walked over and introduced himself to Zoe and Sophie.

"Hello, my name is Kensho Iwata. I am Sam's aikido teacher," said Kensho.

He looked over his shoulder to ensure Ruth was not within earshot and continued,

"You may have heard of me in an email Sam sent to you from my office."

He smiled reassuringly at them.

"Yes. He told us about you in his email. Is Sam going to be okay?" replied Zoe.

"Oh yes, he will be absolutely fine," said Kensho.

Zoe and Sophie looked very relieved.

"It seems he was attacked by some men who wanted to rob him. He will have some painful bruises, and he has a big cut on his head, but he will quickly recover, I am certain."

Sophie was staring at Kensho with a look of wonder.

"You shine so brightly, Kensho," she said. "I've never seen anyone shine like you do!"

Kate had finished talking to Ruth and came back over to join them.

"Kensho says Sam is going to be fine!" said Sophie excitedly.

Kensho introduced himself to Kate, and they all sat down and waited to hear from the doctors. Kensho was sat beside Ruth and, while they waited, he talked quietly to her.

After an hour or so, a doctor entered the room. He spoke to Ruth, explaining that Sam had sustained no serious injuries, no broken bones and no internal injuries or bleeding. Their only real concern was his head injury. They had decided to keep him in the hospital overnight just as a precaution, although all the signs were that he would be absolutely fine.

Zoe asked if they could see him.

"Of course," replied the doctor. "Please follow me."

Leading them into the emergency ward, he pulled back a curtain to reveal Sam sitting up in bed. He had a gash on his left temple that was now sewn up with black stitches. His face looked pale, but it lit up when he saw his sisters. Sophie squealed, ran up and jumped onto the bed hugging Sam. Sam half-laughed and half-cried out before saying,

"Soph, you're hurting me!"

"I'm sorry, big brother. I love you," said Sophie, as she loosened her hug slightly and looked up at him before kissing him gently on his cheek.

"How are you feeling?" asked Zoe as she came along the left side of the bed and leaned in to gently hug and then kiss Sam.

"Oh I'm doing fine, Zo. I'm just a bit sore. But don't worry, I'll be fine in no time."

"Don't put on a brave face for me, Sam Stone. How are you, really?"

Sam smiled and laughed a little, but that made him wince.

"Okay, I'm in quite a bit of pain actually, Zoe Stone. But I will be fine soon. Honestly!"

"Hhhhmmmm. Well, thank you for your honest answer. You've got to take care of yourself, okay?"

Zoe squeezed Sam's hands as she spoke.

"I will, Zo," said Sam, nodding.

Ruth stood on the other side of the bed and asked,

"What happened, Sam?"

Sam recounted the attack as they all listened.

"Well I'm so glad that you're okay. You will be more careful and stay away from alleys from now on, won't you?" said Ruth.

Sam nodded. Then Ruth made an announcement: "Well, I have some good news to cheer you up. Kensho is a very persuasive man. He has said that you have made a commitment to him not to run away or skip school. Is that true?"

Sam nodded and, again, Ruth continued. "Well, Kensho and I have discussed things. He suggested that I allow you and your sisters to meet at his dojo once a week, on a trial basis. If there is any hint of a problem then the deal is off. But for now, as long as Susie agrees, then I have said that I am happy for this to happen."

Sam looked astonished, first at Kensho and then at his sisters. Sophie bounced up and down on the bed in excitement, before diving in to hug Sam once again. Zoe leant in and hugged them both as tears began to roll down her cheeks. Sam didn't even notice the pain of his injuries as he held his sisters so tightly.

When finally their embrace was over, Sam looked at Kensho then Ruth and said, "Thank you. Thank you so very, very much."

Sam was transferred from the emergency ward to a children's ward for the night. Kate had to get home, and so Zoe and Sophie said goodbye, knowing they would see their brother again very soon.

Then Ruth left, saying she would be back in the morning to collect Sam. Only Kensho remained, sitting in a chair beside Sam's bed.

"I know I haven't actually had my first aikido class yet, but do you mind if I start calling you Sensei?" asked Sam.

"Of course not, Sam. Let's call it practice for when you do finally make it to the dojo to train."

"How did you know I was hurt and how did you know how to find me? And how did you know my name was Sam when the name tag said Ray?"

Kensho gazed intently into Sam's eyes.

"Sam, everything unfolds exactly as it should. Can I ask that you just trust me for now and also trust that in time you will come to understand?"

"Of course, Sensei," said Sam, nodding. "I really want to say thank you so much for everything that you have done for me. For us. A few days ago, I had no idea how I would see my sisters. Now you have managed to arrange things so we can see each other every week. That's just amazing."

As he spoke, tears began to well up in Sam's eyes.

"It all unfolds just as it should, Sam. We must trust in that. What may at first appear as misfortune often turns out to be the greatest blessing."

Kensho shifted in his chair and leant in towards Sam, saying, "Actually, Sam, I believe you have had your first aikido class. There is a lesson in today's events. What do you think you might have learnt?"

Sam thought for a minute.

"Well, I shall not go down anymore alleys."

"I can see how you arrived at that conclusion," said Kensho. "But had you not cycled down the alley my dojo was in, we would never have met. Now, think back to the moment you cycled into that alley today, Sam."

Sam thought back and suddenly remembered.

"I sort of felt I shouldn't go down that alley!"

"But you did not listen to your intuition, did you Sam?"

"No, Sensei. I didn't want to be late for my first class."

"That is good, Sam. It is important to approach your training with a good attitude. 'Awareness', and always trust your intuition, those are today's aikido lessons."

"Sam, be aware of what is going on inside yourself as well as around you. Be aware of the quiet voice of intuition that most people no longer hear. When you hear it, trust it and act upon it."

Then Kensho stood up.

"Are you okay if I leave now?"

"Of course Sensei! You must have missed classes because of me. I am sorry."

"My senior students are more than capable of teaching the classes. Besides, they are all probably relieved that the difficult old teacher isn't there to berate them. I will come over to visit you tomorrow and bring something that will help with your recovery. Maybe even some of my delicious tea! Sleep well, Sam. Goodbye."

"Goodbye Sensei."

He watched Kensho as he walked down the ward, saying 'goodbye' and 'thank you' to all the nurses as he left.

Sam lay in his bed trying to get to grips with what had happened in his life. It was as if everything was changing too quickly, and he couldn't keep up. He recalled the phrase Kensho had said,

"It all unfolds just as it should."

"Well, it sure is unfolding," he murmured to himself. He stared at the white ceiling of the ward for quite some time, thinking about what Kensho had said about awareness and intuition before he finally fell asleep.

CHAPTER 18

The Great Guardian of the Osawa Scrolls

When Kensho arrived back at the dojo, he found Hiroshi preparing tea in the kitchen. He had just set a kettle on one of the electric rings at the back of the hob and was switching the ring on.

"Ah, Kensho! Quite the day you have had. I thought that you would appreciate a cup of tea upon your return."

"Thank you, Sensei."

Kensho then walked over to the hob and moved the kettle onto the front ring that Hiroshi had actually switched on, before saying,

"But I think the kettle will boil more quickly on the hot ring."

"Good. I see your awareness is not slipping," Hiroshi immediately replied.

"Another 'test' then, Sensei?" said Kensho, chuckling.

Hiroshi's eyes twinkled mischievously, and then he asked, "So, how is young Sam bearing up?"

Kensho told Hiroshi of the events and of Sam's injuries.

"He has a remarkably strong spirit, Sensei. His anger is easing, and his light is growing."

"Well, that is good news. What of his sisters?"

"Interesting that you should ask, Sensei. They both seem quite unusual. Sophie, the youngest, seems to have remarkable perception. Zoe also seems unusually perceptive, but there is something else about her that I have not yet been able to identify. Why do you ask?" Kensho looked at Hiroshi quizzically.

"Oh, it is nothing," replied Hiroshi waving a hand in the air dismissively.

Kensho looked knowingly at Hiroshi."Sensei, what do you know?"

"I know nothing, Kensho! Now, how is the dojo doing?"

Kensho was all too aware of Hiroshi changing the subject but he didn't persist in his questioning. Instead he began to tell Hiroshi of his student's progress while he made the tea.

They chatted for some time until Hiroshi put his empty tea cup down silently on the counter. Then he turned to Kensho and, smiling broadly, said, "Now I must be heading back soon. But before I do, let's watch a cartoon!"

"Sensei, you are The Great Guardian of the Osawa Scrolls. You stand as the brightest light holding Darkness at bay. And you are like a seven-year-old child obsessed with cartoons," said Kensho, shaking his head and laughing.

Hiroshi grinned and, in that moment, he did look for all the world like a seven-year-old child.

"Kensho, there is no television in 16th century Japan and the nights are long and quiet. Now, spoil your old master."

Kensho turned on a tiny TV that looked like it might have been made in the 16th century and found the right channel. As dusk turned to night outside, the two friends sat happily side by side in the little kitchen watching cartoons.

CHAPTER 19

Shining Bright

The girls were home and in bed, but they couldn't sleep. Just like Sam, they were struggling to comprehend how it was that their lives had changed so quickly.

"Zo, are you awake?" asked Sophie quietly.

"Yes. I can't sleep."

"Did you see how brightly Kensho shone?" said Sophie. "He was so bright and so pure white. It was incredible! I've never seen anyone look like that before."

"I sensed something about him Soph, but I still can't see the light as you do. I think he is a wonderful and lovely man and that he is going to be a really great help to Sam."

"Yes. He is going to help Sam a lot. Sam wanted to get the three of us together, and Kensho's making it happen! I am so excited, Zo!"

"Me too, Soph, me too," replied Zoe with a smile. "Now let's get some sleep."

CHAPTER 20

The Attack in the Woodshed

Hiroshi had returned to the old farmhouse. The fire was almost out, and night had fallen. He lit an oil lamp, but it barely lifted the gloom. He slid open the back door and began to walk up the garden path to the wood shed to fetch some more logs. Hiroshi felt the mountains more full of malice than ever. Though it was night, the nearly-full moon lit the garden. Arriving at the wood shed, he knew that danger was very close by. Waiting for it to reveal itself, he bent over and reached his right hand out to grasp the first log.

What took place next happened with such speed that an onlooker would have seen nothing but a blur. From his left side came something evil, an ill-defined dark form that had lain in wait beside the woodshed ready to attack. Hiroshi didn't see it or hear it, but he sensed it. His response came from tens of thousands of hours of practice over many decades of training. His conscious mind would have been far too slow to process the danger and decide upon the correct response.

But his trained mind reacted in an instant. His right hand, the one that had been about to grasp the log, shifted to grasp the hilt of his sword. He began to draw it. As he did so, Hiroshi's hips lowered, and he span around and back to his right, putting distance between him and the advancing attacker. As he span, he brought the sword down in a diagonal cut. The sword sliced the dark form clean through as it advanced upon him. The dark form let out a penetrating scream that echoed through the valley, and its darkness dissipated back into the forest.

Hiroshi immediately shifted his stance so he was ready for another attack, should it come. His body was completely relaxed, his breathing slow and deep, his mind fluid, and his gaze soft and open. He could have been waiting for Kensho to hand him a cup of tea, such was his calm state. After a few minutes, Hiroshi sheathed his sword. He sensed no danger nearby. Once more he bent down and picked up the logs. Then he made his way back to the house with the logs and tended the fire. He cooked himself a simple dinner of rice and steamed vegetables, before meditating for an hour. Finally, he stocked the fire up one last time for the night and went to bed.

CHAPTER 21

The Old Master

Early the following morning, the doctor came to see Sam. He did some tests on him and asked questions, such as whether he felt dizzy or nauseous, before declaring him ready to go home. A nurse phoned Ruth to ask her to come and collect Sam. In the meantime two police officers arrived on the ward and interviewed Sam. They wanted as much information as possible about the attackers. Sam did his best to recall every detail, even telling them about the attackers' broken and yellowed teeth.

When he was done, one of the officers said, "Muggings and attacks are much more common in that area than where you live. So, if you must travel through it, stick to the main streets, okay?"

Sam nodded and the police officers wished him well before departing.

An hour or so later, Ruth appeared and took Sam home. As she drove him, Ruth told Sam that she had spoken to Susie and that it was agreed that Zoe and Sophie would see Sam at Kensho's dojo on Saturdays. Right now Sam was to have the rest of the week off school while he recovered.

After lunch, Kensho arrived. Ruth showed him up to Sam's room and left.

"How are you feeling, Sam?" asked Kensho.

"Oh, not too bad, thank you Sensei. I ache a lot and woke up lots of times last night. The ward was quite noisy, and the pain kept disturbing me."

"Well, I have some things to help you recover quickly and to help occupy your mind until you can get back on your feet."

First, Kensho produced a thermos from his bag.

"This is my wonderful green tea with some extra special ingredients that will help you feel better."

Kensho poured some into a cup, and Sam began to sip from it as Kensho reached into his bag and pulled out a very small jar.

"This ointment is excellent at healing bruises and cuts. Put this on twice a day," he said, as he passed Sam the jar.

Finally, Kensho pulled out an old and battered book. He handed it to Sam, who put his cup on the little table beside his bed and took the book from him. Then he frowned as he looked at the title of the book, which read Tao Te Ching.

"It is pronounced 'Dow Day Jing', Sam. The rough English translation is 'The Book of the Way'."

Sam opened it and saw that it had lots of short verses in it almost like a poem. "Is it poetry?" he asked Kensho.

"Almost. It was written by someone called Lao Tzu 2,500 years ago in China. Lao Tzu is sometimes called 'The Old Master'. The book is really a guide to living a contented life."

Sam flicked through the pages and then one verse caught his eye, and he read it out loud:

> Become one with the Tao, and the Tao welcomes you
> Become one with goodness, and goodness is within you
> Become one with loss, and you will experience loss willingly.

"What's the Tao, Sensei?" he asked.

"That is a very difficult question, Sam," said Kensho, laughing. "Go to the start of the book and read what it says." Sam did so and read out loud again:

> The tao that can be spoken of
> is not the eternal Tao
> The name that can be named
> is not the eternal Name.

"Well, I'm glad we've cleared that up then," said Sam, cheekily.

"It is confusing at first," said Kensho. "It seems to be so much nonsense. Yet, as you progress through your aikido training, you will begin to see with more clarity, and will find that the words that once seemed so silly suddenly seem so wise."

Sam flicked through some more pages scanning the words. Then he saw a passage that caught his eye and he found himself reading to Kensho once more:

> When a great person learns of the Tao,
> they diligently practice it.
> When an average person learns of the Tao,
> they are interested but quickly forget.
> When a foolish person learns of the Tao,
> they burst out laughing.
> If they did not laugh,
> it would not be the Tao.

"As you read the words, try not to think too much about them, Sam. Try to let them settle into you and allow yourself to feel them."

Sam didn't really understand what Kensho meant any more than he understood much of what he had read so far in The Book of the Way. But he said, "I'll try to, Sensei."

"Very good. Now, Sam, I must be getting back to the dojo, if you will excuse me."

"Thank you very much for coming to see me, Sensei, and for bringing me these things."

"That is my pleasure, Sam," said Kensho, bowing slightly. "Now, drink the tea, rest well and let's see you on the mat for your first aikido class soon!"

Then Kensho took his leave and left Sam to drink the tea and begin to read The Book of the Way properly.

CHAPTER 22

The Search for the Scroll

Hiroshi unrolled yet another scroll. He was searching for an obscure text that he felt sure he had read many, many years before. Though Hiroshi looked old, he was, in fact, far older than anyone would have guessed. Even he had lost track of his age, but in truth he was fast approaching his 113th birthday. There was nothing magical behind his age. As he himself would say, he had simply lived his life in harmony with the way things are.

Hiroshi lived in a farming region that was particularly well aligned with nature's rhythm. In fact, there was no clear distinction between the people and nature. The two had become so closely harmonised over the centuries, the actions of both so tightly integrated, that they were interdependent.

It was mid-morning on an early summer's day. The sun was shining in a clear blue sky. It was cooler up on the mountainside, but in the valley below it would be hot. Soon, Hiroshi would have to set off on his walk down the mountain and into the nearby village to visit his friend and student Daichi. So, he rolled the scroll up and put it back on the shelf amongst hundreds of others. He then went out into the garden and gathered some fresh vegetables, arranging them carefully in a basket made from reeds. Then, with his sword tucked through his belt as always, he began his walk down the steep and twisting path to the village below.

The path was wide enough for three people to walk side by side. At first, it cut its way through the forest, which was a mixture of fir, deciduous trees and groves of thick and very tall bamboo. The insects chirruped, and the birds sang as Hiroshi strode by. It was a beautifully tranquil walk, and although he was aware of the malice in the mountains, it somehow felt a little more distant at that moment.

Hiroshi came upon his favourite corner of the path. Here there was a bridge crossing the same stream that Kensho had meditated beside a few weeks earlier, higher up the mountain. It was a small, very old wooden footbridge that Hiroshi himself had rebuilt with Kensho's help many years before. Standing on this bridge, Hiroshi was afforded an incredible view as he looked south across the sun-filled valley below. He could see a small river meandering through the valley floor, making its lazy way to the lake. He gazed down at paddy fields with people working in them, wooden houses with smoke gently rising and the village that was his destination. The village was on the edge of the lake that stretched as far as the eye could see and Hiroshi could just make out many small fishing boats dotting the lake.

It was no coincidence that the view was south. When Hiroshi had chosen the site to build his house, he had followed a very important and ancient set of rules. To the north, there must be mountains, which, of course, were stretching high up above Hiroshi's house. To the south there must be an open plain. To the east, there must be flowing water, which was the stream that he now crossed. To the west, there must be a path or a road, which was the path upon which Hiroshi now stood. It continued up the mountain to the west of his house to a small Zen Buddhist temple that he also frequently visited.

Hiroshi had enjoyed this view for almost a century and yet each time he saw it, it was as if it was for the first time. He took a deep breath and silently gave a prayer of thanks before continuing on his way. In time the path became less steep, and Hiroshi emerged from the forest into the terraced paddy fields. The area was a hive of activity and Hiroshi waved to the men and women working in the fields as he passed. Occasionally, he would share a brief exchange shouted across the fields. The sides of the path were lined with wild flowers as well as plum and persimmon trees and the air was thick with the sound of bees hard at work.

His path joined a rough road that ran beside the river and he followed it all the way into the village. He stopped more frequently now to talk. Everyone knew Hiroshi and respected him greatly.

The villagers were in awe of Hiroshi for good reason. They knew that the mountains held evil spirits and strange super-natural creatures. Legends of these creatures had been passed down from generation to generation for millennia. Most well-known was the tengu which looked a bit like a small human, although much uglier and with a much longer nose. Some legends cast the tengu as bad and others as good. Whether good or bad, they were most certainly frightening, and the villagers thought that they were best avoided.

Certainly far more dangerous and undoubtedly evil were oni. These were huge troll-like creatures. There were different descriptions of oni. Some had horns on their head, and others didn't. Some were black-skinned, while others brown. But there was a total agreement that they were extremely dangerous, jolly unpleasant and to be avoided at all costs.

Most terrifying of all were the yokai. They were formless evil spirits that supposedly could do terrible things to their victims. It was a yokai that had attacked Hiroshi by the woodshed.

It was the fact that Hiroshi lived alone in the forest on the mountain and in a simple farmhouse that gave him so much respect. That the villagers would sometimes hear terrifying screams echo across the valley from the direction of Hiroshi's home only increased their awe. There had been much discussion about this very thing a few weeks ago, after Hiroshi had had his encounter with the yokai at the woodshed.

The villagers all agreed that Hiroshi was protecting them from the malice in the mountains and so were very thankful.

After much bowing and many polite conversations, Hiroshi eventually arrived at Daichi's home. Though also made of wood it was different to Hiroshi's home with a flatter roof covered in tiles. The snowfall in winter was much less in the valley floor than higher

up the mountain where Hiroshi lived and so the roof didn't need to
be so steeply sloped.

Hiroshi saw Aiko, Daichi's wife, working in the garden and called
out to her. She stood up and waved to him before putting down the
basket she was holding and walking over to welcome him.

Although in her early seventies, Aiko's hair was still mostly black.
She was tiny and had an air of mischief about her. Hiroshi bowed to
Aiko, and she bowed back.

"Aiko, I know that these will never match the quality of vegetables
that you grow, but please accept my humble gift," said Hiroshi,
bowing as he gave her his basket of vegetables.

"Oh, Hiroshi, you know that your vegetables taste far better than
mine!" replied Aiko as she gratefully received the basket and bowed
once more.

Then they both laughed, happy to see each other, and Aiko invited
Hiroshi into the house.

Hiroshi sat beside the fire while Aiko prepared some tea.

"Daichi should be here soon, Hiroshi," she said. "I am so sorry he is
late. There is much to do in the fields, and he is always being called
on for advice."

"Not to worry," replied Hiroshi.

He was quite content to sit with Aiko and catch up on the to-ing
and fro-ing of village life.

"You caused quite a stir a few weeks ago, Hiroshi," said Aiko with
a knowing smile. "The whole village heard the scream, and everyone
guessed what it was. You seem unharmed - as always."

"Yes. I am fine. Thank you, Aiko. But the danger grows daily. That
is why I must talk to Daichi."

Daichi arrived ten minutes later. He was big for a Japanese man,
much bigger than Hiroshi. Like Aiko he was in his early seventies,
had little grey hair and was obviously very fit and strong.

"Ah, Sensei!" said Daichi as he bowed. "I spend so much time
helping the other farmers I have no time to farm for myself! I am so

sorry for making you wait. Please allow me a minute to wash off the dirt from the fields, and I shall join you."

Daichi disappeared into the rear of the house. Along the back of his home flowed a little stream. It created a pool just inside the back wall of the house with stone steps that lead down to it. This was where Aiko and Daichi washed themselves, their clothes and their dishes. Six big lazy carp swam in the pool and tidied up any scraps washed off the dishes. Daichi stripped his top off and quickly gave himself a rinse. It had been hot work in the fields, and he had been out all morning.

"Sensei, shall we sit outside, in the shade of the persimmon tree?" Daichi suggested upon his return.

Hiroshi agreed, and they headed out together. Aiko stayed inside and began to prepare a late lunch.

A breeze gently stirred the tree's leaves. The persimmon fruit were just beginning to appear on its branches, a gift that would help Daichi and Aiko through the cold winter. But winter was still far away. The sun was strong and hot in the valley though it was very pleasant sitting in the shade, cooled by the breeze. At first Daichi and Hiroshi talked about village life, the season's rice crop and news that had come from over the mountains out of the city of Kyoto, the capital of Japan. In particular, they spoke of Hirohito Tanaka, who was the daimyo, or lord, of their region.

"Hirohito continues his political maneuvering. He has built a strong alliance since he betrayed Isamu Noro. Has he returned to visit you recently, Sensei?" asked Daichi.

"Not since last autumn, Daichi," said Hiroshi, shaking his head. "But he will be back soon, and I do not think he will accept my refusal this time. As you so rightly say, his ambition grows constantly. He wishes to have the best trained samurai to fight his battles, and he will demand I train them. He will not rest until the Emperor declares him Shogun."

Hiroshi looked south towards the mountains that stood between them and Kyoto, where the Emperor resided. Daichi changed the subject.

"I am glad to see you looking so well Sensei. I heard you dispatch another yokai a few weeks ago. It is getting more frequent, is it not?"

"There is a shift taking place, Daichi. We are being tested as Darkness begins to grow once more. Tengu, that were once just mischievous but mostly of good nature, are beginning to come under its influence. They avoid me now on my walks through the forest, but they watch me. You should be careful now at night in the village. I think you would be wise to spread the word gently. There is no need for panic, but caution is called for."

Daichi nodded. He might appear the lowly farmer, but he was actually an astonishingly well read and knowledgeable man. His full name was Daichi Hosokawa and he had been in charge of the library at the Emperor's palace in Kyoto for many years. But with shifts in power and political manoeuvring, Daichi was forced to leave his position. So, he had chosen to settle into the simple life of a farmer. He was no ordinary farmer though. Permitted by the daimyo to carry a sword he also had a mind like a library. Once he read something he never forgot it, and he had read an enormous amount.

Of course, it was no accident that Daichi had ended up in the village close by Hiroshi's dojo. He was drawn there by unseen forces that guide the good, just as unseen forces guide the evil. He had become a student of Hiroshi's over 20 years ago. Hiroshi had anticipated Daichi's coming and knew he was a man of the utmost integrity who had been sent to help.

Hiroshi continued their conversation with a question. He asked Daichi about an ancient and obscure text he seemed to recall reading long, long ago. It was the legend of a brother and two sisters who united the three powers – those of man, nature, and ki – to create an immensely powerful force before which all evil was swept away. Hiroshi asked Daichi if he knew of this text. Daichi sat in silence for a long time as he travelled to the farthest corners of his memory to find the answer. A bird landed in the tree and began to sing joyfully. Daichi continued to think. The story sounded familiar to him too, yet he couldn't recall it, which was a most unusual and frustrating experience for him.

Eventually he conceded defeat.

"It is familiar to me too, Sensei. Yet, for some reason, I cannot recall where I have read it. I have been through all the great and lesser texts that I know. I have even recalled the most obscure texts, but nothing matches the tale of which you speak. Yet I know I have read it too, Sensei! How can I not recall it? I am sorry to fail you, Sensei."

"Be gentle on yourself, my friend," said Hiroshi. "This is but the great unfolding taking place just as it should. You cannot recall it because you are not yet meant to. Trust that. Now, let it go, trust, and listen to the song of the bird."

Daichi smiled back at his teacher. As much knowledge as Daichi possessed, it was as a leaf in the great forest compared to the simple wisdom of Hiroshi. Then, he left his mind to babble on and joined Hiroshi in listening to the song of the bird as he felt his breath come in and go out.

Sometime later, Aiko joined both men carrying lunch on a tray. It was a simple lunch of rice and fresh vegetables from the garden. As simple as it was, the food tasted wonderful.

"Aiko your food is the most delicious food I have ever tasted, and do you know why?" said Hiroshi, as he smiled at Aiko.

Aiko smiled and looked down shyly as she shook her head.

"Because," continued Hiroshi, "it is made with such love, and that love fills every morsel."

"Hai!" said Daichi in loud agreement, his heart swelling as he looked at his beautiful wife.

Aiko laughed a laugh so delicate and lovely that it matched the beauty of the bird's song.

"It is easy when I make it for two such magnificent men."

After lunch, Hiroshi bid Daichi and Aiko farewell. Daichi said he would keep thinking about the ancient text, and if he remembered it, he would tell Hiroshi immediately. He also said that once this busy time in the fields was done, he would be back to his training at the dojo in earnest.

Hiroshi told Daichi to take his time.

"I think you are now more than half my age, Daichi. As you approach middle age, you need to take more care of your body!" he joked as he walked back out of the gate and onto the road.

"Go carefully, Sensei! I expect you to still be teaching me when I am twice my age!" said Daichi, laughing as he spoke.

Hiroshi gave a final wave and then strode out through the village. He had only gone a few paces, when he sensed something malevolent coming towards him. In the distance, he saw three figures entering the far end of the village. He saw that they had two swords at theirs sides, which meant that they could only be samurai. However these were no ordinary samurai. They were ronin. Samurai are known as samurai only when they are in the service of a daimyo. When samurai are no longer in service, then they become known as ronin. Ronin are samurai without purpose. Powerful men who are without purpose are liable to become destructive. It was for this very reason that Hiroshi felt the malevolence from these three men, men who were without purpose. He felt great compassion for them but knew that compassion would not head off conflict. If they encountered him, they would attack him. They were descending into Darkness, and his light would fill them with such hatred they would be bound to attack.

Hiroshi quickly slipped between two houses and made his way out of the village between the paddy fields. The villagers were surprised to see him coming that way, but it was Hiroshi, so they expected to be surprised by his strange antics. They greeted him with kindness and watched as he strode quickly back onto a little path that ran parallel to the road that the ronin had come in on. Before long, Hiroshi rejoined the path that lead up past his house. Though the gradient steepened, his pace never relented as he strode quickly home. He paused only once on his journey and that was on the little bridge once again. He absorbed the view, the beauty and the peacefulness that lay spread out before him. The innocence of the farmers in the fields, the fishermen in their boats and the children playing in the groves of trees, all made his heart sing. This was what he protected. This was his purpose. A purpose that gave him enormous strength and that continued to toughen his resolve as each year passed. Come what may, he would give himself completely to the protection of them all.

CHAPTER 23

The First Class

Whether due to his youth or Kensho's special tea and balm, Sam's recovery was incredibly quick. The bruising went down in just a few days, and the pain he felt when he moved also quickly subsided. He was back to school on Friday but was very disappointed not to see the girls on Saturday. Susie had already made arrangements for the girls to go for a hike that day. Ruth also refused to let him go to the dojo since she was worried he would do something silly and injure himself again. So, their weekly get together at the dojo would begin next Saturday. So it was Monday after school before Sam finally did make it to the dojo. He would never forget his first aikido class.

Sam arrived before any of the other students and Kensho was there at the door to welcome him. He showed Sam upstairs to the changing room and presented Sam with a brand new training uniform that was called a 'gi' in Japanese. Kensho told Sam to put it on and then come back downstairs to find him. When Kensho left Sam looked more carefully at his gi. The top was like a large, heavy white shirt but without any buttons. Instead the right side of the shirt overlapped the left side at the front and then Sam had to tie a knot using the ties at the side to keep it from flapping open. The trousers were also white and quite short with a tie at the front to keep them tight around Sam's hips.

Once he'd changed, Sam rather self-consciously came down the stairs and looked for Kensho. There was no sign of him so he stood by the mat for a while not sure what to do. Then he remembered what he had seen the other students do when he had first visited. So he stepped onto the mat, knelt down and bowed towards the picture of O'Sensei, hoping he was doing it the same way he had seen the students perform the bow. Just as he began to do some warm ups,

Kensho reappeared from the back of the dojo, smiling broadly at Sam.

"Excellent! Get straight into it and don't feel hesitant. This class will be a challenge but just do you best."

Then Kensho handed Sam a very long white belt. It was cotton, about three centimetres wide and quite stiff. Kensho showed him how to wrap it around his waist twice and then tie a knot at the front.

"There," said Kensho. "Now you have your belt. You will keep this same belt for the rest of your life. Take care of it, as it will be your companion on this aikido journey, but never wash it!"

"Why shouldn't I wash it?" asked Sam, looking puzzled.

"I'm sure you have heard of martial artists being given a black belt when they have been tested and attained a certain standard," said Kensho. "This is not how it used to be. A black belt signified an accomplished martial artist simply because it indicated many years of training. The belt was actually a white belt that had turned black through many years of handling without being washed. In modern days people want lots of different coloured belts to motivate them to keep training: yellow belt after so many months, orange after so many more. Everyone wants quick results or they get bored. This is not the traditional way."

"Yes Sensei," said Sam, looking down at his brand new white belt and wondering how many years he would have to tie it before it even became a little grey, let alone black.

Sam's first aikido class was far, far harder than he had expected. After warming up with the other students, he had to do his first ukemi, a technique that teaches you how to roll safely out of a throw. Seeing others do it, Sam thought it looked easy. However, when Sam tried to roll it felt as though he was a square. He smashed his head, then his shoulder and then his lower back, ending up in a heap on the floor.

Then things got worse. In aikido, one trains with a partner, and each takes turns at being the attacker and the defender. Sam would watch Kensho demonstrate the technique, and then he would stand up with his partner and try to copy it. He was hopeless. He had his left foot forward when it should have been his right. He grabbed with his right hand, when it should have been his left. He turned the wrong way, and he stepped with the wrong foot. He punched with the wrong fist too inaccurately and too weakly. If it was possible to do it wrong, then he did.

By the end of the class, he was exhausted and bruised and felt utterly useless at aikido. He'd never felt as much of a fool in all his life. Every sport he had ever tried, he had just picked up immediately. But this was completely different somehow. It looked so incredibly simple and completely effortless when Kensho did it. But even when Sam did get his hands and feet in the right places, he still couldn't get the techniques to flow. He kept colliding with his attacker and ended up trying to use all his strength to get his attacker to go where he wanted them to go. He was embarrassed and ashamed.

To Sam's relief, the other students, whether beginners or advanced, were very friendly and very patient. When Kensho came over, he was stern, but he never got angry. He kept telling the students to "relax, relax, relax". He said that they had to sense the ki in the attacker. If they waited until they saw their attacker begin the attack, it was too late. They must learn to sense the attack at the moment the attacker decides to commit. Sam had a vague idea of what Sensei meant, but the harder he tried to sense the attack the slower he reacted.

It would have been so very easy for Sam to give up there and then. Later, he saw many people do just that. They would come to one or two classes and then give up and never be seen again. But Sam's passion never waned even if his frustration was deep. The worse he did, the more determined he became to improve. So, improve he did. Each class that week, his ukemi got a little better. He began to roll a little bit more like a ball than a cube. He got a little less confused as to how he was to stand and move. It still felt ridiculously hard, but not quite impossible.

CHAPTER 24

The Sword that Kills

All week Sam looked forward to Saturday. When it finally arrived, Kensho drove by Sam's house and picked him up before driving to Burnaby to fetch the girls from their home. When they all arrived back at the dojo, Zoe and Sophie were very excited. Kensho told Sam to show them around, so Sam gave his sisters a tour. Then Sam got changed into his gi and with Kensho he gave the girls a demonstration of aikido. The girls were as amazed as Sam had been the first time he had seen Kensho's demonstration. Because Sam was still an absolute beginner, his attacks were slow, and Kensho was very careful with Sam. But the essence of aikido was still there for the girls to see.

Sophie could see the ki flowing around and between Kensho and Sam. She could see Sam's intention appear, like a burst of light, moments before he launched his attack. She could also see Kensho respond to Sam's ki and draw it into his own ki as he lead Sam's attack.

Sophie loved the authenticity of it. She found the normal world very difficult since people's intentions and their words rarely matched. But in this physical interaction, there were no words: just lots of amazing circles of energy as Sam's ki was drawn in and redirected by Kensho. She was also absorbed by the amazing beauty of Kensho's ki. In particular, she was in awe of the purity of the whiteness of his ki and its incredible power. She also noticed the first signs of a shift in Sam's ki. Where once it had been quite dull and grey, now it was a little whiter and a little brighter.

When they had finished the aikido demonstration, Sam knelt at the side of the mat, and Kensho fetched a metal training sword from a drawer beneath the rack of wooden sticks.

"This is called iaido. It is a martial art that uses the Japanese samurai sword. This is not a real samurai sword so it is not sharp," said Kensho.

Then Kensho began to demonstrate iaido. Though iaido didn't look as dramatic and dynamic as aikido, the girls were still impressed by it. Sophie saw the way Kensho's ki flowed into the sword, so that the sword literally became an extension of his arms. Kensho moved with incredible precision. Even the practice of putting the sword back into its sheath was done in a very specific and precise manner. While Sam sat utterly absorbed by it all, both Zoe and Sophie were unsettled by the sound of the sword slicing through the air.

After a few minutes Kensho bowed out and both he and Sam came over to where the girls were sitting. Sophie couldn't contain her excitement any longer and jumped off her chair to hug Sam.

"You were amazing, Sam!" said Sophie as she let go her embrace. "This is what you were meant to do. I can see it! You shine when you do aikido!"

"She's right, Sam," said Zoe. "You looked incredible. I loved the aikido - it looked amazing. Kensho, do you think one day I might be able to try?"

Sam looked at Zoe with a surprised expression. He never expected her to be interested.

"That would be awesome!" said Sam.

"One day, with your foster mother's approval, of course!" said Kensho. "But let's take things one step at a time. With all these changes, not least arranging this Saturday visit, we have stretched both sets of foster parents as far as they will go for now I think."

"Kensho, do you see people's energy?" asked Sophie.

"Perhaps a little, Sophie. We call people's energy ki. You see ki, don't you?"

"I've always been able to see it, though the older I get the clearer it is becoming."

Sophie was glad to have an adult to talk to who understood her.

"I find it very confusing, Kensho. I can see what people really want, but when they talk, they often say something different. It seems most people are lying, and I find that really hard."

"People can be very confusing, Sophie," said Kensho, nodding. "Sometimes they are lying. But sometimes they don't know what they really want to do. Sometimes what they say is what they think they mean. Or what they think they ought to say. So, rather than think everyone is lying, perhaps think that most people are just very confused."

As Kensho said that, he gave Sophie a reassuring smile. Sophie smiled back. She liked Kensho because she never sensed a mismatch between what he said and what he felt or intended to do.

Zoe looked at the sword in its sheath by Kensho's side.

"That sword looked very dangerous."

"And swords are very dangerous," confirmed Kensho. "Real samurai swords are very, very sharp, and they are very deadly."

"But then, why do you use them?" asked Zoe, frowning. "They seem so nasty. Would you really chop someone up with one?"

"No Zoe. Let me explain a little about the sword. You are quite right. It is a weapon that can be used to do quite dreadful things. It can kill or maim a person with great efficiency. In that respect it is 'nasty' as you say.

"However, as one trains with the sword diligently, so one improves as a person. Eventually, with long and hard training, one becomes the best person one can possibly be. This is called self-mastery. One has mastered oneself. When one masters oneself, one no longer does bad things but only does good. In this way the sword is a wonderful thing that brings good into the world. That is why there is a saying in Japan that goes:

'The sword that kills, the sword that saves.'

"The sword has the potential to do either," continued Kensho. "It can take a life or it can save a life. It saves a life by helping the person who trains with it to achieve self-mastery. That is why we train with the sword. Do you understand?"

Zoe nodded, and Kensho said, "Good! Now let us go and eat some lunch. I have prepared lots of delicious food, even ice cream! Lead the way upstairs, Sam!"

The four of them squeezed into Kensho's small kitchen where they were met by a table of interesting food to try. The girls had a taste of everything and even tried to use chopsticks but without much success. Kensho was being silly, making the girls laugh endlessly. He picked up a strawberry with his chopsticks and brought it up to his mouth before dropping it and catching it again with his chopsticks. He kept doing this while exclaiming, "It's alive! Help! I can't keep hold of it!" Sam and the girls began to laugh so much, they couldn't stop. Tears were running down their cheeks, and Sophie ended up sat on the floor because she was laughing so much.

Sam felt like he had died and gone to heaven! He couldn't remember the last time the three of them had had so much fun together: it felt like they were a little family and he wished it could go on forever.

CHAPTER 25

Everyone Struggles

Though he found the training very challenging, Sam practised diligently. He was young, fit and healthy, and so he was able to train five times a week. His attitude was always positive, and he was always smiling. The other students liked him and enjoyed training with him. After class, he would always throw himself into the cleaning of the mat and any other tasks around the dojo that Kensho would give him.

Sam discovered that in aikido, while they didn't use a real sword, they used a wooden replica made of white oak called a 'bokken'. These were on the rack that Sam had noticed the first time he entered the dojo. At first, Sam thought it was like a child's toy. But Kensho reminded the class that the bokken is a real weapon. He said that there were many stories of samurai killing their attackers, who were armed with real swords, just using a bokken. So, the students treated the bokken with the same respect one would treat a real sword.

Training with the bokken began with learning how to hold it correctly. Even something as simple as that was actually difficult. Then Sam was taught how to cut properly with the bokken. He was no longer surprised to discover that it was far more challenging than it looked. After learning how to handle the bokken, Sam trained with a partner who also had one bokken and he began to learn something called 'tachi-dori', a really challenging set of techniques to disarm an attacker who is using a bokken while Sam himself was unarmed. As he faced the attacker, Sam imagined what it would be like if this was a real attack with a real samurai sword wielded by someone highly skilled and utterly determined to take his life. He got a taste of the fear that could overwhelm you in those circumstances.

On the same rack with the bokken were the 'jo' – long wooden sticks, perhaps 1.3 metres in length, similar to a walking staff.

Kensho once again emphasised the danger of the weapon, making it clear that a firm blow to the head would be fatal. Because it was longer than the sword, it had a greater range. Also, because one could use either end of it to attack, it was more versatile. Despite these attributes, Sam still found that he preferred the bokken. His dream was to have his own samurai sword and he felt that his bokken training was preparing him for that day.

Finally, they used a wooden replica of a knife called a 'tanto'. While there was little danger of getting hurt by it, Sam still found training very difficult. It was extremely hard to evade a determined and well executed knife attack. Attacked with a tanto, Sam kept getting painful pokes in the ribs, arms or whatever bit of him didn't get out of the way. He knew if that had been a real knife, he would likely have been on the ground, bleeding to death. He was very glad the men who attacked him in the alley hadn't used knives.

Occasionally after class, Kensho would go to a nearby cafe with some students for tea and perhaps a little snack. Sam had always wanted to go along, but he felt he was too new and didn't want to be presumptuous. It was a warm evening in late August when Kensho beckoned Sam over and invited him to join them. Sam enthusiastically accepted.

The cafe was a short walk away, and the old Japanese owner knew Kensho very well. He welcomed them all in and set up tables for the five of them. The other students that came with Kensho were Jonathan, the man Sam had seen on the very first day, Tomoko, a Japanese-Canadian woman, who, Sam guessed, was about 30, and Fumi, a tiny Japanese-Canadian woman who was ten years older.

They all sat down, and Kensho indicated to Sam to sit beside him. The five of them chit-chatted about all sorts of things, not just aikido. Kensho was very interested to hear about his students' lives outside the dojo.

"So, you are almost three months into your aikido training, Sam," said Kensho. "How are you finding it?"

"I'm loving it!" replied Sam.

Suddenly he worried that Kensho might have invited him along to tell him he wasn't good enough and that he would have to leave. So he quickly continued. "Of course, I know I am hopeless and always make mistakes, and I never seem to relax, and as hard as I watch what you show us, Sensei, I never seem to be able to do it like you do it, but that doesn't mean I am not trying my very best because I certainly am, and I really, really want to keep training!"

Kensho and the other students all burst out laughing. Sam turned beetroot red thinking they were all laughing at him for being so useless.

"Sam," said Kensho, his voice soft and reassuring. "Everything you just said is exactly the same thing we all experienced when we first began and most of us still experience even in the last class we ever take."

"Sam, I have been doing aikido for eight years now and still feel hopeless sometimes," said Fumi. "I hear Sensei telling me the same things over and over again, and I think I must be the world's worse aikido student."

"I so vividly remember my first few months of training, Sam," said Jonathan. "I was forever getting everything the wrong way round. I'd watch what Sensei demonstrated, stand up and then completely forget what I had just seen. I had to look around the class at the other students and what they were doing to remind myself. I'm twelve years into my training, and I might not forget what I am shown, but now I just see even more little mistakes that I constantly make. Sensei used to come over and say, 'put your left foot forward', and I would, and then he would say, 'No, your other left foot', and I'd realise I had my right foot forward. I still look at Sensei and think that I'll never even come close to doing the aikido he does."

Sam began to laugh. He realised just how much tension and worry he had been carrying, fearing that he was the world's worst aikido student and that the whole dojo wished he was gone. At last, he was seeing that he was just experiencing the same thing every beginner experienced.

"Wow. Thank you. I've been waiting for the day Sensei kicked me out because I was so bad I was beyond even his skills to teach!"

They all laughed again.

"Sam, if I can learn aikido, then anyone can," said Kensho. "You are doing fine. Continue to train regularly and with the enthusiasm you have been showing, and you can't help but make steady progress."

As they left the cafe, the students all went their separate ways until it was just Kensho and Sam stood together in the last rays of the setting sun. Finally Sam plucked up the courage and asked Kensho a question he'd been dying to ask.

"Sensei, when might I be considered for training with a real sword? I really, really would like to start training in iaido."

"In good time, Sam, in good time."

CHAPTER 26

People's Approval

S am had given Kensho his word that he would not skip school, and he stuck to it. But he thought school was a total waste of time, apart from getting to play sports and hanging out with his friends. Well, and maybe seeing the cute girls. Not that he got anywhere with them. His clothes were all from charity shops and he knew he looked a total loser.

His best friend was Jake. Not only was Jake being fostered but he too was from England. As Jake had lived in Vancouver since he was five he had lost his accent. But he certainly didn't sound like a Canadian. Jake insisted on talking like a surfer dude from SoCal. Or at least what Jake thought a surfer dude from SoCal would sound like. Jake's dream was to move to California and surf. Not that he'd ever surfed or actually been to California. But he sure watched a lot of surfing movies and, as Jake would say, "Dude! The babes!" The upshot was that Sam had no idea what Jake's real accent was. Still, with so much in common, it was inevitable they were going to be friends.

Mostly Sam got by unnoticed but there was always one person who made his life miserable. That person was Kevin Jones. One lunch break, he came up to Sam and said: "So, I hear you've taken up dancing."

Sam looked at him confused and then responded: "You mean aikido …"

"Aikido. Dancing. Same thing," said Kevin.

Sam began to explain that aikido was a martial art, but Kevin cut in: "Aikido is dancing. It's all pretend. It's nothing like real fighting. It's not realistic. You wanna do a martial art, a real man's martial art, you do something like kickboxing. There's no dancing in kickboxing. Just kicks and punches to the face, broken ribs, broken noses. It's real fighting. Like that time you got beaten up. Remember? aikido isn't real fighting: it's dancing. You know, almost all the mixed martial arts guys have done kick-boxing. How many mixed martial artists do aikido? Zero."

Kevin held his thumb and finger together in a circle to emphasise the zero as he walked off laughing with his buddies.

Jake had been standing beside Sam and shouted after Kevin, "Dude, why are you such a downer, man?"

Then Jake turned to Sam: "Dude, don't listen to that loser. He's trying to take your mojo, dude!"

Sam nodded and said, "Yeah, what does he know anyway, right?"

But Sam was actually pretty taken aback and what Kevin said played on his mind for days. Maybe aikido wasn't realistic? Maybe it was more like dancing? But what he had seen Kensho do in the demonstration hadn't looked remotely like dancing. Still he couldn't shake what Kevin said. It wasn't helped by the fact that whenever Kevin saw him, he would grab someone nearby and imitate doing ballroom dancing with them, before laughing at Sam.

So, eventually Sam decided to mention it to Kensho after class at the cafe. When there was a lull in the conversation Sam summoned up the courage and said, "Sensei, one of the guys at school says that aikido isn't realistic and that it is just dancing and that things like kickboxing are proper martial arts. He said that is why mixed martial artists never use aikido."

Kensho laughed long and deep. "Sam, do you care what this boy thinks about you? Do you want this boy's approval?"

Sam had never really thought about it. He considered Kensho's question for a few moments before replying. "I guess so. I mean, I don't want people to think I'm stupid." Sam paused again before continuing. "I guess I want people to be impressed by what I do. So yes, I guess I do want his approval, though, I'd never thought about it that way before. Doesn't everyone want approval?"

"Yes Sam, most people do seek the approval of others. But if you care about someone's approval then that person controls you. They imprison you. Most people are living lives controlled by others. Prisoners of their parents, prisoners of their friends, prisoners of society as a whole. They don't live their own truth, they don't act from the core. Is it possible to live one's life and never care about the approval of others? Yes it is. That does not mean that one ignores the advice of others. Far from it. One listens carefully before deciding whether to heed it or not. It also does not mean that one does not act with great compassion and love. In fact, when one cares not for the approval of others, then one is truly free to act with compassion. Compassion for others and compassion for oneself."

Kensho paused to take a sip of his tea before continuing. "As for this boy's comments, they have no truth to them. No martial art as it is practised today is 'realistic'. If one wants realism, then stand unarmed before a skilled swordsman whose entire intent is to end your life. Then it will be real. Then you will be facing your own death squarely. Then it will not matter whether you have trained in aikido, kickboxing, karate, jujutsu, kung fu or whatever. Every martial art is just a different path up the same mountain, Sam. The peak of the mountain is not defeating one's external enemies. It is simply defeating the enemy that lies within oneself. It is self-mastery. The rest is nonsense."

The server came over with a fresh pot of green tea. Kensho smiled at her and said,

"Thank you Sarah. You do take such wonderful care of us. Now who would like some more tea?" Kensho topped up everyone's cup and then continued: "But what do I say all the time in our training? We must always practise with the same intensity as we would were we facing a skilled swordsman intent on killing us. We must bring this focus to our training. When you receive an attack, receive it as though the attacker wishes to end your life. Do not see Fumi or Jonathan or David. Do not see your fellow students, but rather see an attacker who is utterly focused on your death. This is the way to train. And when it is your turn to attack, then bring that intensity to your attack. Do not simply go through the motions. Do not telegraph your attack. If we train in this way, then when you stand in front of someone who truly is intent on your death, it is familiar to you. But our training is not about that moment. It is about training with such intensity. Because it is through such intense training that we move towards self-mastery.

"True aikido is true bushido. Bushido is 'Spirit of the Warrior'. The true warrior is not intent on taking life, on killing or maiming people, or on showering himself in glory. That is not the true warrior. The true warrior is intent on saving life, on protecting people. He is humble and will avoid fighting at all costs. When he must fight, he does so gravely, and he does so while doing all that he can to protect his attacker. This was the gift that O'Sensei gave us through aikido. A way to protect life. He gave us true bushido. He gave us the Art of Peace."

Sam felt like a fool. He realised how little he knew and understood, and he felt embarrassed.

Kensho then told him and the rest of the students a story about O'Sensei. "I know that my senior students have heard this story many times, but it is one we should always keep in mind for it is the heart of aikido. O'Sensei was famous throughout Japan as a great martial artist and swordsman. One day, a British naval officer challenged him to a duel using bokken. The naval officer was a very gifted swordsman and felt sure he would beat this tiny Japanese man. But O'Sensei knew he would defeat the naval officer and did not want to fight him and risk injuring or even killing him. The naval officer decided to force O'Sensei to fight him by attacking him anyway. O'Sensei did not use his bokken. Instead, each time the officer attacked, O'Sensei simply evaded the cuts and thrusts. In the end, the officer, exhausted, simply gave up. And so it was that O'Sensei saw how it was possible to defeat an enemy without ever fighting him.

"It was one of his great moments of enlightenment that eventually lead to the creation of aikido.

"The true master does not fight. He refuses to fight unless his life is truly in danger. This is not just the aikido way. This is the way of all great masters. In Okinawa, there is Shorin-ryu karate. It was created by the great Master Chosin Chibana, who lived during the same period as O'Sensei. He became very famous in Okinawa as a great martial artist. One day, he was set upon by a bunch of thugs who wanted to become famous for defeating this great master. They began hitting and kicking him, but he never fought back. They beat him up very badly, but still he refused to fight them because he knew that his karate blows would cause serious injury or even death. Eventually, the thugs stopped beating him and apologised. They realised they were in the presence of a great master. When Master Chibana was asked why he never fought back, he said it was because his life had never been in danger. That is self-mastery. That is true courage. That is true bushido.

"So Sam, while I have immense respect for the hours of training and the physical skills of those who would fight in competitions, I am afraid that they are very, very far from true bushido, from the Spirit of the Warrior. They may be very skilled, but their spirit shares nothing with true bushido. They are caught up in their own egos. They teach the world violence, but they teach nothing of the true warrior spirit. Masters Chibana and O'Sensei are true bushido."

Sam left the cafe that evening with a very heavy heart. He felt like he was with the MMA guys - miles from true bushido. He couldn't imagine standing there and letting some thugs beat him up if he had the skills to take them out. The satisfaction he would feel from laying out a bunch of thugs was immense. If he let them beat him up, he'd feel like a total loser. What would Kevin Jones say then? Why was he learning aikido anyway if it wasn't to protect himself? The samurai warriors of old Japan fought. The most famous samurai warrior of all, Miyamoto Musashi, killed 60 men in duels throughout his life and had had his first duel and killed his opponent when he was only 13 years old. He didn't understand how not fighting was the Way of the Warrior. Warriors fought. That was what made them warriors, wasn't it? It made no sense to him.

However what occupied his mind for days to come was what Kensho had said about seeking the approval of others. Was he really a prisoner? How could he live life and not care about people's approval? It seemed impossible to him.

CHAPTER 27

It is Time

Though he hid it, Kensho watched Sam very carefully. Sam's mettle was being tested, and Kensho wanted to see how Sam would respond. Finally, just as early spring was bringing the first cherry blossoms to line the streets of Vancouver, Kensho felt it was time to talk to Hiroshi about the next step. Although Sam might not have felt he had a natural aptitude to aikido, his ability was coming on in leaps and bounds. Even more important than that was his attitude. Kensho saw the struggles Sam was having: the doubts, the confusion, the sense that a martial art should be all about defeating others and basking in glory. He understood those struggles as he had had them when he was Sam's age. It was the overcoming of these struggles that was the true training that Sam was undertaking, and he was doing so with total commitment and trust. Kensho was also well aware that Sam was frequently asking to train with the samurai sword.

Kensho visited his master regularly, though he would time his visits carefully so that his students would not notice his absence. His students knew not to enter his quarters unless Kensho specifically invited them. Travelling to 16th-century Japan was no ordinary matter and required extraordinary help.

That help was the special powers of Kensho's samurai sword. Not only did it enable Kensho to make this amazing journey, but it also enabled him to stay in 16th-century Japan for a long time without raising suspicion. Somehow, it seemed like time would pass at a slower pace while he was away. So, if he spent two hours with Hiroshi, it seemed he was only gone from his dojo in Vancouver for fifteen minutes. This allowed Kensho to spend a lot of time with Hiroshi with no one noticing he was gone. If Hiroshi visited Kensho (though he rarely did), the same would be true for Hiroshi - two hours with Kensho would only seem like 15 minutes back at the old farmhouse.

After the evening's class had finished, Kensho said goodbye to his students and then went up to his office. He stood quietly for a moment, listening to the sounds in the dojo, before sliding the hidden door open and climbing the secret staircase. Once again, he took the special sword from the cabinet before moving in shikko over to the altar to meditate. It was not long before the familiar humming sound began to grow louder, culminating in Kensho's disappearance.

When Kensho appeared at Hiroshi's house, he went out into the garden and saw Hiroshi up at the woodshed.

Because it was early afternoon, Hiroshi would not be teaching in his dojo for another few hours, so Kensho knew they had time to talk. It was March, and winter in this region of Japan was beginning to give way to spring. As Kensho made his way up the narrow path to the woodshed, he noticed the first green shoots had begun to appear in the garden. Hiroshi was organising the logs and the kindling. It took a lot of wood to keep the house from becoming icy cold over winter, and the woodshed would soon need replenishing. Despite the thick thatched roof, there were still the thin doors and the uninsulated floor that drew the cold deep into the house. The little fire did its best, but it was no match for winter's icy bite.

"Kensho!" called Hiroshi, without looking up.

Every living thing has an energy field around it. Typically people's energy fields only extend a foot or so away from their body. But through his years of training, Hiroshi's energy field stretched out vastly further. Thus he could sense things far beyond what he could hear, smell, feel or even see.

Hiroshi could also sense people's emotions, intentions and, to a certain extent, their thoughts. This was especially true with Kensho, whom he had trained for over 40 years.

"So, you think it is time, Kensho?" Hiroshi said as Kensho drew near.

"I do," replied Kensho.

"Very well," said Hiroshi. "I sense that it is time also. He has faced the challenges of his training as well as a young Kensho did. Perhaps even better!" laughed Hiroshi.

"He has done very well, Sensei, but you and I both know this is just the beginning, and what lies before him is far more difficult," said Kensho.

"You are right, Kensho," said Hiroshi. "But let us not forget how well he came through his close encounter with death. This boy has shown a rare strength of character. Now, let us drink tea and warm up!"

The pair walked back down the steep path to the house. Kensho, carrying as much wood as he could, observed that the air was still, and their breath hung in a long cloud lit by the low, pale sun. Once inside the house, Kensho stoked the fire and got the kettle boiling. He made them both tea, and they sat together beside the fire holding their cups in their hands to extract the warmth.

"So, he has been consistent in his request for iaido training?" asked Hiroshi.

"Yes, Sensei. From the very beginning, it has been something he has been determined to do. When do you think he should come?"

Hiroshi sat quietly for a while before saying, "In a week. I will tell my students that we will stop training for two weeks. They will be surprised, but it is good to keep them on their toes anyway."

"Very well," said Kensho. "I have Sam's foster parents' agreement that he can go away for a weekend out into the forest as part of his training. So that will allow him to stay for just over two weeks with you, Sensei."

"That will be ample time."

The following evening, once Sam had finished cleaning the dojo mat, Kensho took him to one side. He told him that they would be going into the forest for a weekend of intense practice. He said that he had the agreement of Sam's foster parents and gave Sam a list of things he would need for the trip. He also told him not to mention the training trip to anyone other than his sisters and foster-parents.

The following Saturday, Sam told Zoe and Sophie that he would be away the next weekend with Kensho training in the forest. Sophie nodded as if she already knew.

"It will be very hard Sam, but trust him," she said.

Sam looked at Sophie and then at Zoe with a puzzled look. Zoe nodded. Then he asked,

"What do you mean, Soph?"

"It will be very hard, but trust him. I was told to tell you this, Sam. I know that you will struggle and even despair. Don't worry. Trust him."

Sam knew Sophie well enough to listen to what she said.

"Ok, Soph. I hear you. I will trust him."

"Everything will turn out fine, Sam," said Zoe.

"What do you two know?" asked Sam.

"We don't know any more than that. But we do know that you must trust him," said Sophie.

"Trust who? Do you mean Kensho?" asked Sam.

"You will know," said Zoe.

"Okay you two," said Sam, nodding. "I will trust him, whoever he is."

CHAPTER 28

The First Journey

Kensho had told Sam they would be leaving for the forest on Friday afternoon. Sam didn't know where they were going, but he was excited and a little nervous. He knew that this was going to be an intense time of training because Kensho had warned him to prepare.

So, it was straight after school that afternoon that Kensho invited Sam up to his quarters to help him to prepare. Once upstairs, Kensho directed Sam into his office. Sam noticed that Kensho had a more serious air about him than usual. Kensho slid the door to the office closed behind him and sat down at his desk. He indicated to Sam to sit down on the other chair. Sam took a pile of papers off the chair and placed them on the floor before sitting down. Kensho looked at Sam for some time before he finally began.

"Sam. It was no accident that we met and that you became my student. Your arrival at the dojo has been long foretold. For well over a thousand years, our meeting has been foreseen. The journey that you and I are about to take is one that you will find very difficult in many different ways. It will challenge much that you believe. It will also force you to challenge much that you think you know about the world and about yourself. There will be times when you will feel utterly forsaken. I know because I experienced those feelings too as a young student. I ask only one thing of you, Sam. I simply ask that you trust me. Will you do that?"

Sam was scared. The tone of Kensho's voice and his demeanour were quite unlike anything Sam had seen before from Kensho. He knew that this was something very serious, and he knew that, should he agree to trust Kensho, he would be setting something in motion far greater than anything he had experienced before. He knew instinctively that once set in motion, whatever it was could never be stopped. Quite how he knew, he wasn't sure. He just did. There would be no going back from this moment.

Sophie's voice echoed in his mind, "Trust him." So, Sam did. He looked Kensho in the eyes and said, "I trust you, Sensei."

Kensho looked at Sam. He remembered his own innocence as he had sat opposite Hiroshi all those years before. He felt a tinge of sadness as he thought of how this decision had now changed Sam's life irrevocably. Yet, he knew that this was Sam's purpose, a path that he had to walk.

"Then, let us begin. Follow me," said Kensho, smiling softly.

Kensho stood up and went over to a panel in the wall and, to Sam's astonishment, gently slid it open to reveal a staircase. Kensho gestured for Sam to go in. As Sam began to climb the staircase, Kensho stepped in behind him and slid the door shut.

"Mind your head when you enter the room above, Sam. Stay in shikko," said Kensho.

Sam had been practicing shikko in aikido, so he knew what it was, and he was reasonably proficient at it. He pushed the door at the top of the stairs up and open, before pausing briefly to look around. He saw a simple wooden cabinet in the middle of the room and an altar at the far end. He then climbed the last few steps and moved to the side of the door to allow Kensho to enter the room.

Kensho shut the door and went over to the cabinet. He unlocked it, opened the drawer and unwrapped the sword. After sliding the sword through his belt and locking the cabinet again, he said to Sam,

"Follow me over to the altar, Sam, and kneel beside me on my right-hand side, please."

Sam did as Kensho said.

"Sam, I would like you to close your eyes and begin to meditate. Just focus completely on your breathing. In a little while, you will begin to hear a sound, a hum. Notice it but just keep focusing on your breathing."

"Yes, Sensei."

So the two of them sat in seiza side by side and began to meditate. Sam focused on his breathing, following his breath in and following it out. He began to hear the hum, which he assumed was being made by Kensho, and he continued to focus on his breath.

Sam felt himself change a little. He felt as though he was becoming lighter, almost as if his physical being was dropping away. He tried not to get caught up in the thoughts his mind was raising. The thought occurred to him: Perhaps this is enlightenment? But he let the thought pass and returned to his breathing. Another thought: Am I falling asleep? But again he dismissed it and focused on his breathing.

Then Sam found himself flying through a dark sky. That was the best way he could describe the sensation he felt. He was weightless, and images began to appear in his mind in a constant stream. The images were grey. It was as if he was seeing them in the last light of dusk when all colour has been drained from them. He saw the outline of mountains. He saw islands in a sea. He saw an eagle, a bear and then a hawk. Then fear enveloped him. Suddenly, he saw a fierce and terrifying face emerging out of the darkness. As it drew closer he realised that it was a samurai warrior wearing a red mask that covered his face from just below his eyes down to his chin. He also wore a helmet with what appeared to be golden metal horns. As the samurai continued to emerge from the darkness Sam could see his whole body. He wore full samurai armour that was red with gold stitching and he had two swords by his side. Drawing ever closer, the samurai's right hand began to stretch out towards Sam, grasping at him, overwhelming him with the malice that poured forth.

Just as it seemed certain the samurai's hand would reach him, Sam was jolted out of his meditation and opened his eyes wide. He felt just as he did when he awoke from nightmares. That sense of disorientation and the brief panic as his mind tries to work out what is real and what was the nightmare. He assumed that he had briefly fallen asleep while meditating and had somehow fallen straight into that nightmare. He looked at the altar in front of him, his mind searching for familiar sights to confirm he was back to reality. But though there was an altar, it looked different to the one he had been in front of when last he closed his eyes. He knew he should keep meditating as Kensho had told him to, but he couldn't help but look around to confirm he was in the low room above Kensho's office. However, the more he looked, the stranger things became. The room was totally different. He turned his head to his right, and panic and confusion began to grip him. Sam's mind was rejecting what he was seeing because it couldn't make sense of it. Was he still dreaming? He must be dreaming, his mind concluded, as it was the only answer that made any kind of sense.

Suddenly, Sam felt a hand take hold of his left shoulder. He wheeled around expecting to see the malice-filled face of the man who had been trying to grab him. Instead, he saw the kind face of Kensho.

"It is okay, Sam. I am here with you. Remember to trust me. Everything is okay. It will just be a little confusing and overwhelming at first. That is okay. Now, let us stand up."

Kensho helped Sam up. Sam felt very unsteady on his feet. His mind was whirring at an incredible pace trying to grasp what had happened and where he was. He was looking around a poorly lit room made from large timbers. It had a wooden floor with a fireplace in the floor at the other end from where they stood. Sam became aware that it was cold.

"Did I fall asleep, Sensei? Where are we? I don't understand!"

Sam felt panic building in him now, and he took a deep breath.

Kensho took Sam by the shoulders and looked into his eyes.

"Sam, everything is okay. We took a journey when we meditated. This is the house of my master Hiroshi Nagato Sensei. I understand how unsettling this is for you, Sam. It was unsettling for me the first few times I took the journey too. But come, sit with me by the fire and let me make some tea. Then I will tell you all about the journey we just took, where we are and what it all means. Trust me."

Sam nodded. Kensho, with his hand still on Sam's left shoulder, turned him and guided him over to the fireplace.

"Sit down on that mat there, and I will put the kettle on," said Kensho.

Sam watched him go to the side of the room, where there was something like a small kitchen. Kensho poured water from a jug into a large, black kettle and returned to hang the kettle over the fire for the water to boil. Then, he sat down beside Sam and grasped Sam's right shoulder firmly.

"Sit quietly and observe your thoughts, Sam," whispered Kensho. "Become aware of the turmoil in your mind, the fear that is in you. Observe them but let them be."

CHAPTER 29

The Divine Swords

They sat quietly together. Sam stared into the embers and tried to do as Kensho asked. But he couldn't help but get caught up in his thoughts. He had to figure out what had happened. Had he passed out at the dojo, and then Kensho driven him out to the forest? Was this a house that Kensho had built out in the wilderness? It certainly reminded him of a Japanese house from hundreds of years ago. He looked around and saw no lights hanging from the ceiling or on the walls. He saw what looked like an old oil lamp on a table. Well, that must be it, thought Sam. They must be out at the cabin that Kensho had built in the forest, and Kensho's master must live here. But how come he had never mentioned his master before? And how had he got here?

The kettle began to boil, and Kensho got up and prepared the tea. Once they were both sat down again, tea cups in hand, Kensho began to explain.

"As I said, we are in the home of my master Hiroshi Nagato. He has been my master since I was 12 years old, and he is a very wise man. Nagato Sensei is one of a long line of masters who are known as The Guardians of the Osawa Scrolls. The Guardians have been protecting a secret for nearly 1,400 years. The importance of this secret cannot be overestimated. It is a secret that protects the world from a danger beyond imagination. For you to understand the danger, I must tell you the story of how it all began all those years ago.

"Swords have existed in Japan for thousands of years. It is thought that the first Japanese swordsmiths learnt their skills from China. So, Japanese swords were like Chinese swords with a cutting edge on both sides. However they were poor quality and easily broken in battle.

"History records that the first samurai sword, as we know it, was forged by Amakuni Yasutsuna in 700AD. He was swordsmith to the Emperor of Japan. He was forging his swords using the methods learnt from China. However, he was deeply ashamed when he saw the Emperor's soldiers returning from battle with so many broken swords. Amakuni and his son Amakura resolved to forge a sword that would never break in battle. They locked themselves in the forge and prayed for divine guidance. They prayed for six days, never once leaving the forge. On the seventh day, the guidance they sought came to each of them in a dream, and together they forged the first single-edged, curve-bladed samurai sword."

Kensho paused to stoke the fire, and then continued, "But history is wrong, Sam. The first and finest samurai swords ever made were forged one hundred years earlier by the greatest swordsmith ever to have lived, Master Mitsunari Osawa. Master Osawa was swordsmith to a daimyo, or Lord as you would say, who ruled a region of southern Japan. Master Osawa was a very spiritual man, and he was a very good man. He devoted his life to forging swords and had begun learning his skill from his father when he was only eight years old.

"His father had travelled to China, when Master Osawa was a young man, seeking to learn the skills of sword making. When he returned to Japan, he not only brought back those sword-making skills, but he also brought the Tao Te Ching. It greatly influenced both his father and later, Master Osawa himself. As you know, it emphasises harmonising with the way things are, not thinking too much, and allowing one's actions to simply arise from within oneself."

As he said that, Kensho tapped his hand against his chest as if pointing to where these actions arise from. Sam shifted his weight as his legs were beginning to hurt from sitting in seiza all this time.

"It's okay if you sit cross-legged, Sam," said Kensho, "I want you to be comfortable because what I am telling you is very important, so you need to listen well."

Sam shifted to sit cross-legged, and Kensho continued. "The Tao

Te Ching was what helped Master Osawa to become the greatest swordsmith Japan has ever known. As he sought to improve his swords, he didn't spend time thinking and analysing. Rather, he sought to harmonise with the metal, the forging process and with the sword. Many, many of the swords he made could be described as failures. Some were too brittle and broke easily. Others were too soft and would go blunt and lose their edge too quickly. But each failure taught Master Osawa an important lesson, and he never became discouraged or gave up.

"As well as studying the Tao Te Ching, he would also practice Zen Buddhism and Shinto. During his father's travels in the mountains of China he had encountered Dazu Huike, the 2nd patriarch of Zen Buddhism. Huike was a master of the Tao as well as of Zen Buddhism. During the year that Master Osawa's father spent with Huike he learned much. Shinto is a type of religion in Japan that believes in living in harmony with nature, and that nature and all living things are sacred and filled with the divine spirit. Shinto emphasises 'misogi' or ritual purification. Master Osawa knew his spirit must be pure if he was to be allowed to forge the sword he sought. So he would practice lots of purification rituals. Waterfalls are thought to be especially sacred. So, one of the rituals he would practice daily was standing under an ice cold waterfall and chanting purifying mantras for long periods of time. This, he believed, would both purify his spirit and strengthen his resolve.

"Misogi lead him to realise that, just as he himself must be pure, so the steel he used must be pure. If he started with steel that was full of impurities it would weaken the sword no matter how well he tried to make it. So he heated the steel and repeatedly hammered it and folded it to remove any remaining impurities. This was like misogi for the steel.

"Now he had the purist steel. His next challenge was to make a sword that was flexible so that it would not break, but also incredibly hard so it would not go blunt. At first this seemed impossible to achieve. But Master Osawa learnt the techniques necessary. He combined two separate parts of the blade. The core of the blade was made from softer, more flexible steel. This was inserted into the outer part of the blade that was very hard. This all took place while the metal was red hot. Once combined, he would then plunge the blade into cold water and the two pieces of metal became one. Finally he sharpened and polished the swords until he held in his hand the finest samurai swords ever made. Each sword took him four months to make.

"When a master swordsmith forges a sword, his spirit flows into the sword. Master Osawa's spirit became so pure that the swords he began to forge not only contained his spirit but also the divine spirit that flowed through him and into the swords. Thus, the swords became know as the 'Divine Swords', and they had powers well beyond that of a normal sword."

Kensho took a deep breath before concluding the most important part of his story. "Master Osawa realised the danger of these swords falling into the wrong hands. Master Osawa knew that his daimyo, Yoshio Tatsuya, was an evil man and he was determined not to let Tatsuya get the swords. So he hid them and made no mention of the work he had been doing, and he continued to produce the old, inferior swords for Tatsuya. But Tatsuya had been spying on Master Osawa and knew that he had made some special swords. Tatsuya was a very ambitious man who craved power. He wished to be the ruler of Japan, and then to spread the empire beyond the islands of Japan, defeating neighbouring countries. He had murdered his older brother in order to become daimyo and take power over the region. He knew these swords would help him to achieve his ambition.

"So, he came to see Master Osawa and demanded that he give the swords to him. Master Osawa refused to yield. Tatsuya became furious and drew his sword to strike down Master Osawa."

As Kensho said that, the fire cracked loudly and sparks spiralled up towards the hole in the roof. Pausing only briefly, he continued,

"But Master Osawa read his intentions, and before Tatsuya had fully drawn his blade, he used one of the Divine Swords to banish him. Then, Master Osawa gathered the rest of the Divine Swords and left.

"He travelled deep into the mountains and found refuge near a Buddhist temple. While there, he hid one of the Divine Swords. He then continued to travel throughout Japan, hiding the rest of the Divine Swords and writing the Osawa Scrolls, which detailed how he made the swords and where they were hidden. Though he had banished Tatsuya, he knew that one day he might return. So, before he died, he chose two men who were also of pure spirit to continue to be Guardians of the Osawa Scrolls and to be on guard for Tatsuya's return. Since that time, there have been Guardians continuously. Master Hiroshi is a Guardian. I am a Guardian. Now you too will begin your training to become a Guardian of the Osawa Scrolls."

As Kensho had predicted, Sam was utterly overwhelmed. An hour ago, he had been preparing to head out for a weekend with Kensho into the North Shore Mountains for some intense aikido training. Now, he was, well he didn't know where. He was being told about 'divine swords' with incredible powers, evil daimyos and ancient secret scrolls of which he was to become a guardian.

Then Hiroshi entered.

CHAPTER 30

Meeting Hiroshi

Upon seeing his master enter, Kensho immediately stood up."Hello, Sensei," he said, and bowed deeply. Sam wasn't quite sure what he should do but decided to follow suit. He stood up as quickly as his stiff legs would allow him and also bowed deeply.

"Kensho, it is good to see you. I see you have brought Sam with you."

"Hai!" replied Kensho loudly before introducing them. "Sensei, this is Sam Stone. Sam, please meet Hiroshi Nagato Sensei, The Great Guardian of the Osawa Scrolls, and my master."

Sam bowed again, and then Hiroshi walked up to Sam and stood before him. Sam was a little taller than Hiroshi, so he looked down slightly as their eyes met. Hiroshi's brown eyes were the most incredible Sam had ever seen. They were intense like Kensho's, but the light that burned behind them was even brighter and more powerful. Sam felt as if Hiroshi was looking straight through him, and after a few seconds, he had to break his gaze.

"Welcome to my humble home, Sam," said Hiroshi in a soft and kind voice. "I do hope that you are not feeling too confused by these events that have unfolded for you. No doubt, Kensho has been explaining a little to you."

Sam didn't dare to speak but nodded, and Kensho said, "I have told Sam about Master Osawa and the Divine Swords, and he now knows that he is to be trained as a Guardian."

"Very good," said Hiroshi as he invited them both to sit down. Sam decided to sit in seiza in the presence of Hiroshi.

"Would you like some tea, Sensei?" asked Kensho.

"Yes, thank you, Kensho," said Hiroshi. "The air still has the last of winter's chill, and my old bones feel as frozen as the bamboo."

Kensho busied himself by tending to the fire. He then got the kettle going before selecting some ingredients and beginning to prepare some soup.

"I can see you have lots of questions. Perhaps you would like to ask some of them, and I will do my best to answer," said Hiroshi to Sam.

Sam was a little awestruck and also a little scared of Hiroshi. Much like Kensho, he had a quiet power about him. However, Hiroshi's power felt more ancient, timeless even, yet simultaneously overflowing with vitality. Sam struggled to understand precisely what he felt but whatever it was, it made him feel very small and insignificant.

As Sam looked at him, he felt as though he was looking at the universe itself. He took a deep breath and asked, "Where am I?"

"That's easy!" replied Hiroshi. "You are in my home! But where is my home, you wonder. Well, you are in the Kyoto region of Japan on the shores of Lake Biwa. A long way from home, I know. You are also a long time from home, for the year here is 1537." Hiroshi's warm smile was full of such compassion, the like of which Sam had never felt before. Still Sam's mind was refusing to comprehend what he had just heard. He shook his head as he tried to grasp this incredible information, but he could not.

"Well, how did I get here?"

"Ah!" said Hiroshi. "This is where it becomes interesting!"

Sam thought that things were quite interesting enough actually and didn't want things to get any more interesting. But more interesting they got.

"Kensho explained that we are Guardians of the Osawa Scrolls. Well, as Guardians, we take care of the Divine Swords. Did you know that these swords have special powers?"

Sam nodded but said, "I don't know what those special powers are though."

"Yes, you do!" insisted Hiroshi. "You are in Japan, in 1537! That is one of their special powers. That is how you came to be here,

Sam. Kensho brought you here with the power of one of the Divine Swords."

Sam thought his mind was going to tear itself apart. He just couldn't grasp what was being said to him. He suddenly jumped up and ran to the door. He slid it open and looked outside. The garden sloped steeply up the mountain, and as Sam looked up, he saw the forest behind. But it wasn't a forest of Douglas and Cedar trees he was familiar with on the mountains at home. This forest was a mixture of evergreen and deciduous trees, their leafless branches looking stark against the frosted ground lit by the late afternoon sun. As he scanned the forest he also noticed a grove of tall bamboo, just inside its edge.

He ran out and around the side of the house and stopped. Before him lay a valley and a huge lake stretching far into the distance, cradled by mountains all around its edge. This looked like nothing he had seen before. It certainly didn't look like the North Shore Mountains or anywhere else he had seen in British Columbia. He could see smoke rising from all the little houses in the valley. He couldn't see any roads, street lights or cars, just small tracks. He couldn't see any electricity lines or telegraph poles.

Kensho came up behind Sam and, once again, put his hand on Sam's shoulder. Sam looked at him with pleading eyes as if hoping Kensho would come up with some explanation his mind could cope with. But Kensho simply said, "Isn't Lake Biwa beautiful? Come, let us go back inside."

Sam sat back down beside the fire. He felt exhausted, and he began to shiver, more from the shock of it all than the chill air. Kensho ladled some vegetable soup from the big iron bowl above the fire into a small wooden bowl and handed it to Sam along with a little wooden spoon. Sam gratefully took the soup and began to eat.

When Sam had finished, Hiroshi came and sat beside him to show him the sword that was tucked through his belt.

"This is one of the Divine Swords. You will be training to become a

Guardian of this and the other swords. Would you like to take a close look?" asked Hiroshi.

Sam nodded and Hiroshi slid the sword, still sheathed, out of his belt and held it before Sam. Sam thought it didn't look very special, but it certainly looked beautiful. The sheath was a shiny dark grey, verging on black, and was quite plain-looking. It had no markings, no designs and nothing elaborate or ostentatious like jewels or gold leaf. It was really quite unremarkable.

Then Hiroshi slowly drew the sword. As he did so, Sam began to feel a power emanate from it. It was very hard to describe, but Sam felt it moving through his whole being. It was like a vibration in response to which his cells, his muscles, his bones, even his own ki, began to vibrate. It reminded him somehow of the low hum he had heard when Kensho and he had begun to meditate.

Hiroshi drew the sword completely and, laying it across his hands, held it up so Sam could look at it closely. Sam noticed something else odd about the sword. Again, he struggled to grasp exactly what it was, but there was some kind of a light or a glow - something almost ethereal about the sword. He wasn't sure if he was really seeing it or if he was imagining it. If he tried to look at the glow, it wasn't there. But if he looked directly at the sword's blade, he would see the glow surrounding the blade in his peripheral vision. Or so it seemed.

The sword was, thought Sam, the most beautiful thing he had ever seen. Like the sheath, the sword had no ornate design. Were it not for the light and the vibration, it would seem ordinary. He studied the curve of the blade. The top of it was thick and completely blunt, like the backbone of the blade. From there, it tapered towards the cutting edge of the blade. As it tapered, he could see a thin wave-like line that ran from the hilt all the way to the tip. It seemed to mark the transition from one type of steel to another. It was perfectly polished and shiny, with not one mark or blemish along the entire sword's length. Sam very much wanted to hold the sword and to feel its weight in his hands. He had dreamed for so long now of wielding a real samurai sword. But he sensed that to ask to hold this one was inappropriate, and so he just studied it as Hiroshi held it.

"It is a simple sword. Simplicity creates purity. Purity holds the Divine Spirit. Divine Spirit completes all things," said Hiroshi.

Then Hiroshi slid the sword back into its sheath and then slid the sheath back through his belt. "Kensho," he said, "I will leave you two to talk. There is much still for you to share with Sam."

Hai!" said Kensho loudly, and bowed to Hiroshi. Once again Sam jumped up and bowed to Hiroshi as Kensho did.

Then Hiroshi disappeared, presumably returning to wherever he had come from.

CHAPTER 31

Tatsuya's Spirit Grows

"**H**ow are you feeling, Sam?" asked Kensho, as he filled their cups with some more tea. Sam took a deep breath. Focusing on the sword seemed to have helped him re-centre himself. Or, he wondered, if perhaps the sword itself had done that. Perhaps that was why Hiroshi had shown it to him, knowing that it would help him. Whatever the reason, he felt much better.

"I feel a great deal more settled, thank you, Sensei," he replied. "Sensei, I wonder if I could just run through what I understand to see if I have this clear in my mind?"

"Of course, Sam."

"So, right now I am in Japan in the year 1537 in the house of your master on the shores of a lake called Biwa. We arrived here through the powers of The Divine Sword, which you have. You are a Guardian of The Divine Sword as well as of a secret scroll, the...." Sam paused trying to recall the name.

"Osawa," said Kensho helpfully.

Sam nodded and continued, "...the Osawa Scrolls. I have been chosen, or was destined or something, 1400 years ago to also become a Guardian of the Osawa Scrolls. The Guardians protect the swords and the scrolls and keep them secret. They also guard against the return of Tatsuya, who has been banished somewhere though I didn't quite understand where. I think that is all?"

From Kensho's expression, Sam could see that maybe that might not be 'all'.

"Yes, Sam, you have understood well. However, I have not begun to scratch the surface of what you will learn."

"Sensei, is this how you knew my name the first day that we met?"

"Yes, Sam," said Kensho. "I knew of you long before we met. But how I knew is best left to a later discussion."

Sam thought some more and then asked, "So, where was Tatsuya banished to? And, if it happened fourteen hundred years ago, how could he possibly return?"

Kensho leant back and said, "Well firstly we have to be clear that it happened 1400 years ago in our time. The time we are in now, it happened just under 1000 years ago. Master Osawa never took anyone's life in protecting The Divine Swords and their secret. It is strictly forbidden to kill or maim another human being unless the secret itself, or a Divine Sword, would otherwise certainly be lost. To kill or injure runs contrary to Tao, to the Divine Spirit. In fourteen hundred years, only three times has a Guardian had no alternative but to take a life."

Kensho paused for a moment to take a drink of tea before continuing, "However, Tatsuya was no ordinary man. What exactly he was we do not know. But he could best be described as Darkness in physical form. Like a yokai that had taken the form of a human being."

"What's a yokai?" asked Sam as he swapped his crossed legs around, rubbing his sleeping ankle.

"It's an evil spirit. So, Master Osawa didn't kill Tatsuya, but rather he banished Tatsuya into the shadows. Tatsuya's spirit lives on in Darkness, and his spirit is forever seeking to rise up from the shadows and seize the Divine Swords and their secrets. Were he to ever succeed, then the consequences would be dire. This is the purpose of the Guardians. We must constantly be vigilant and do all that we can to keep Darkness at bay. Darkness is growing, and in these mountains evil walks in ever greater numbers. It is drawn to the light of the swords though they hate it and wish only to destroy it. There have never been more dangerous times, Sam. We may be approaching a great battle, a battle that we must not lose."

Sam sat quietly thinking. Then he said, "But, Sensei, surely we know that the battle, if it comes, will not be lost. Because if it had, then we would know that in our time, in the future. Had Tatsuya succeeded, then we would surely know it in our time, wouldn't we? So we know that nothing bad happens, don't we?" Sam looked at Kensho with both hope and confusion.

"You are a bright boy, Sam. But your thinking is linear. In matters such as these, the threads are a great deal more complex. Each decision that we make takes us on an ever branching path. There is not just one single thread, but an infinite number of threads for every decision made or not made. You and I come from one thread, but we arrived at an unknown thread long, long ago and our very presence creates more threads that previously did not exist. This is a complex and confusing topic, Sam. For now, please, just trust me when I say that the battle between Light and Darkness depends upon our courage, dedication and trust. We must take nothing for granted and take no hope from events as they seem in our time."

Sam remembered watching a TV progamme with his dad about quantum physics. The show talked about the possibility of infinite universes with infinite versions of ourselves, all living different lives as our decisions, and those of others around us, shaped our lives differently. Suddenly, he smiled as he remembered Sophie's comment. She had been playing and hadn't seemed to be paying attention to the TV. Then, at the end of the show, she announced, "We shouldn't call it the universe. I think it should be called the multichorus. It sounds much brighter, happier and more colourful." It was classic Sophie.

Kensho watched Sam break out into a smile and asked, "What is it, Sam?"

"So, not a universe at all, but actually a multichorus," said Sam.

"I like that, Sam. Yes - a multichorus. And all we need to do is sing our part in it with all our hearts."

They fell silent again. Kensho stoked the fire as Sam sipped the last of his tea. He looked at the old wooden cup he held in his hands, so simple yet so right somehow. He looked around at the old house: it too so simple yet so right. If he ever built his place in the forest back home, then he wanted it to be just like this. Then Sam thought back to the journey he had made.

"Who did I see when we were…well…when we were meditating and got from your dojo to here?"

Kensho immediately stopped stoking the fire and turned to look at Sam with a very serious expression.

"What do you mean, Sam? You saw someone? Describe to me as accurately as you can exactly what you saw."

"Well," said Sam, trying to recall the images he had seen. "At first, I saw lots of different images like mountains and islands and some animals. It was all quite dark, and none of the images had any colour. Then suddenly a samurai appeared."

"Please, describe the samurai to me, Sam."

"Well," said Sam, "He was quite frightening to be honest, Sensei. He looked, well, angry. No. More than angry, he looked…evil, I guess. His face was hidden beneath a red mask that had a scary expression, kind of twisted and….well.. scary. As he got closer I could see he had red armour on and lots of gold stitching. He was looking right at me, and he was coming towards me from underneath me, it seemed. Like a shark coming out of the depths of the ocean. He had his right arm outstretched as if he was trying to grab me." Sam demonstrated by reaching his right arm out. "I vividly remember his right hand grasping at the air."

"What did his helmet look like, Sam?" asked Kensho, with urgency in his voice.

"It had horns," continued Sam, "gold horns. Oh and he had a ring on his right hand. A ring with a black stone on it."

"Tatsuya!" said Kensho as he jumped up. "We must find Sensei immediately. Quick, come with me, Sam."

Kensho strode over to the shoji and slid it open. Sam stepped through, and Kensho followed him out before quickly but gently closing the shoji behind him.

"What's the matter, Sensei?"

"We need to talk to Nagato Sensei, Sam. Up the path. Quick as you can."

Sam climbed the steep path up the garden as it weaved between the terraced vegetable plots. He noticed the beds were neatly prepared and, in some, vegetables were already beginning to grow.

Eventually, the path entered the forest and continued to weave its way through the trees. Sam could hear the sound of rushing water and then saw, away to his right, a fast flowing stream, skipping and dancing over a steep rocky bed. Still Sam pushed on, his breathing becoming more laboured with the strain of the steep climb. Kensho's breathing was so quiet and light behind him that he couldn't hear it over his own.

Finally, Sam spotted Hiroshi. The incredible sight filled Sam with amazement. There stood Hiroshi under a powerful waterfall, an icy cold waterfall, thought Sam. Hiroshi was only wearing big white shorts. He had the palms of his hands pushed together in front of his chest with his fingers intertwined except for his index fingers that were pointing up. He was chanting loudly with his eyes closed, his body motionless under the pounding water. Sam could see his sword carefully placed on a rock within close reach but out of the water.

Kensho strode past Sam effortlessly, and Sam was almost as surprised by Kensho's fitness as he was by Hiroshi's feat of endurance. Kensho stopped beside the waterfall and faced Hiroshi, but he didn't say a word. Sam joined him, and they both stood side by side, patiently watching and waiting for Hiroshi to acknowledge their presence.

Recalling what Kensho had told him about Master Osawa, Sam presumed this was misogi or ritual purification. It looked like some form of dreadful torture to him. It was bad enough when his elbow accidentally knocked the shower lever and he got a short blast of cold water. Standing under this constant torrent of ice cold water on a chilly day seemed horribly painful and impossibly hard to Sam. Yet, Hiroshi wasn't shivering or moving at all. The only movement came from his mouth forming the sounds of the mantra and his chest rising and falling as he breathed.

Sam and Kensho must have stood there for ten minutes. Knowing the urgency that Kensho felt, Sam was surprised he did not call out to Hiroshi. But Kensho stood quite still and silent the whole time that they waited. Finally, Hiroshi raised his hands above his head, palms still pushed together, and stretched his arms straight up. Then he lowered them to his side, and, opening his eyes, he turned and smiled at them both. Then he stepped from under the waterfall and, picking up his sword, came over to them.

"I know why you are here, Kensho. I saw Sam's vision in my meditation. Tatsuya's spirit grows ever stronger. Let us return to the house."

CHAPTER 32

The Story is Found

In the village below, Aiko was tidying around the house. Daichi was sitting in a small room, overflowing with scrolls and papers, going through his own collection of obscure texts. After so many months, he had still not been able to find the text about the brother and two sisters that Hiroshi had spoken about during the previous summer. He had never been unable to recall a text before, and he was utterly determined not to let Hiroshi down. He was completely immersed in his research, and Aiko, as she worked, did not disturb him. However, Daichi had been training for a long time under Hiroshi. He had learned to focus, but he had also learned to maintain awareness of what was going on inside him as well as around him.

So, while Aiko busied herself around the house, Daichi became aware of a tune she was gently humming to herself. He didn't know why, but the tune seemed important. He kept trying to silence the gentle voice that nudged him towards the song. His thinking mind was intent on focusing on the important scrolls spread out before him, and it told him to ignore the silly song. He had to keep searching, keep trying to find the answer in these dusty old bits of paper. But the quiet yet insistent voice told him he must pay attention to Aiko's tune. Daichi was a wise man, and in his heart he knew to listen to that voice. So, subduing his thinking mind, he got up and walked over to where Aiko was working.

She was brushing the wooden floor around the fire. Ash had collected under the mats that she was now washing, so she gently swept it back into the fire.

"What is that tune you are humming, my love?" asked Daichi.

"Oh, I'm not sure," said Aiko, looking surprised. "It's an old song I've known since childhood, I think. I don't know why I started humming it. Am I disturbing you?"

Daichi smiled at his wife who loved him so. "No, my love. Do you remember the words?"

"Oh, my dear, it has been a very long time since I last sung it." Aiko frowned as she struggled to recall them. "I was only a young child. It's just a silly child's song. I remember I learnt it from a great aunt who had lived with us for a while. She would sing the song to us, and I remember thinking how beautiful it was, so she taught it to me. Let me see now."

After a brief pause, Aiko began to sing. She was surprised that as she did so, the song just flowed through her, and she did not stumble over any of the words as she sang it to her husband. Daichi felt his heart fill with love as Aiko sang. It seemed to him that he had never heard a more beautiful song. The words and the tune harmonised into something vastly more powerful than a 'silly child's song'. Aiko seemed to shine, to vibrate almost, as she sang it, and they both found themselves lost in the song.

When finally Aiko stopped singing, they both had tears rolling down their wrinkled cheeks. Their hearts ached - so full were they with love. Neither wanted to say a word. They simply embraced one another and stood there feeling their hearts close to each other. Eventually, they parted, and Aiko spoke first.

"Daichi," she paused searching for the right words, "I felt filled with love as I sang. It felt as though an amazing power and light flowed into me and then out through the song. Did you feel it?"

Daichi nodded. Never had his wife looked more beautiful, and never had his love felt so deep.

Then Daichi began to laugh. Quietly at first, just a little chuckle. Then Aiko began to chuckle too. Before long their chuckles had grown into full laughter, and tears once again rolled down their cheeks. They both ended up lying on the floor - they were laughing so much. Finally, the laughter was done, and they lay on their backs, holding hands and looking into one another's eyes.

"This world we live in is wonderful beyond words, beyond

imagination, Aiko. It all unfolds so perfectly if only we let it, if only we stop trying and start trusting. Sensei is so right, of course. This is his wisdom. The wisdom of the Tao. All we need to do is trust and let go. That song that you sang, Aiko. Not only was it the most beautiful thing I have ever heard, but it is also the story for which I have been searching all these months. It is the story that Sensei asked me if I knew."

Daichi was about to ask Aiko to write the words of the song out, but something stopped him. The story must be sung. As a scholar of the written word, Daichi believed in writing things down. But once again, though his thinking mind told him he must write it or it will be lost, the quiet voice told him he must learn it. So it was that this old husband and wife sat side by side, and Aiko taught one of Japan's great scholars a child's song.

CHAPTER 33

The Great Unfolding

Hiroshi, Kensho and Sam were all back at the house. Hiroshi had put on warm dry clothes, and once again they were all sat together around the fire. The fire really was the heart of the house. It warmed them, cooked their food, boiled their water, provided light and even entertained them with its dancing flames and glowing embers.

"Sam's encounter with Tatsuya tells me little more than I already knew, Kensho," said Hiroshi. "I have felt the malice in the mountains growing. Tengu that were once our friends have begun to avoid me, and I expect soon they will begin to attack me. I also sense that oni are gathering, too, though they have not revealed themselves yet. I have had more frequent encounters with the yokai. Sam's vision of Tatsuya confirms that we are entering very dangerous times, Kensho."

Sam was listening quietly, but talk of tengu, oni and yokai was a little too much for him. They didn't sound very nice and he had to know what they were. So, he asked Kensho, "What are tengu and oni? And what is a yokai? I know it is an evil spirit, but what does that mean exactly?"

Kensho looked at Hiroshi, and Hiroshi nodded.

"Tengu are creatures that inhabit the forests in the mountains of Japan," explained Kensho. "Usually they are the size of a small man or large child, though sometimes they can be much larger. They have much longer noses than any human though. They have always been mischievous, but they were friendly to us until recently.

"I have never seen an oni, but legend has it they are fierce creatures, a bit like an ogre as you might know it, Sam.

"Yokai can best be described as evil energy that coalesces into a dark presence. Sam, these are things which I had not expected to tell you about for some time. I do not want you to become too frightened. I know that it all must seem very unpleasant. Or perhaps it sounds too incredible to you. Trust me when I say that though these things are real, we are very capable of protecting ourselves from them."

Sam knew there was nothing too incredible about the creatures Kensho described. Perhaps before, he may have had doubts, but given the events that had already taken place that day, he none now. Despite his fear of the mysterious creatures of the Japanese forest, he did feel safe in the company of these two humble men. He knew that their skill, their power and their courage wasn't some thin and fragile facade. These qualities were the very core of their beings. He felt profoundly honoured to be with them. He also wondered how he could possibly follow in their footsteps and become a Guardian like them. The very idea seemed absurd.

"Kensho, there is no time to lose," said Hiroshi. "We must begin Sam's training in earnest. Please talk to Sam about the training he must now undertake. I sense Daichi's approach, so I will meet him outside and talk to him in the dojo. He must have urgent news if he is coming to see me. I told him that I was not to be disturbed for two weeks. He could join us, but I think that Sam has had enough encounters for today."

Hiroshi got up, his sword by his side as always, and left the house.

"Sam, I am sorry," said Kensho. "This was not how I expected the day to turn out. But expectations are dangerous things. They tie us to a course that prevents us from embracing reality as it unfolds. That causes us pain. We must flow, Sam, flow with whatever unfolds, bending as the bamboo bends in the storm's wind. It bends; thus, it never breaks. We must be as bamboo, Sam."

Sam thought he understood or at least had an inkling. He had had to be like bamboo today. He had had to let go of rigid beliefs of how the world worked and flow with this new reality that was taking place. Either that, he reasoned, or his mind would explode with all the new information it was absorbing.

"Sam, I am your teacher. Sensei Nagato is my teacher, and he is also your teacher. Our purpose is not to fill you with knowledge; it is to help you lose that which blocks you. The Tao Te Ching will be another of your teachers. One of the verses says:

For the student of learning, something is added every day.
In the practice of wisdom, every day something is dropped.

"Sam you are wise beyond all reckoning. As your teachers, we will work with you to help you drop your beliefs, ideas, and judgements so that you may perceive reality with total clarity. Perceiving with total clarity is awareness. Awareness is wisdom, wisdom is awareness. Awareness is love, love is awareness."

Kensho paused for a moment looking at Sam and then smiled before continuing. "My master told a story to me when I became his disciple. Now, it is my turn as your master to tell this story to you, my disciple."

Again Kensho paused before telling the story: "The master said to his disciple, 'You are only a disciple because your eyes are closed. The day you open them, you will see there is nothing you can learn from me or anyone.'"

"The disciple asked, 'What then is a Master for?'"

"'To make you see the uselessness of having one,' said the master."

Then Kensho fell silent.

Sam wished he understood. But he did not. It seemed to him he had an enormous amount to learn.

"I don't understand Sensei," Sam said eventually. "I am trying to, but I don't understand." Kensho nodded. "Nor did I Sam, nor did Sensei Nagato when he became a disciple to his master. Nor did any student in the beginning. That was why we all have needed a master."

"Do you wish to learn iaido, Sam?" asked Kensho.

"More than anything, Sensei," said Sam, his face lighting up. "It was amazing to see a real samurai sword, especially a sword so special. I want more than anything to learn iaido."

"Learning the Way of The Sword is a very difficult path, Sam. The training is severe. Because you are destined to become a Guardian, it is far more severe than anything you have previously experienced. Do you feel you are ready?"

"I feel I am ready, Sensei," said Sam confidently.

"Very well. Sensei Nagato will be your teacher for a while now, Sam. I know this will be another difficult thing for you to understand, but the time you spend here does not flow at the same speed as time at home. So, when you will return to the dojo late Sunday afternoon, you will have spent 16 days training with Sensei Nagato. Please, do not underestimate just how difficult these 16 days will be, Sam."

Sam didn't like the feeling he was getting.

"Are you leaving, Sensei?"

Much to Sam's dismay, Kensho nodded. Kensho saw Sam's expression and sensed the fear within him. He put his hands on Sam's shoulders.

"You have great courage, Sam. When your eyes are opened, you will know that courage is no longer necessary. But until then, courage will be your great ally. I see the courage that you have even though you do not. What did I ask you in my office before our journey here?"

"To trust you," said Sam, quietly.

Kensho nodded and said, "Then that is still what I ask of you, Sam. I ask that you trust me. You will never meet a wiser nor more compassionate man than Sensei Nagato. Even if his wisdom and compassion may at times run contrary to your understanding. Trust, Sam! Trust the Divine Spirit. Trust the Tao. Trust the Great Unfolding. This is what you were meant to do. This is your purpose. Trust that and let go. All will be well, Sam. All is well. Though you may not yet have the eyes to see it."

Then Kensho got up. Sam stood up too.

"Farewell, Sam. Trust!"

And with that, Kensho bowed slowly and walked over to the altar. Sam sat back down beside the fire, but he did not look over to where Kensho sat. He couldn't bear to see him depart. He knew when Kensho had gone as the hum stopped the moment he left. Sam was left on his own. He felt as far away from courageous as he could possibly to be.

CHAPTER 34

The Story is Shared

As Kensho and Sam talked, Hiroshi was meeting Daichi. Having left the house, Hiroshi walked along the short path to the dojo. Standing on the porch of the dojo, Hiroshi could see Daichi climbing the steep path up towards the house. Daichi saw Hiroshi and waved, and Hiroshi waved back. After a few minutes, Daichi reached the entrance to the dojo, where Hiroshi was waiting.

"Forgive me, Sensei, for disturbing you, but I have great news, and I felt certain that you would want to hear it immediately," said Daichi, bowing deeply.

"I knew that you would only come to see me on important matters Daichi. Let us step into the dojo and you can tell me your news."

Hiroshi slid the shoji open, and the two men stepped into the dojo. Hiroshi then slid the door closed behind them, and they both knelt on the tatami.

"Now, please tell me your news, Daichi," said Hiroshi.

"Sensei, you remember our conversation under the persimmon tree? You asked me if I knew of a story about the brother and two sisters who united the three powers - those of man, nature, and ki - and swept evil before them."

Hiroshi nodded, and Daichi continued. "Well, Sensei, I have searched long and hard. I have sat quietly for long hours racking my mind, going through all the many thousands of texts I have read. I have searched through the most obscure scrolls that I keep stacked around the house, much to Aiko's frustration!"

Hiroshi smiled and nodded. Daichi smiled back before carrying on. "But I could not find anything that matched your story. Nearing the end of the search through my scrolls I began to think I should pay a visit to the Emperor's palace in Kyoto to search the library. It would be very dangerous, as you know, but I was determined not to let you down, and I knew I had read the story somewhere. Ah, but I was wrong Sensei. I was wrong."

Hiroshi stretched out his arm and patted Daichi on the arm reassuringly.

"Daichi, my old friend. You have not let me down. How could you, as you have always been a friend to me like few others."

"No, Sensei," said Daichi, shaking his head. "I was wrong that I thought I had read it somewhere. I did know the story, but I had never read it. That was why I couldn't remember it!"

Hiroshi looked quizzically at Daichi.

"Sensei, what have you always told me?"

Hiroshi thought for a moment and then, looking very serious, said, "Never eat yellow snow?"

Daichi burst out laughing, and Hiroshi joined him. When they had both settled back down, Hiroshi continued: "Well, other than that, I may also have said, 'Trust Daichi. Let go of your thinking mind and trust that the right action will arise at the right moment'.

"That you have helped to get me out of my dusty and stiff mind, and to feel the right action has been a gift beyond measure, Sensei, a gift that brought me the answer to your question. As I sat staring at scroll after scroll, I heard Aiko humming a tune. I tried to ignore it, but right action kept prodding me, and so I got up and asked her about the tune she was humming, and she sang me this song."

Then Daichi began to sing the song that Aiko sang. Though his voice was not even close to the beauty of Aiko's, still the power of the song shone through. When he had finished, Hiroshi leant forward and, stretching out his arms, grasped the side of Daichi's shoulders.

"Daichi, you have brought to me a gift beyond measure," said Hiroshi, looking deep into Daichi's eyes. "One day, my dear friend, you will know your part in the defeat of Darkness. For now, please make do with my sincerest gratitude for your hard work and for doing the thing that you find the hardest: letting go of your thinking mind and trusting."

"Sensei, it has always been my greatest pleasure to serve you in whatever small way I might. I am full of gratitude for the opportunity to help you in this great battle. Now, I would have written the song down, but that did not feel like the right action."

"No," said Hiroshi, shaking his head. "You did well. I have the song in my head now, Daichi, and it will not leave me."

"Would you think me rude if I bid you farewell and headed for home?" asked Daichi. "Dusk is close at hand."

"Of course not, Daichi!" replied Hiroshi. "Come let us head out now and get you on your way."

"Thank you, Sensei," said Daichi as they both got up to leave the dojo.

CHAPTER 35

The First Night

After Daichi had said his farewell and began his walk back down the mountain, Hiroshi returned to the house. He found Sam alone, dozing in front of the dying embers of the fire.

Hiroshi silently sat on a wooden bench just inside the door and watched this boy at peace. Hiroshi reflected on where Sam found himself. The boy had lost his mother and his father in the most tragic of circumstances. Hiroshi imagined the sense of abandonment that must have filled Sam, and the subsequent pain of being separated from his sisters.

Recently, with the help of a new father figure in Kensho, he had been reunited with his sisters and found a direction and purpose to his life as he trained in aikido. Now he had been taken away from that wonderful new life that had just began to blossom. He was with a formidable old man who he didn't know, in a strange land far away, both in time and distance, from his beloved sisters. Kensho, his most trusted friend, had left him. How could this not revive feelings of abandonment for Sam? And to make matters even more difficult, this was only the beginning. The ordeal that lay before Sam over the next few weeks would push the very strongest men to their limits. Yet Sam must endure. To forge the finest steel the metal must be heated and hammered repeatedly to remove the impurities. This was the beginning of Sam's forging and he was to be thrust deep into the fire.

Hiroshi stood up and coughed loudly, waking Sam from his slumber. Together they prepared a simple dinner before Hiroshi showed Sam to the bath house, a small wooden building beside the main house, where Sam could bathe and prepare for bed. When Sam returned Hiroshi showed him to the makeshift bed that he had prepared for Sam by the fire. He knew Sam would find the nights bitterly cold and if he were to get any sleep at all he would need to be near the fire. Then Hiroshi wished him good night and went into his bedroom that was off of the large room, taking the oil lamp with him.

Sam pulled the blanket tighter over himself. Despite the warmth of the fire, it was still quite chilly, so he didn't get undressed. Sleep was a long time in coming. His mind was going over the day's incredible events. Try as he might he could not block out thoughts of the evil that lurked out in the forest. Would the wooden walls of the house be enough to keep Darkness out, he wondered? Eventually, despite his fears, exhaustion overcame Sam, and he fell into a deep, settled sleep.

CHAPTER 36

The Ordeal Begins

Hiroshi rose at 4.30, as he did every morning. It was still dark, but he knew exactly where everything was and had no need for light. He got up, rolled his sleeping mat up and folded his blanket neatly. Then he knelt on the floor of his room and meditated in the darkness for an hour. At 5.30 he silently slid open the shoji.

Sam lay under the blanket beside the embers of the fire fast asleep.

"Sam!" called out Hiroshi loudly.

Sam sat bolt upright, his eyes wide open. He looked around for a few moments utterly confused as to where he was. He had been dreaming he was camping in the mountains outside Vancouver, and a landslide was bearing down on him. But as the dream left, he remembered where he was. He jumped to his feet and the blanket, saved in the nick of time, nearly fell into the fire.

"Your training begins now," said Hiroshi. "Roll up your sleeping mat and fold your blanket. We will go to the dojo and begin our morning meditation."

"Yes, Sensei," said Sam, and did as Hiroshi instructed.

As he rolled up his mat, he thought how different Hiroshi seemed this morning. Last night there had been a softness about him, but this morning he felt stern and hard.

"Now stoke the fire and add some logs," said Hiroshi once Sam was done.

While Sam did so, Hiroshi lit an oil lamp.

"Follow me," said Hiroshi as he opened the shoji and slid back the outer wooden door.

Sam put on his shoes and stepped through into the crisp early morning air. Hiroshi followed Sam, then slid the shoji shut and began walking, with Sam following, to the dojo. It was still pitch dark, and Sam stumbled a few times despite the light from the oil lamp that

Hiroshi held. It would be some time before the first light of dawn began to brighten the eastern sky.

When they arrived at the entrance to the dojo Hiroshi slid open the shoji and stepped in, before taking off his sandals and leaving them by the door. Then he bowed and walked into the dojo. Sam followed suit. Hiroshi hung the oil lamp from a hook in one of the rafters and then fetched two cushions and blankets, one of each he handed to Sam. Finally Hiroshi sat in seiza on the cushion, and wrapped the blanket around his shoulders. Then he told Sam to do the same.

So began Sam's first ever early morning meditation. It was not pleasant to say the least. He sat for an hour with only a short break halfway through to stretch his legs. He had no idea for how long they were to meditate, and time seemed drag on forever. Despite the blanket he began to shiver uncontrollably.

When it was finally over, Sam slowly stood up and stretched his stiff legs.

"Go and wash and meet me back here," said Hiroshi.

The sky to the east was just beginning to lighten as Sam made his way to the bath house. Once inside, he fumbled around in the gloom to find the jug of cold water and to wash himself.

Sam left the bath house and began to walk back to the dojo just as the first of the sun's rays filled the garden. He was wondering whether breakfast would be soon and what it would be. As he turned the corner of the house, suddenly Hiroshi appeared in front of him and in an instant hit him on his left shoulder with something hard. Sam tried to block the blow with his left arm, but he was far too slow. He screeched in fear and pain and grabbed his shoulder while leaping back and looking at Hiroshi in shock. Hiroshi said not a word and simply turned and walked back to the dojo.

As Sam watched Hiroshi walk away, he strained to see what it was that Hiroshi had hit him with. He managed to make out a shinai in Hiroshi's left hand. A shinai is a bamboo training sword, the blade end of which is made of split bamboo. When used to hit hard, it hurts and bruises, but it does not break any bones. Or so Sam had been told at Kensho's dojo. As he felt his shoulder, he now questioned if that were true.

Reluctantly, Sam set off after Hiroshi. As he walked, he wondered what he had done wrong to deserve such harsh punishment. Why would Hiroshi have struck him? Sam concluded he must have taken too long in the bath house.

Upon their return to the dojo, Hiroshi explained what Sam's next training exercise would be. He pointed to the edge of the dojo's wooden floor. Sam could just make out an inlay of thin wood, lighter than the rest, which went around the edge of the floor.

"Walk around the edge of the dojo following that line. Do not step off the line. Begin."

Sam began to walk. As he turned back towards the entrance he realised that Hiroshi had gone. Sam didn't know for how long he had been walking round the dojo. He only knew that it was now fully light outside and that he was getting very tired, hungry and thirsty. He supposed that at some point Hiroshi would come in and tell him it was time to stop. His mind was wandering when suddenly he was aware of something in front of him. He looked up, and there was Hiroshi, shinai raised above his head ready to strike. Sam lifted both his arms, but it was too late, and once again Hiroshi landed a blow, this time on his right shoulder. Again Sam shrieked, grabbed his shoulder and quickly tried to ease the pain by rubbing it better.

Again Hiroshi said nothing of the attack.

"Go to the well and fill the jug with water."

Then Hiroshi turned and left.

Sam felt awful. He was tired, he was hungry, he was thirsty, and both his shoulders hurt. Worse than that, he felt Hiroshi was testing his aikido training, and Sam had completely failed. He had failed to be aware of Hiroshi's attacks, and he had failed to defend himself.

"I must try harder," thought Sam, "or Hiroshi might decide I am not worthy to be trained."

He left the dojo with care in case Hiroshi attacked again. He went to the well, where he found the jug waiting for him. He lowered the bucket and filled the jug before cautiously approaching the entrance to the house. Hiroshi was waiting inside with breakfast and cups of tea. They ate in silence. When they had finished, Hiroshi instructed him to wash the dishes.

"Now return to the dojo and continue your practice as I instructed," said Hiroshi once Sam had finished the dishes.

As Sam walked around the edge of the dojo, he wondered what on earth this had to do with iaido. Once again he didn't know for how long he walked, but suddenly there was Hiroshi beside him. He tried to turn and block the attack, but he was far too late, and the shinai struck him hard behind the left leg.

Sam tried not to cry out this time, but he couldn't help rubbing his leg to ease the pain.

"There is an axe and some logs up by the woodshed. Split all the logs and then carry a bundle down to the house."

Then Hiroshi turned and left.

Log splitting is hard work, but Sam threw himself into it. He was determined to prove his strength to Hiroshi. Nonetheless, he kept his guard up at all times so as not to let Hiroshi take him by surprise. He knew he could evade Hiroshi if he could only stay aware. This time, however, he didn't even see Hiroshi. He had pulled the axe out of a log, and as he stood up and lifted the axe above his head, the shinai blow struck him in the ribs under the right armpit. It was the most painful blow yet. The axe tumbled to the ground as Sam grasped his ribs letting out a terrible cry of pain and falling to his knees.

When Sam looked up, Hiroshi was gone. He felt an increasing feeling of despair but his determination to show Hiroshi that he had the skills to become a great samurai warrior was still strong. Then he noticed the food that Hiroshi had left for him. As he ate the meal he marvelled at the ability of this old man to deliver food, attack him and then depart all without him seeing a thing. He ate quickly and then went straight back to splitting the logs with renewed vigour. He would show Hiroshi.

Dusk was falling fast by the time Sam had finished splitting all the logs. He wiped the sweat from his brow and looked into the forest. The shadows were deepening, and in them he imagined terrible things watching him. He shivered and quickly collected an armful of split logs before hurrying back down to the house.

He was halfway down the garden, when he was struck from his left side. This time the blow landed on his left shoulder, and all the logs tumbled to the ground. Once again Hiroshi was nowhere to be seen, so Sam silently and methodically collected all the logs and continued to carry them to the house. As he stacked them neatly by the fire, Hiroshi came in.

"It is time for evening meditation. Meet me in the dojo."

Sam's legs hurt even more during this meditation. If meditation was supposed to allow one to find peace and detachment from one's thoughts, then Sam was far, far from meditating. It was simply a test of endurance. All he could focus on were his screaming legs and the recurring thought: How much longer? How much longer? Time seemed to crawl by and when Hiroshi eventually bowed, thus indicating the sitting was over, Sam felt like they had been there for days, not an hour.

With dinner eaten and the first day finally over, Sam got to lie down on his sleeping mat by the fire. He was in pain and he was utterly, utterly exhausted. He felt all the bruises that now covered his body. The tension of the day, the fear of being attacked and his humiliation at failing to evade even one blow had taken a toll on his spirit. He began to question whether he was really ready for this. But still, his determination to prove his worthiness was strong, and he resolved to evade Hiroshi's next attack.

The next few days followed the same pattern as the first: meditating, walking for hours around the dojo and doing chores. Many times a day Sam was attacked, and every time, despite his best efforts, he was not even close to defending himself. He could never even detect Hiroshi's approach.

On the morning of the fourth day, Sam was fetching water from the well. He felt like he was slowly being beaten into a pulp. The blows had kept coming, and they kept hitting the same parts of his body that were already bruised. His determination was fading. He was beginning to become convinced that he just did not have the skills necessary to learn iaido. As hard as he tried, he could not detect Hiroshi's approach nor evade the shinai.

He was sure that Hiroshi was testing him. Either it was a test to see if he had the necessary skills or a test to see if he had the resolve to put up with the attacks. Either way, he was failing. He was beginning to hate this man. He remembered Kensho saying that Hiroshi was kind and compassionate. Well, there was nothing kind or compassionate about him now, of that Sam was certain.

He had just got the bucket to the top of the well and was about to pour the water from the bucket into the jug when the blow struck. The bucket tumbled out of his hands and covered him with icy cold water as it bounced off the edge of the well wall and fell back down into the darkness. Sam's resolve tumbled with it. He collapsed to his knees and fell forward onto his hands sobbing. He had failed. He knew he had failed. He didn't have what it took to be a warrior. He couldn't evade the blows, and he couldn't continue suffering the pain. He was done. He had nothing left in him. He knelt on the floor, his face buried in his hands and his body shaking as he cried.

Eventually the crying eased. He unfolded himself and stood up. Hiroshi was standing before him, saying nothing.

"I am sorry Sensei," said Sam, at last. "I give up. I have tried to be aware of your approach, but I have failed. I have tried to evade your attacks, but I have failed. I thought I had what it took to learn iaido, but I do not. I have nothing."

"Excellent," replied Hiroshi approvingly, "At last you are ready to learn iaido."

Sam couldn't comprehend what Hiroshi had just said. He stood there looking confused.

"Let us go into the house," said Hiroshi, warmly. "I have some balm that will help those bruises heal quickly."

Hiroshi turned and walked towards the house. Sam stood still for a while, trying to make sense of what was happening. Eventually, he accepted it didn't make sense and followed Hiroshi into the house anyway.

Hiroshi was waiting for him.

"Come, sit by the fire."

Sam took off his top and t-shirt and rolled up his trousers. Then Sam took the balm Hiroshi handed to him, and began to apply it to all the huge black and yellow bruises that covered his body.

"You need a bath to help the healing. I will light the fire to warm the water."

In a while, Hiroshi returned with some traditional Japanese clothes for Sam to wear. He also had a gi, which he laid out for Sam on a shelf nearby.

Then Hiroshi lead Sam out to the bath house. The wooden bath was full of water, with a fierce fire burning beneath it. The base of the bath was shielded by metal, and already steam was rising from the water. Hiroshi tested the water temperature, then extinguished the flames.

"Not as hot as I'd like it, but for you I think this is plenty hot enough."

Sam dipped his fingers in and snapped them back out it was so hot.

Hiroshi added some salts and other mysterious substances to the water saying, "These will also help your healing and aid the recovery of your aching muscles. Now wash yourself off and then climb in. I will go and prepare us an early dinner. Stay in the bath for as long as you can so the healing waters can do their work."

Hiroshi left, and Sam did as he was told. The water was incredibly hot, so Sam slowly lowered himself in. But once immersed he found the bath very soothing. For the first time in many days, Sam really began to relax.

When Sam finally returned to the house, Hiroshi had finished preparing the meal. They sat in their usual places by the fire and ate.

As they did so, Hiroshi talked.

"Sam, have you heard of 'beginner's mind'?" he asked.

"Yes, I have heard Iwata Sensei say it, but I am not sure I really understand what it means."

"Beginner's mind," explained Hiroshi, "is very important for correct learning. It means having an empty mind, free from one's own ideas. It is like an empty canvas upon which one begins to paint. The great artist does not start to paint with a canvas already covered in brush strokes. So it is with learning martial arts. If a student comes with a mind already filled with ideas of how the martial art is then the teacher cannot teach proper technique. The student will not see the techniques that teacher shows but rather will see those techniques in relation to his own ideas. The student will think it looks like this thing or that thing he already knows."

Hiroshi paused and took a drink of his tea before continuing,

"Your mind was a canvas covered in brush strokes. You had to let go of all your ideas. You had to know that you did not know. Words will only get us so far. It is through training that we really learn. So, I had to teach you that you did not know. I am sorry it was such a painful lesson.

"Kensho has taught you aikido. In aikido you use bokken. But it is aikido bokken not iaido bokken. The bokken is the same, but the training is different. If the training was the same, then aikido and iaido would be the same. The training is different. If you bring aikido bokken to iaido, then you do not have beginner's mind.

"But now you are a blank canvas. Now you are ready to learn. Tomorrow, we begin iaido practice."

After dinner, Sam washed up and tended to the fire as was becoming his routine now. Then Hiroshi said goodnight, and Sam lay down on his sleeping mat. He was excited. Tomorrow he would finally hold a samurai sword. He wondered if it would be a Divine Sword. If he was to be a Guardian, surely he would have a Divine Sword. He wondered what other powers the sword had.

He felt his bruises and was surprised to feel how much better they already were. In fact, it almost felt as though they had healed. He began to read the Tao Te Ching by the fire light. As usual, he didn't manage to read very far before sleep overtook him. But these were the last words he read before he could no longer keep his eyes open:

Therefore in leading the people,
the master empties their minds but fills their bellies,
Weakens their ambition and toughens their bones.
He helps them to be without cunning, to be without desire,
and ensures that those with cunning dare not to act.
Practice non-action,
and all will be in order.

CHAPTER 37

Misogi

The following morning started much the same way as previous mornings at Hiroshi's. However, Sam felt like a new person now that the pain of the bruises was gone. He also felt much more settled, having received Hiroshi's explanation about what he was expected to do and how he was to do it. He got dressed in the gi that Hiroshi had given him, and they went to the dojo to meditate. This time Hiroshi told Sam to sit in whatever way he would be most comfortable.

"Meditation is not a feat of endurance. We must be comfortable and relaxed, but not lazy and sleepy. Do not fidget. If you find yourself in discomfort then move to a more comfortable position. Do not try to stop your thoughts. That is like trying to stop the clouds. Just observe them and let them go. Focus on your breathing. If you get caught in a thought do not worry. Simply become aware that you have become attached to a thought and return to your breath. In time there will be no more clouds in the sky. Now begin."

When meditation was over, Sam went and bathed. He was still feeling excited as he walked through the chill morning air back to the dojo. Surely now was the time when Hiroshi would present him with the sword that he would train with. But instead, Hiroshi met him outside the house.

"Follow me," said Hiroshi, as he began walking up the garden.

In the early morning light Sam saw the first buds beginning to appear on some of the trees. They entered the forest and followed the footpath that Kensho and Sam had walked when they had gone to find Hiroshi. Sam looked anxiously around him as they ventured deeper into the forest. He wondered if tengu were stalking them at this very moment or if oni were lying in wait, hidden in the gloom. He noticed the groves of bamboo that were in amongst the trees and thought how very different the forest felt to those back home.

When they reached the waterfall dawn was breaking and the first shafts of sunlight penetrated the forest and lit the tumbling water. The sun felt warm on Sam's back and he basked in it for a few moments.

"Now we begin your iaido practice," said Hiroshi.

Sam looked confused and began to look around to see if his sword was already waiting for him. Or perhaps it was hidden somewhere here.

"In order to practice iaido, one must purify the spirit," said Hiroshi. "A pure spirit leads to pure iaido. Let us begin."

Hiroshi reached within his gi and pulled out two white pieces of cloth. He folded one and then tied it around Sam's head like a head band before tying one around his own head.

Then Hiroshi began to do an exercise that looked a bit like rowing while standing up. He stood with his left leg forward, extended his arms out straight with his fists closed, and shouted "Ei" as he did so. Then he brought his arms back to almost his armpits and shouted "Ho". He repeated the rowing exercise rapidly with Sam trying to copy what he did.

Then Hiroshi stopped, cupped his hands together in front of his belly button and shook them vigorously. Then he stood with his right leg forward and repeated the rowing exercise. They did this for ten minutes or so. Sam could feel the heat building in his body. He could also feel the power of Hiroshi's shouts. His sounded pathetic in comparison, but he did his best and tried not to worry about it.

Then Hiroshi said the words that Sam had been dreading to hear.

"You are now ready to begin purification beneath the waterfall. Take your top off."

Sam looked at the torrent of water. He simply could not imagine standing underneath it. But he did as he was told. Despite the sun, it was still a very chilly morning. Sam once again looked at the waterfall and imagined how numbingly cold it must be.

Hiroshi showed Sam what he was to do. He brought his hands

together in front of his chest with his palms touching, and all his fingers interlaced except for his index fingers that were pointing up. Sam copied, and Hiroshi made some adjustments to the position of his hands before nodding.

"Stay under the waterfall until I tell you to step out. When I do so, raise your hands above your head and then separate them and bring them to your side. Then step out. Now, begin."

Sam took a deep breath and stepped down the little bank into the bed of the stream. His feet submerged beneath the water. As dire as his imagination had been, the water was actually even colder than he had predicted. He walked on, and the first splashes of the waterfall stung his skin. Still, he walked on until he was standing under the full force of the waterfall in the spot he had seen Hiroshi standing a few days before.

The water pounded his neck and shoulders with an incredible force. At first, he found himself completely unable to breathe. His entire body was tense in a way he had never experienced. He remembered to bring his hands together and up to his chest, and he forced himself to take a breath. It was a short, sharp inhale but more followed, and Sam somehow managed to keep breathing.

His whole body began shaking, not just from the power of the pounding water but from the shivering that had begun. Hard as he tried, the shivering would not stop but became more and more violent. Finally, he heard Hiroshi shout, "Hai!" It was a signal for Sam to raise his arms above his head. He couldn't extend them straight because his muscles were convulsing with the shivering. Then he dropped his arms to his side and staggered out from under the waterfall.

He could barely walk, so he stumbled up the low bank to where Hiroshi stood waiting.

"Good," said Hiroshi. "Put on your top and let us head back down."

When they returned to the house, Hiroshi gave Sam a dry gi and a towel. Hiroshi then tended to the fire, before preparing some tea.

They sat by the fire so Sam could warm up.

Once they had finished their tea, Hiroshi stood up and said, "Let us go to the dojo."

Sam followed Hiroshi to the dojo. As he walked, he looked out over the lake and village below. It looked so tranquil. He reflected on how 'right' this life seemed to him: its simplicity, its harmony with nature, and its timelessness. It made Sam feel a profound connection to the earth, the forest and to life itself.

They entered the dojo. Much to Sam's great disappointment, Hiroshi took a bokken from the rack.

"This is your bokken, Sam. It is quite old as you can see." Hiroshi pointed out all the dents in the oak. "You must treat it as you would treat the finest samurai sword."

Then Hiroshi handed it to Sam, bowing slightly as he did so.

Sam bowed and took the bokken. He looked at the dents and thought what beauty they gave the bokken. It had been used by others before him in this very dojo, and each dent represented a cut or a parry. This kind of beauty through imperfection the Japanese call 'wabi sabi.'

For the next few hours, Hiroshi taught Sam the basic fundamentals of iaido. He showed Sam the proper grip on the hilt of the sword, the proper stance, the way his feet ought to move when the sword is brought from Sam's left side to be held in front of him, how to hold his head, and the position of, and relaxation in, his shoulders. Everything was to be incredibly precise, and Hiroshi corrected even the tiniest of errors.

By the time they finished, Sam was completely exhausted. He had done almost nothing. He hadn't done any cuts or parrys. He had just taken the bokken from being held by his left hand at his left side, as though it were in its sheath, to being held in front of him in both hands ready to cut. He repeated this movement of drawing the bokken over and over and over again.

The concentration this simple act required in order to satisfy

Hiroshi's demands was total. Yet Sam never even got close to doing any of it correctly. On top of this, Hiroshi was telling Sam the Japanese words for everything, so Sam was trying to learn those at the same time.

"I have been training in iaido for nearly 100 years," said Hiroshi with a smile. "Now, let us meditate."

At the end of the day, after they had eaten, Sam began to ask Hiroshi some questions.

"How did you find Iwata Sensei? He was such a long distance and time away. Is that what usually happens?" asked Sam before quickly adding, "Iwata Sensei and I met in the same place and time."

Hiroshi shook his head.

"Kensho was a most unusual Guardian. We Guardians are guided by our meditations, Sam. When we meditate, the right action is revealed to us. Every disciple is revealed to his master through meditation. Usually the disciple has been close at hand. Kensho was very different. It took a lot of trust for me to undertake the journey to find him. But there was a reason for this journey to find Kensho. That reason was aikido.

"Of course, you know that when O'Sensei created aikido, he created a martial art unlike any that had existed before. O'Sensei tells of the moment when he was practising misogi and suddenly forgot all the martial arts techniques that he had ever learnt. Instead, he saw the techniques of his teachers in a completely different way. Instead of techniques to kill and maim, they were techniques to save and protect. You know this, now that you have been training in Aikido."

Sam nodded and Hiroshi continued: "The aikido that O'Sensei was shown and that Kensho has learnt is perfectly aligned with the principles of Master Osawa, the Divine Sword maker. Of course, it is aligned because it comes from the same Divine source. It was the purity and dedication of O'Sensei that enabled him to create aikido just as it was the purity and dedication of Master Osawa that enabled him to create the Divine Swords. Both aikido, when practised correctly and the Divine Swords have the Divine in them.

"So I found Kensho when he was 12 years old, and I became his teacher. I guided him, and I also taught him iaido. He travelled from Vancouver to Japan in your time and practised aikido under O'Sensei at the Iwama dojo. Now he passes O'Sensei's aikido to you."

"Can you travel anywhere with the Divine Sword?" asked Sam.

"No," replied Hiroshi, "we can only travel to those times and places that are revealed to us in our meditation."

"Why do I have to stand under a freezing cold waterfall and do misogi? I don't understand what it is going to do," said Sam.

Hiroshi replied,

"The Tao Te Ching says:

> In settling your mind in stillness
> can you be steadfast, never leaving the Way?
> In focusing your breath-power
> can you remain as supple as a newborn child?
> In cleansing your inner vision of darkness
> can you see nothing but light?

"Our meditation settles the mind in stillness. Our training focuses our breath-power, without tension. Our misogi cleanses our inner vision, so we see nothing but the Light. Each one is an important step towards self-mastery. Each one might not seem 'normal', but normal people are far from self-mastery. It takes strength to walk one's own path, to separate from what is deemed normal. Master Osawa, O'Sensei, Lao-Tzu, Buddha, any person who has achieved greatness has never been 'normal'."

"Why would you not want to harm tengu if they are evil creatures?" asked Sam pleased with how forthcoming Hiroshi was being.

"The tengu are coming under the influence of Darkness. They have always been on the border of light and dark. O'Sensei used to go up into the mountains alone, and it was said that he would practice with the tengu using his bokken. There is a legend in Japan that a tengu taught iaido to Minamoto no Yoshitsune, who is one of Japan's most famous warriors. My own encounters, until recently, have been good. Indeed, it was a tengu that first warned me of the growing Darkness deep in the mountains.

"So, though tengu have also been known to cause trouble, by trying to lead Buddhist priests astray for example, rarely have they been associated with injury or death. That may now be changing as they fall under evil influence. Nonetheless, they are not wholly evil and would return to themselves were the evil influence defeated. For that reason, it would be a very grave situation before I injured or killed a tengu. I very much hope no such situation arises."

"But oni and yokai are different from tengu," said Sam.

"Yes," replied Hiroshi, "very much so. I am yet to encounter an oni, but I sense their spirit, and it is wholly dark, though it lacks the depth of malice that yokai possess. I have had too many encounters with them over the last few years."

Then Hiroshi went quiet, and Sam felt he shouldn't ask any more questions.

"We have talked a lot," said Hiroshi, after quite some time. "It is time for sleep."

Once Sam was in bed, he tried to read a few passages of the Tao Te Ching before he slept. There was a simplicity to it that he very much liked, even if he couldn't grasp a lot of what he read. He found one of his favourite bits and read it over and over:

Content with who you are, not trying to prove your superiority,
you will be at peace with everybody.

CHAPTER 38

Taka and the Temple

Sam awoke with a start. A terrible feeling of dread filled him, and he sat up and looked around. The fire had died down and was just glowing embers, but, in the darkness, Sam could just make out the figure of Hiroshi standing a few feet away. His sword was drawn.

"What's wrong?" asked Sam.

"Do not worry," replied Hiroshi in a reassuring voice, "we just have a visitor outside. We are safe in here."

Sam wanted to feel safe, but Hiroshi had his sword drawn, which would seem to indicate otherwise.

"Who is it?" asked Sam, before realising that he should probably have said "what" not "who".

"I am not sure. I have not felt this presence before," said Hiroshi.

Oh good, thought Sam. There's something deeply unpleasant outside, and Hiroshi doesn't know what it is.

Suddenly, the wooden doors outside the shoji began to shake violently. Sam cried out in fear. But Hiroshi raised the sword above his head and let out a terrible shout of incredible power. As he did so, the sword glowed white filling the room with light. The doors instantly stopped shaking.

Steadily Sam felt the dread ease.

"We are quite safe Sam," said Hiroshi, lowering his sword. "There is no need to be afraid. The power of Darkness is, as yet, no threat to us here. Our visitor has gone to lick its wounds and will not return. But I will sit beside you while you go back to sleep."

Sam lay back down as Hiroshi stoked the fire and put some more logs on.

"Sensei, what did you do to wound the thing outside?" asked Sam.

"That was a 'kiai', Sam. It is like a very loud shout, but it comes from the 'hara' or one's centre as a focused projection of ki energy."

"I saw the sword shine too," said Sam.

"Yes," said Hiroshi. "The Divine Sword's power combined with my ki. Our visitor would have taken a mighty blow, Sam. He will not come back. Now let me dispel the energy our visitor left." With that he began to chant quietly.

Sam lay awake for a while, but quite soon the fear left him and his mind stopped racing. Hiroshi's quiet chanting was very soothing, and before long Sam fell into a peaceful sleep once more.

When the wooden doors were opened the following morning, Sam expected to see some sign of the night's visitor. It was still dark, but from the light of an oil lamp, Sam could see nothing to indicate anything had been there.

After breakfast, Hiroshi said they were going to go up to the waterfall. The sun was rising in a cloudless sky, lighting the mountainside. As they walked up the path through the dew-covered garden, Hiroshi stopped and turned to look out across the valley. Sam stood beside him, and the pair absorbed the beauty laid out before them. Sam could see the little fishing boats heading out from the village. Mist hung in the valley floor, and cutting through it Sam could see tiny figures heading out to the fields. He closed his eyes and turned his face to look directly at the sun and feel its warmth.

"Hai," said Hiroshi quietly, turning to carry on walking up the path with Sam following. This time when they did misogi, Hiroshi stood beneath the waterfall with Sam. Once again Hiroshi called out a loud "Hai!" when Sam was allowed to step out. However, Hiroshi stayed in the waterfall for, what Sam guessed, was another ten or fifteen minutes. Sam could not believe that this old man could stand rock steady for so long and show no signs of cold as he stepped out to join Sam on the bank. Sam had been doing exercises to warm up, but he was still shivering.

"Today, we will go to the Zen Buddhist temple farther up the mountain," said Hiroshi after they had returned to the house and had breakfast, "I wish to speak to the head priest."

Hiroshi prepared for the visit by gathering together some dried persimmon fruit as a gift. He told Sam to change out of his gi and into the other traditional Japanese clothes he had given to him.

"Won't they think I look a bit odd and ask questions? I don't suppose there are many westerners in Japan in 1537," asked Sam.

"You are quite right," said Hiroshi. "You would be very unusual and cause quite a stir if you were to be seen. However, in this matter, you have my help. I am able to make you appear as a Japanese to those whom we might encounter. Even so, it would be best to avoid meeting strangers, so we will take the hidden path that carries on past the waterfall to the temple. If we walk on the main path, we are more likely to encounter visitors to the temple. When you meet the head priest, he will see you as you are. He is a man whom we can trust."

They set off up the mountain on the path past the waterfall.

"Stay close by me, Sam. If you start to get tired, just tell me, and we can stop for a rest."

Sam was confident in his fitness and had no doubt that he would be quite capable of keeping up with Hiroshi. The path ran alongside the stream and occasionally crisscrossed it as they climbed. The sun was rising steadily, and the day was growing warmer. Though the first leaves were beginning to appear, the trees were still mostly bare so the sun filled the forest with light.

After an hour of steep climbing, Sam began to flag. Hiroshi's pace was steady but relentless. He seemed to move with an uncanny efficiency that Sam was far from emulating. Sam knew he wouldn't be able to keep this pace up much longer and eventually asked Hiroshi for a break. They sat side by side on large rocks on the bank of the stream. The sound of the water was soothing, and Sam dipped his tired and hot feet into a little pool. Insects buzzed about in the warmth of the sun, and birds hopped along the bank of the stream, trying to catch their lunch.

Hiroshi reached into his bag slung over his back. He pulled out a ball of rice about the size of a cricket ball wrapped in some cloth and offered it to Sam. The rice had been mixed with miso, and Sam gratefully broke off a half. They also drank some water from the stream, and once Sam felt ready, they set off again.

After another hour or so Sam, began to notice stone markers with Japanese writing on them and guessed they were approaching the temple. Then in the distance, still some way above them, he could make out a wall made from large stones and the edges of roofs above the wall. The little path wound its way up through the trees before eventually arriving at a very old looking small wooden gate in the wall.

Hiroshi knocked on the gate, and they waited. It wasn't long before they heard sounds from behind the gate, and then the gate swung open. An old man dressed in long dark blue robes stood before them. He was clean shaven, even his head, and he wore a huge smile as he greeted Hiroshi. He put his hands together at his chest and bowed deeply to them both. Hiroshi and Sam bowed back. Then Sam began to rise but realised that the other man was still bowing, and so he lowered his head again, hoping no one would notice his missed step, and continued to bow. The bow seemed to last a long time before finally Hiroshi and the man rose back up with Sam following.

"Hiroshi!" said the man. "It is so wonderful to see you. Please come in, come in! I see you have a companion with you."

"And it is wonderful to see you, Taka. I would like you to meet my student, Sam Stone, disciple to Iwata Sensei. Sam, this is Reverend Taka Kokushi, Head Priest of the Zenrin-ji temple."

Taka put his hands together once again and bowed to Sam. Sam also bowed and this time stayed bowing until he was aware that Taka had arisen.

"It is a great pleasure to make your acquaintance, Sam," said Taka, with a warm smile. "Please come with me and let me offer you both some food and something to drink."

Sam looked around as they walked into the temple complex. There were a number of single-story wooden buildings that looked similar to Hiroshi's dojo. Between the buildings ran paths made from flat irregular-shaped stones. Between the stones of the path grew moss. It reminded Sam of the entrance to Kensho's dojo.

Some parts of the garden had large ponds; others had shrubs and little trees. The most unusual part of the garden had gravel that was raked, which looked like little waves that ran perfectly straight. In the gravel, large rocks stood tall, and around the rocks the gravel was raked with lines running in circles. Monks in robes were tending to the garden, and they bowed as the three of them passed by.

Taka stopped at the entrance to one of the buildings and bowed a little as he invited Hiroshi and Sam to enter before him. Hiroshi removed his shoes at the entrance and then went in and sat on a cushion inside. Sam followed suit and sat to Hiroshi's left. Finally, Taka came in and sat opposite them. The room was very simple with smooth wooden floors and cushions for seating. Large windows in the walls allowed the sun to stream in, lighting the tiny specks of dust that hung in the air.

Hiroshi gave Taka his gift for which Taka was very grateful. Then a monk brought them tea and some food. With the formalities over, the conversation could begin.

Taka and Hiroshi discussed simple things at first such as the weather, how things were at the temple, life in the village and so on. But after a little while, the discussion became more serious.

"Things are shifting fast, Hiroshi," said Taka. "I sense the growing malevolence, of which I know you are all too well aware."

Hiroshi nodded, and Taka continued: "The daimyo is coming under its influence too. Where once he was benevolent and fair to his people, I see him changing. He is getting drawn ever deeper into the power struggle that rages in Kyoto, and his craving for power is growing.

"There are rumours that his tolerance of you is coming to an end. I have heard that he will soon make one final demand that you teach his samurai. I know that you will not, and you know what the consequence of that will be. He sees this as a matter of honour, Hiroshi. If you decline once again, then he will see it as dishonouring him. He will only feel his honour has been restored when he has killed you."

"What do I do, Taka? I cannot take a life. Yet, I also cannot fail in my responsibility as a Guardian. I have tried to reason with Hirohito. I have tried to reach the light that still lies within him. But I have failed."

"You may find no alternative but to take his life, Hiroshi," said Taka, looking compassionately at Hiroshi. "I know that must be inconceivable to you. Yet, with the burden that you carry, I do not see a choice for you. Life is rarely black and white. Look at us, a temple of Buddhist monks. What more peaceful people could one imagine? Yet we find ourselves with no choice but to take up arms to protect ourselves from attacks by other Buddhist temples. This is the madness wrought by this malevolence.

"Please remember my friend that you find yourself in this position through the work of Darkness. Hirohito has made his choices that lead him to his fate."

"It won't be long now until I have to leave this valley," said Hiroshi. "Will all your temples be safe refuges still, Taka?"

"Yes, Hiroshi. We are still some way off from the corruption of our temples. But you must be ever vigilant of those who visit the temples. They will be your greatest threat."

Sam was shocked to hear what Hiroshi was saying. It seemed Hiroshi was being squeezed from both sides. In the mountains, the evil was growing, and now he was threatened by the powerful lord who controlled the lives of Hiroshi and everyone who lived in the valley. Sam wondered when Hiroshi would leave and where he would go. He also wondered what would happen to Hiroshi's home while Hiroshi was away. He hoped it wouldn't be destroyed.

"You enter this story at a very difficult time," said Taka, turning to

Sam. "I see you are a young man with great compassion. This is your great strength. This is your light. Your role in this will be vital. This I also sense. Listen well to your teachers. Trust your truth. I will pray for you and for all who seek to bring light where there is darkness."

"I am sorry, my friend," said Taka, now turning back to Hiroshi, "but would you please excuse me? I have duties to which I must attend."

"Of course. I have taken up too much of your time and hospitality already," said Hiroshi.

"Not at all," said Taka. "It is always such a pleasure to see you. I will pass word to those that I trust in the temples along your route to let them know that you may be in need of their shelter in the coming months. I pray that we will see each other again before you leave. But it seems to me that we will not. Please know that you are always in my prayers."

"Thank you for your guidance and friendship," said Hiroshi, bowing. "I pray that we will meet again when times are not so dark, my friend."

Taka showed them back to the gate.

"Farewell, Hiroshi. Farewell, Sam. In all that you encounter, do your best."

"Farewell, my dear friend," said Hiroshi.

With that Hiroshi and Sam stepped through the gateway back into the forest and Taka closed the gate behind them.

CHAPTER 39

Oni and Awareness

Sam followed Hiroshi back down the mountain. He was feeling very unsettled by the conversation between Hiroshi and Taka. The way they had parted felt very much to him as though they never expected to see each other again. He felt profoundly sad that he may have witnessed the last farewell of two very old and close friends. He hated the feeling of loss that rose up in him. Nothing seemed to last.

They were perhaps halfway home when suddenly Hiroshi stopped. Sam snapped out of his melancholy thoughts and returned to the present moment. As he did so, he began to feel a sense of foreboding.

"Stand close behind me, Sam," said Hiroshi, quietly but urgently.

Sam closed the gap between them and stood within arm's reach of Hiroshi's back. Hiroshi drew his sword, and Sam's heart began to race and his mouth felt dry as the fear grew ever stronger in him. He knew that something very evil was approaching.

They were standing on the path at the bottom of a little shallow valley. But for the sense of dread, it was a beautiful scene with the rays of the early afternoon sun filtering through the branches.

Sam scanned the ridge above, which was the direction Hiroshi was facing. Hiroshi stood motionless and quiet. Then Sam began to hear, and maybe even feel, heavy footfalls approaching through the forest. Whatever was approaching was huge, and it was noisy. He could hear grunts as it crashed through the trees, snapping branches. But still, he couldn't see it.

Then he noticed a branch violently shake at the top of the rise, and the creature appeared. It was indeed huge, standing perhaps twice the height of a large man and three times as wide. It had dark brown leathery skin, little neck and a low wide head with little ears. But it was its eyes that Sam fixated on. They were very narrow and wide, and they shone a yellow golden colour. The creature stopped, sniffed for a moment and then spotted them below it. It snorted loudly and then raised a huge club that it held in its left hand before beginning to rush down upon them. Sam involuntarily began to back away.

"Stay close behind me Sam," directed Hiroshi, who was still facing the creature with his sword raised above his head.

As the creature got closer and drew its club back, ready to strike, Hiroshi moved with incredible speed towards it, letting out a piercing kiai as he did so. Seeing Hiroshi's advance, the creature tried to swing the club at him. But it was far too slow, and in two cuts that happened in an instant, Hiroshi cut the attacking arm at the elbow and then brought the sword around in an arc and cut the creature's left leg at the knee. The club fell to the ground, taking the creature's lower arm with it. The creature fell onto its right knee and let out a bellow of rage. But the bellow was short lived as Hiroshi plunged the sword through its chest from behind. The creature's lifeless body fell forward onto the ground barely a metre from where Sam stood.

Hiroshi immediately returned to stand in front of Sam again, his sword ready to receive another attack. But no attack came. After a minute or two, Hiroshi shook the blood off the sword before sheathing it.

"Are you alright?" asked Hiroshi.

Sam was in a state of shock but managed to nod, as he began choking on the foul stench of the creature.

"Well, that is a first for both of us. I too have never seen an oni before. I have heard tales and read stories, but now we have both had our first encounter with this foe. It will not be our last. Come, let us head home quickly before dusk begins to fall."

Sam looked one last time at the creature, watching the black blood ooze from its body, before turning and beginning to walk alongside Hiroshi. They travelled the rest of the journey quickly and in silence.

It was with great relief that Sam finally emerged into the garden, leaving the forest behind. Hiroshi immediately instructed Sam to go into the house, light the fire and get it blazing strong while he remained outside.

Hiroshi eventually came in.

"I do not sense any particular danger tonight. This house may not look very strong to you, Sam, but there are powers protecting it that you do not see. You are safe in here, and it is important that you get your rest. There is still much training for you to do over the coming days."

Sam sat quietly before asking,

"Sensei, where did that creature come from?"

"I don't know Sam," replied Hiroshi. "Just as I don't know the origins of tengu. What I do know is that if oni have hearts, they are quite black. I think the best way to try to understand their origin is to just accept that they come from Darkness. What is the origin of any evil? It is beyond our comprehension. We must simply recognise evil for what it is. Sometimes, it is obvious such as an oni. Other times, it is subtle such as turning a blind eye. It is the subtle that is truly dangerous and that erodes one's goodness little by little. That is why awareness is our greatest ally. If we are truly aware, we are truly light."

Sam thought for a while and then asked, "What do you mean by 'awareness', Sensei?"

"Let us take a little journey, Sam. Let me show you one aspect of awareness. When we take this journey, it will seem as though we are physically there, but fear not, we shall never leave this spot, and we will be quite invisible to those we observe."

Then Hiroshi drew his sword, and it seemed to Sam that the room faded around them and a different room began to come into view slowly. Two old Japanese men were sitting at a table talking. One man was telling the other how his sons were progressing in their martial arts training. Each was coming on well, he said, but one was making the greatest progress. He then decided to demonstrate to his guest their differing skill levels.

He balanced an empty clay pot on top of the door, which he left ajar. Then he called the first son to join them. The first son pushed the door open, and the pot began to fall, but before it could hit him, he stepped to the side and cut it with his sword. His father then asked him to clean up the mess and dismissed him.

Then, he balanced another pot and called his second son. The second son pushed open the door, and the pot began to fall. But he moved as quick as lightning and caught the pot before placing it carefully on the table beside the door. Again, his father dismissed him. Finally, after he had balanced the pot once more, the father called his third son. As the son arrived at the door, he noticed the pot, reached up and took it down before pushing the door open and saying, "Yes, father?" The father dismissed him and turned to his guest and said, "You see how close to mastery my third son is?"

The room began to fade again and Sam found himself back in Hiroshi's house.

"Mastery of the martial arts is not being the strongest or the fastest," said Hiroshi. "It is about awareness with perfect clarity. That is not just awareness of that which is external to us. It is awareness of what goes on within ourselves.

"If we are not aware of what goes on within ourselves, then what is in us controls us without our knowing. People are controlled by their feelings of shame or anger or pride or whatever fills them, yet they are not aware. They do not even know those feelings are in them, let alone that they are controlled by them. It is as if they are asleep. If they became aware, then they would begin to see through those feelings and no longer be controlled by them. Sam, you will never master iaido, aikido or master yourself if you do not know yourself. You must wake up."

Sam thought for a while and then said,

"But isn't anger a good thing sometimes? If I see someone being hurt that makes me angry, and I step in to help them. Otherwise, I'd just ignore them and walk away."

"No, Sam," replied Hiroshi. "Stepping in to satisfy your anger is not a good thing. The anger might arise within you, but you must simply be aware of it but not be driven by it. Then you step in because it is the right thing to do, not to satisfy your anger. If you respond through anger, then you might do something in that moment, driven by your anger, that you later regret. One does not have to be angry to act.

"It is not a question of suppressing or never having feelings of anger. Those feelings may be present. It is about being aware of those feelings but not being controlled by them. This is hard to understand, Sam. This is why you must train with great dedication. Through dedicated training comes awareness. Awareness of what is inside as well as what is outside."

Sam thought some more and then said, "What about love? That is a feeling. Doesn't that control us?"

"No, Sam," said Hiroshi, laughing. "Love is not a feeling. Love is our natural state. It is innate to us when we are born into this world. It is what we return to when we find awareness.

"Awareness is love. Let me explain. You are on a bus in Vancouver, and a man gets on and starts screaming with rage at the other passengers. He pushes people out of the way, he starts to smash the windows, tear at the seats, he throws passengers' belongings. People are scared, someone might get hurt by this violent man. One's natural response might be to dislike this man, to hate him even. One might even think this man is evil. One might become angry and want to step in and beat this violent and evil man.

"But what if you learnt that some great tragedy had befallen this man? His mother and father and siblings had all just died in a fire at his home. He had been careless in some way that had lead to the fire. He was full of guilt at his mistake. He was full of rage at himself and the injustice of life that such innocent people would be taken, yet he had survived. He was full of pain. He was on the bus to go to the morgue where the bodies of his loved ones lay. His world was collapsing around him and he was completely unable to cope.

"How would you then see that man? In awareness how would you now feel for him? Should you step in to prevent him from injuring anyone on the bus, as well as himself? Of course! But you would step in with love and with deep compassion. The nature of your response would be quite different.

"Do you understand, Sam? Do you understand that we must also become aware of what emotions control us? If we are full of anger or guilt or shame and we are not aware, then they control us. The effects might not be as dramatic as they were for the man on the bus, but controlled we will be. In awareness, we see those emotions. We don't deny them or seek to get rid of them. We just observe them. We might say, 'Ah look, this situation is bringing up feelings of guilt.' Just that simple observation begins to free us from the control of that feeling.

"This is why we train, Sam. That is the true purpose of martial arts, true budo. Not for fame or to have power over others. We train for awareness. This is why we stand under an icy waterfall. This is why we meditate for hours. That is why we practice iaido and aikido, because this training will bring awareness. Only then can we bring light to the world.

"But that is enough talk. If talking brought awareness, then we would not need to train. Let us prepare dinner. All this talking is making me hungry!" With that Hiroshi let out a big bellowing laugh.

"Remember to be gentle on yourself, Sam," said Hiroshi. "We are all imperfect. We always will be. We will always make mistakes, we will always fail. All that we must do is dedicate ourselves to our training and trust. That and laugh often and long!"

That night as Sam lay beside the fire, his thoughts were not on the incredible events of the day. He had been attacked by a dreadful creature that most people would never even believe existed. Yet his thoughts were about the emotions that were in him. He remembered the rage that drove him to pick up the brick that he was going to throw at Kensho's windows. How could he not have seen that rage before? It seemed incredible. Well, he thought, I am making progress at least. And I've seen an oni. Though no one would believe me if I told them. He laughed quietly to himself and then rolled over and drifted off to sleep.

CHAPTER 40
Motsugai and Humility

For the next eight days, Sam continued his rigorous training of meditation, misogi and bokken practice. Slowly, he began to find more peace and less pain in the meditation. Each time under the waterfall, he seemed to be able to stay a little longer and shiver a little less violently.

His bokken practice was very intense, and he really wondered if he was making any progress at all. But he knew from his aikido training that progress often seemed imperceptible, and sometimes it came in great leaps after long periods of apparent stagnation. So he kept his spirits up and simply applied himself as best as he could.

Towards the end of the eighth day, as they completed the afternoon's bokken training, Hiroshi said to Sam, "It is time for you to begin handling a sword. Wait here."

As he sat waiting for Hiroshi to return Sam couldn't quite believe that the moment he had dreamed of was finally here.

After a minute or so, Hiroshi entered the dojo with a sword in its sheath. He sat before Sam and unsheathed the sword.

"This is not a Divine Sword. Nonetheless, it is a very fine sword. It was made over 200 years ago by Gorō Nyūdō Masamune, one of Japan's great swordsmiths and a man with a pure spirit. I give it to you now, Sam. It was passed to me by my master's master, and now it is passed to you by your master's master."

Hiroshi bowed and held the sword out in the palms of both his hands. Sam took the sword and held it in the palms of his hands, blade facing toward him and then bowed to Hiroshi.

"Good," said Hiroshi. "Now let us begin your training with your sword."

Sam had dreamt of this moment for a long time. Hiroshi showed Sam how to correctly sheath the sword and then how to slide the sheathed sword through the belt of his gi. Everything, as always, was done with the greatest of precision, and no movement was unnecessary.

Then for the first time in his life, Sam drew a real samurai sword. His practice with the bokken had helped, but this was something completely different. He slightly fumbled drawing the sword, and then he held it out in front of him. The balance of the blade felt perfect. Sam was acutely aware he was holding something incredibly powerful and dangerous. He knew this blade was sharper than a razor and must be treated with enormous respect. But more than anything, it felt right. It was almost as though he had held this blade before, so familiar was it to him.

For another hour or so Hiroshi taught him how to draw the sword and then sheath it correctly. Sam realised he could practice this one simple movement alone for years and never get it right. One of the trickiest parts was the shaking of the sword before sheathing it. Hiroshi explained this was to shake your opponent's blood off the blade. It was what Hiroshi had done after he had cut down the oni. His own efforts seemed laughably bad to Sam. In truth, he very much hoped he would never have need of this anyway. The thought of cutting another person with this blade seemed impossible to him.

When they headed back to the house for the evening, Hiroshi began to teach Sam proper care of the sword. There was much to learn, and Sam was fascinated. He realised he had a treasure in this sword, and he felt great responsibility to maintain it well. It was not just a matter of keeping the blade clean and polished, but it was also about maintaining the other parts of the sword as well as the sheath itself.

That evening, they were sitting beside the fire as usual. Sam was appreciating these moments all the more since he had heard Hiroshi talk of having to leave the house.

"Are you a samurai warrior?" asked Sam.

"No, I am not samurai," said Hiroshi, continuing to clean his sword.

"To be samurai one needs to be in service to the daimyo. Samurai is a class in Japan. I am a simple farmer. I am not in the service of the daimyo. It is usually only samurai who may carry a sword. In fact, samurai carry two swords: a long one, like the one we have been using, called a katana, and a shorter one called a wakizashi. It is a status symbol for the samurai and only they are allowed to wear the two swords.

"However, some farmers are also granted the right to carry a sword. I am one of those farmers. That I also teach iaido is not usually tolerated. However, the daimyo for this region has, until now, accepted it. I teach very few people, and I am not generally known as a teacher. As you heard during our visit to Taka, the daimyo wishes me to teach his samurai."

Hiroshi fell silent, and Sam thought it wise not to question him anymore. Hiroshi didn't speak again that evening. They prepared the evening meal together and ate it in silence. Sam was slowly getting to grips with the chopsticks. It actually struck Sam just how easy it had been to fit into life in Japan nearly 500 years ago. Unlike Europeans of that time, the Japanese washed regularly and usually bathed every day. Europeans of the same period bathed once every few months and ate with a knife and their fingers. By comparison, the Japanese were much more sophisticated. It made it easy for Sam to fit in, even if he did have to learn so much etiquette. Simple things, such as where one sat beside the fireplace, were in fact governed by very clear rules. But Sam was at ease with this way of life. He loved the simplicity and the timeless feel of things. It was more peaceful and far more connected to the environment within which they existed. Were it not for the malevolence that constantly threatened them, Sam would have felt quite content.

The following morning, as they trained in the dojo with the sword, Hiroshi stopped Sam. Whenever Hiroshi did this, Sam immediately sat in seiza and focused completely on what Hiroshi said or what he demonstrated.

"Your progress has been excellent, Sam. You are an exemplary student. You have entered into your training with dedication, and you have maintained the 'beginner's mind' of which we spoke."

Sam smiled with pride as Hiroshi continued: "However, you are very young, and you are in danger of becoming arrogant. The pride that fills you can easily lead you astray."

Sam's smile fell away.

"You are not superior to anyone, Sam, nor are you inferior," said Hiroshi. "Everyone you encounter is no better or worse than you. The only difference between you and another man is the path that each of you have walked upon. Had you walked the same path, you would be little different. When you return to your home, you are at risk of returning with arrogance and a feeling of superiority. This is a great danger to you and will set you on a path towards Darkness. Remember, Sam, that it is the subtle things that slowly lead one astray. It is these subtle things of which we must be so aware. You must be aware of your arrogance and your feeling of superiority, and you must see through them.

"Let me show you a great Japanese martial arts master and priest, a master with amazing strength and skills, who could easily defeat any man who would challenge him. If ever there was a man who should be arrogant and feel superior, Motsugai Fusen would be such a man."

Hiroshi knelt beside Sam, the room began to fade, and Sam found himself in a beautiful garden much like Taka's. There was a man who was perhaps 50 years old, tending to the garden and sweeping up the leaves that had fallen on the path. As the man worked away a samurai warrior entered through a gate. He had his two swords tucked through his belt, and he strutted up to the man and asked,

"Where is Motsugai? I wish to challenge him to a duel."

The man did not answer but kept on sweeping. The samurai raised his voice and put his hand to the hilt of his sword. "Do not dare to ignore me! Are you Motsugai?" he asked angrily.

The man gave no response to the samurai. Instead he calmly bent down and grasped the bottom of a huge rock. With one arm he lifted the side of the rock up and swept the leaves under it before carefully lowering the enormous rock back to the ground.

"Who are you?" asked the samurai, stepping back in astonishment.

"I am but a lowly student," said the man as he turned to face the samurai. "Motsugai is unavailable today but perhaps if you come back tomorrow he will accept your request for a duel."

The samurai saw the huge strength and the lack of fear that Motsugai's student showed. He thus thought better of issuing his challenge to Motsugai, turned and quickly departed.

As the man returned to his sweeping, Hiroshi turned to Sam and quietly said, "That is Motsugai."

Then the garden began to fade, and Sam found himself in a busy street.

"We are in a street in Kyoto, one of Japan's largest cities," said Hiroshi.

Then Sam spotted Motsugai walking along the street towards them. He was dressed in very simple clothes, looked rather poor and was noticed by nobody. Then Motsugai stopped outside the building next to Sam and Hiroshi.

Sam became aware of the sounds of martial artists training inside and realised it was a dojo, and Motsugai was obviously stopping to observe.

"This is the dojo of Kondo Isami, and the men who are training inside are very dangerous. They are killers and are responsible for many assassinations," said Hiroshi.

Suddenly a man appeared at the entrance to the dojo.

"That's Isami."

Isami challenged Motsugai. "Who are you, and why do you dare to watch our training?"

"Please excuse me, sir. I am just a lowly country fool, and I was interested by the sounds I heard," said Motsugai.

"You are interested, are you? Then come inside and let us show you what we do!" said Isami as he grabbed Motsugai and dragged him into the dojo. He threw Motsugai into the middle of the training mat and said, "We have someone who wishes to train with us!"

The other five men in the dojo all laughed at the sight of this simple old man who looked so poor and helpless.

"I apologise if I have offended you. I do not wish to cause any trouble. Please let me go on my way," said Motsugai.

"Why leave now when you were so interested in what we do? Let one of my students give you a demonstration," replied Isami.

At that, Isami pointed to one of the men who quickly drew his sword and attacked Motsugai. Motsugai, armed only with a short walking staff, easily defeated the initial attack and disarmed the swordsman. He then defeated the next attack and gave the attacker a little nudge and the attacker sprawled ignominiously onto the floor. Isami looked furious and pointed at another of his students, who also attacked and who met the same fate. As each of his students was humiliated with such ease Isami became ever more furious.

Eventually, it was only Isami left to challenge Motsugai. Rather than using his sword, he took a long spear down from the rack on the wall. This was obviously going to be far harder for Motsugai to defend against as he would not be able to get close to Isami. So, Motsugai took two little wooden bowls out from the sack he had slung over his shoulder. As Isami thrust the spear at Motsugai's chest, Motsugai trapped the spear's blade between the bowls. Try as he might, Isami could not break the grip Motsugai had on the spear. Isami pulled with all his might and suddenly Motsugai released his hold on the spear. Isami tumbled in a heap against the wall of the dojo.

Isami, accepting his defeat, stood up and bowed to Motsugai.

"We have encountered a great master. My name is Kondo Isami. Might I know your name?"

Motsugai bowed and then walked to the door, where he paused briefly and said, "My name is Motsugai," before leaving.

Shock and astonishment filled the faces of Isami and his students.

Then Isami's dojo began to fade, and Sam found himself back at Hiroshi's dojo.

"Please learn from Motsugai, Sam," said Hiroshi. "He was one of Japan's greatest martial artists."

Sam nodded, his pride now gone. Thinking of Hiroshi, Kensho, O'Sensei and Motsugai, he realised how little he knew and how far he still had to go. He was just beginning to understand how much more to his training there was than simply mastering the techniques.

"Come, Sam. Let us go and practice misogi," said Hiroshi as he stood up and walked to the dojo door.

That evening Sam and Hiroshi talked once again. At first Sam tried to find out more about the powers of the Divine Swords, but Hiroshi would only say, "In good time."

Then Sam asked, "Where is Tatsuya? I know he was banished, but to where? How did I see him on my journey here? And why is he growing stronger? And why did he try to grab me? And are the oni and tengu and the other evil things under his control?"

"That was six questions at once, Sam," said Hiroshi, laughing. "You are getting bolder!"

"Sorry, Sensei," said Sam, looking down. "I try not to pester you with too many questions, but there is so much I don't understand."

"I understand Sam," replied Hiroshi. "I know how hard it is not to know everything. Remember I once sat where you now sit, full of the same questions that you now ask. Tatsuya is caught in the gap between worlds. You travelled through that gap to arrive here. Quite why you saw him, I do not exactly know. It may be that it is just an indication of his growing power. But then Kensho and I would see him as well as the other Guardians, and we do not."

Sam's eyes opened wide at the mention of other Guardians, but Hiroshi continued before he could interrupt.

"So it is perhaps something special about you, Sam, though I am not clear yet what. As for his growing power, it was predicted in the scrolls that he would return. Master Osawa knew that Tatsuya's banishment would not last forever, and thus the Guardians have long been seeking the key to finally rid the world of his influence.

"As to why he is growing stronger now, I am not entirely sure. However, I suspect he draws much of his power from the evil energy that is created by men and women. Japan has been going through a very violent and evil period for some time now. Most people are simple and only wish to live in peace and harmony with each other and with nature. But there are a few men who crave only power and will take it at any price. So much violence, so much death, so much deception and treachery has taken place. I suspect that this is giving Tatsuya power, and I also suspect that he lies behind it, constantly fanning the flames of violence and drawing strength from it.

"But the Guardians cannot be drawn into the politics and warring between the daimyos. That is not our path to walk."

Sam had been trying to listen, but really he was bursting to ask his next question.

"There are other Guardians?" he asked excitedly. "How many? And where are they?"

"Well done, Sam," laughed Hiroshi. "That was only three questions. Yes, there are other Guardians, and they are spread throughout Japan. But I have not yet answered all of your earlier six questions, Sam."

Sam apologised, and Hiroshi continued, "I don't think that the oni and tengu are yet directly under Tatsuya's control. However, he is influencing the tengu and drawing them deeper into Darkness, of that I am certain. I also do not think it is a coincidence that the number of oni is on the rise. Where they come from is a mystery, other than that they come out of Darkness.

"As with all evil, they are drawn inexorably towards the light. They are drawn towards it because they wish to destroy it. This is true of those creatures as much as it is true of men and women who have been lost to Darkness. But do not forget, Sam, that good is also drawn to the light. The brighter the light, the more good is drawn. Light can pass from one person to another like a flame that may be passed from candle to candle. One candle may look lost in the darkness, but from that one candle ten candles can be lit, and from those ten another thousand, and from those thousand another ten thousand.

"We are those candles in the darkness, and we must keep burning fierce and bright. Now it is getting late, and you must prepare for bed."

CHAPTER 41

Time to Return

Sam knew he was becoming more aware of his surroundings though he didn't realise quite what a transformation had taken place. He walked with his head up, and his vision was softening and becoming more diffuse. Instead of allowing any one thing to capture his whole attention, he allowed his awareness to rest upon all that his eyes saw. He felt the uneven surface beneath his feet. He noticed his breathing, and he became aware of tension that he carried in his body. He began to move in a more relaxed and easy manner.

After another morning's training in the dojo, Sam caught sight of his first tengu. Spring was really underway, and the garden was beginning to grow quickly. One of his other major chores was helping Hiroshi keep on top of the weeds. As he made his way up to the woodshed he looked at the vegetable plots to see which needed weeding. Though he was looking down he still caught a glimpse of some movement deeper in the forest. Sam had his sword by his side, so he decided to keep walking without giving any indication that he had seen the movement. As he continued up the garden, the movement became more defined. Sam realised it was the shape of a small person. He guessed it was a tengu, but still he continued towards the woodshed while giving no indication that he had seen anything.

As Sam reached the woodshed, he was aware that the tengu had moved nearer towards him through the forest. It was probably 30 metres away. Sam walked behind the woodshed out of the tengu's sight and paused for a moment before suddenly looking around the side. Sure enough, he had caught the tengu sneaking between the trees. It spotted him, and quick as a flash it threw a large stone with amazing accuracy. Just avoiding being hit, Sam ducked behind the woodshed and nearly bumped into Hiroshi.

"I see we have a visitor," Hiroshi said as he stepped out from behind the woodshed and effortlessly side-stepped another stone that came flying out of the forest. Hiroshi let out a powerful kiai, and the tengu fled.

"They are getting bolder, but as yet they are not too dangerous. That could change very quickly. Next time you see or even sense any danger, please come to me, Sam. Tengu might be small, but they have the ability to be dangerous."

"Yes, Sensei. I will."

"Good," said Hiroshi. "Then let us gather some logs and head back to the house."

The days seemed to be flying by now. Sam had settled into the daily routine and was feeling much more comfortable in Hiroshi's presence. He understood the boundaries and requirements of the relationship. Hiroshi's demands were exceptionally high, and if Sam slacked even in the slightest then Hiroshi would reprimand him immediately. But Sam began to appreciate Hiroshi's exacting demands. He knew that it was because Hiroshi cared so deeply about him that he pushed him to excel. Sam also knew that this wasn't a game. His life probably depended upon him quickly mastering the skills Hiroshi taught him.

On the morning of his last day, Sam awoke before Hiroshi had finished his meditation and emerged from his bedroom. In the chill of the early morning, Sam silently rolled up his sleeping mat and folded his blanket. He quietly stoked the fire and placed a few more logs on. Then he sat and waited patiently. Before long, Hiroshi slid the shoji to his room open. In the dim light cast by the fire, Sam saw Hiroshi nod to him. Sam stood up and followed Hiroshi to the dojo.

Morning meditation was getting steadily easier, but misogi remained very difficult and not something Sam remotely looked forward to. It was true that he was staying under the waterfall a little longer than when he had started, but it seemed to him his progress was rather pathetic. He very quickly began to shiver uncontrollably and still marvelled at Hiroshi's ability to stand for so long and so steady.

As they walked down from the waterfall for the final time, Sam felt sadness rising up in him. Though his time with Hiroshi had been incredibly challenging, he had found that he really enjoyed it here. He enjoyed the training, he enjoyed learning from such an incredible man, and he enjoyed living so simply in the farmhouse in ancient Japan.

They walked silently down the little path under the growing canopy of young green leaves and emerged from the forest to the view across the valley. Hiroshi stopped. They stood side by side, the teacher and his student, filled once again by the beauty that was laid out before them.

Sam could see that the paddy fields were all flooded and they were a hive of activity. He wished he could go down, meet the people and help them in the fields. He really wanted to become part of this community. But then his thoughts turned to Zoe and Sophie back home. Though to them it had only been a couple of days, for Sam these two weeks or so seemed a very long time to be out of contact with them. He wished he could bring them here to see this incredible place and to meet Hiroshi.

Hiroshi patted Sam on the back before continuing down the garden path. When they entered the farmhouse, they were met by Kensho.

"Hello, Sensei," he said, bowing.

"Hello, Kensho!" replied Hiroshi, bowing as well.

"Hello, Sensei," said Sam to Kensho as he bowed long and deep. Sam was overjoyed to see Kensho and immediately wanted to tell him everything that had happened and all that he had learnt, but he managed to bottle it up.

"Hello Sam! Well, you appear to be in fine shape. I very much look forward to hearing the tale that you no doubt have to tell."

"He is a fine student, Kensho. You have taught him well at your dojo, and so he has made good progress here," said Hiroshi, happily.

"Thank you Sensei. Well done Sam. I knew that you would rise to the challenge. Have you managed to enjoy it?"

"It has been an incredible two weeks, Sensei. Nagato Sensei has been very patient with me, and I have done my best to learn all that he has taught me. I see I have a very, very long way to go."

"Good. Sensei, I have water boiling ready for tea, and I have also prepared some lunch."

"Wonderful, Kensho!" said Hiroshi happily. "You are a great student indeed!"

As they ate lunch together, Hiroshi told Kensho of the encounter with the oni and also of his visit to Taka. Sam listened intently as Hiroshi spoke. When he reached the part about having to leave the house, Hiroshi said, "I am not sure exactly when I will have to leave, Kensho. It may be in weeks, months or yet still in years. However, both Taka and I foresee that my departure from this valley will be inevitable one day."

Kensho nodded and asked, "Do you know where you will go?"

"Tokin-ji temple," replied Hiroshi.

"Hai, Sensei," said Kensho, nodding.

Then Hiroshi turned to Sam. "It is time for you to go home for now, Sam, though you will return. While you are only just beginning your training, you have done well. Remember to keep your awareness strong. Look inside yourself and recognise the feelings that arise. Do not judge them. If anger arises, then simply notice it, but do not judge it as bad. If compassion arises, simply notice it also, but do not judge it as good. Just be aware. With awareness will come self-mastery. In awareness, you will naturally and effortlessly act properly. In awareness, you will shine, and as you shine, so you will light others around you. This is the true way to drive out Darkness."

Sam nodded. He was starting to grasp what it was that Hiroshi and Kensho were trying to teach him.

"Thank you, Nagato Sensei. I am deeply grateful that you have had the patience to teach me. I will do my best to stay in awareness, and I very much look forward to training here with you again soon."

Hiroshi stood up, and Sam and Kensho followed. Hiroshi bowed to Sam, and Sam bowed back. Finally Hiroshi bowed to Kensho."I must do some work in the garden. Goodbye, Kensho. Goodbye, Sam." Then he turned and left the house.

"Let us head home, Sam," said Kensho.

"What should I do with the sword?" asked Sam.

"It is your sword now, Sam. Bring it to the dojo with you, and I will look after it for you."

"Thank you, Sensei."

Sam gathered his things together. Then he took one final look out of the shoji at the dojo and the garden. There was Hiroshi bent over working in the vegetable plot. Beyond lay the forest giving no hint of the malice hidden within, lit as it was by the bright spring sunshine. Here was the place that had so deeply, so profoundly, altered his life. He knew that a good part of him would forever remain here on this mountain in 16th century Japan.

Then Sam turned and walked over to join Kensho by the altar. They knelt side by side, their swords by their sides, and began to meditate. Before long, they were gone.

Sophie felt Sam's return. She was in the bedroom with Zoe when it happened.

"Zo, he's back! Wow! He feels so different!"

"How does he feel different, Soph?" asked Zoe.

Sophie paused, trying to find the words that adequately captured the change she felt in Sam before replying.

"He's softer yet stronger. There is a peacefulness to him. The anger has almost all gone. He's shining brighter than ever, Zo!"

"That's awesome! Wow. He is changing so much and so quickly, isn't he?"

"He is becoming a man. It is awesome!"

Then Sophie's face became more grave. "But I sense danger is closer than ever, Zo."

"Yes, even I feel that. That the danger is getting stronger. What is the danger? Do you know?"

"No. I can't figure it out," said Sophie, shaking her head. "When I try to look, all I see is black. I'd really like to talk to him. I can't wait until next Saturday!"

When Sam arrived back at Kensho's dojo he was relieved that he hadn't encountered Tatsuya during this journey. He went over to the wooden cabinet with Kensho. Kensho took Sam's sword and, after carefully wrapping it in a cloth he retrieved from the bottom drawer, put it in the drawer with his Divine Sword. Then the pair went down the secret staircase to the office.

It was early evening, and Kensho told Sam that he would have to take him home soon. But, before that, he asked Sam to tell him about his training with Hiroshi. He nodded as Sam told him about his first few days of training and being attacked by Hiroshi.

"That was my experience with Hiroshi's master too, Sam. I knew that you would have to go through that, but I also knew that you would be fine. You are a stubborn young man though! You lasted much longer than I did before giving in and admitting you were not able to defend yourself!"

"You went through exactly the same thing?" said Sam in astonishment.

"Every Guardian has been through the same experience. We all are so full of our own ideas, and it takes this to empty us and prepare us to learn. It is not a pleasant experience, but it is necessary."

Then Sam told him about misogi, the night the doors shook on the house, the trip to the temple, the attack by the oni and the encounter with the tengu.

"Well, Sam, you have had quite the adventure. I know you will want to tell your sisters and friends about it. But unfortunately you must not. I know it will be hard, but you must not breathe a word of any of this to anyone. Do you understand?"

"Yes Sensei."

"Good. Now go and get changed in the changing room and then let us get you home."

When he arrived home, Sam emailed Zoe and Sophie and told them that his weekend away with Kensho had been amazing and that he couldn't wait to see them on Saturday. Then he headed up to his bedroom and stood looking out of the window as the last light disappeared from the sky. The sunset caught the top of the snow-capped mountains, and they seemed to be aflame in the orange rays.

He thought of Hiroshi in his house so far away and so long ago. He wondered if Hiroshi was lonely. The whole thing seemed such a surreal experience now that he was home again. Had he really been attacked by an oni and a tengu? As he stood in his bedroom in East Vancouver with cars driving by, it seemed faintly ridiculous. But the fear he recalled as that huge creature charged them was still vivid, as was the memory of the stench of its blood.

He turned from the window and folded up a rug to make a little mat, placed a cushion on it and sat in seiza to meditate. He wanted to reconnect with that magical place so far away. After he had finished, he got ready for bed and then he read the Tao Te Ching. It didn't take long for his eyes to become heavy and for sleep to come. But just before he closed his eyes, his question as to whether Hiroshi was lonely was answered in the words he read:

To be 'lonely', 'orphaned' and 'worthless'
is what ordinary people hate.
Yet the sages embrace these, calling themselves by these terms.

CHAPTER 42

Trapped

Going to school on Monday morning was an incredible experience for Sam. The school was the same, but he was a completely different person. Before his time in Japan, he had felt immersed in all the social politics, caught up in the gossip about who was seeing who. The teachers had seemed so powerful, and the whole school experience so all-consuming.

Now, it was as if he was observing all that was happening, but he was no longer caught up in it. He looked at the people who had previously had so much influence over his life and realised they now had none. Clearly aware of all his past judgements and prejudices he realised just how badly his view of people had been distorted by how he felt about them. He recalled Kensho's words, "if you care about someone's approval then that person controls you."

It was so blindingly obvious now. He had cared and they had controlled him. But now he thought that those cares were gone.

There was also a complete shift in how people responded to him. Everyone sensed the change in Sam, the confidence and calmness that he now exuded, none more so than Kevin Jones. Gone was the mickey-taking about aikido, and Kevin's pirouettes with his buddies. Now Kevin kept his distance, all his bravado and feigned confidence gone.

Jake took Sam aside at morning break: "Dude, what's going on with you? What happened this weekend? It's like you're a different person. Not in a bad way. But dude, you're...well like you're... Dude I don't know. But you're way different."

"I guess some intense martial arts training can really have an effect, eh?"

"Dude, I should take this martial arts stuff seriously. Have you seen the way the babes are checking you out? Whatever it is, you got it, dude. You got it!"

"Dude! Like, that's crazy dude! The babes are like checking me out dude? Dude!" said Sam, laughing.

"What ho sir. Why don't you have some afternoon tea with the ladies? Tell them about queen and country, what ho!"

Laughing together Sam and Jake headed off to their next class. As they walked, Sam had to admit to himself that he had noticed a lot more glances and smiles in his direction from girls who previously had barely noticed him. He thought how good it felt to be noticed.

At lunch, Sam became aware of Kevin looking at him and quickly turning away whenever Sam looked back. As Sam sat eating he suddenly felt a huge surge of energy course through his body. He felt the delicious taste of power over others. He had seen things these people would never believe. He had been somewhere they would never believe. He had done things they would never believe. He was being trained by two of the greatest martial artists that had ever lived. He would become one of the greatest martial artists that had ever lived, wielding a sword of incredible power. He looked at all these little people around him, people who once had power over him, who now appeared so weak, so insignificant, so frightened.

Sam actually began to reel as this power flowed through him. He grasped the edge of the table. Suddenly the words of Hiroshi came to him: "You are not superior to anyone, Sam, nor are you inferior. When you return to your home, you are in danger of returning with arrogance and superiority. This is a great danger to you and will set you on a path towards Darkness."

Sam looked around the dining hall. The power that filled him began to subside. He looked at the people around him and he was filled with compassion for them. He saw himself in them: their fears and their confusion. He turned to Kevin and once more caught him looking over. Sam stood up and began to walk over to Kevin's table. Kevin was trying to look nonchalant but was failing miserably.

By the time he reached Kevin's table, Kevin and all his buddies had stopped talking and just sat looking at him. In fact, Sam noticed that the entire dining hall had gone silent. He squatted down beside Kevin, so Kevin might feel a little less threatened.

"I want to say thank you," said Sam, looking Kevin in the eyes. "You were so right, Kevin. aikido is just like dancing. You've got to show the same love and compassion to your attacker as you would to your dancing partner. Know what I mean? I'd never have got that without your help. You're a top man Kevin. Thanks."

Kevin just looked at Sam quite unable to articulate any kind of clever response.

"You're welcome," he said quietly after a few moments thought.

"You really should come down to the dojo with me one evening. See for yourself," said Sam. And he meant it. He knew that it was very unlikely Kevin would come, but his suggestion was genuine.

Then Sam stood up and bowed a little to Kevin.

"Take it easy gentlemen," said Sam to Kevin and his friends, before turning and walking out of the still silent dining hall.

Monday evening he had to work at the cafe, so he wasn't able to go to the dojo to train. However, he did receive an email from Zoe saying that they too couldn't wait to see him and hear all about his weekend's training.

He went to aikido on Tuesday night and was stunned to see how much he had improved following his two weeks with Hiroshi. That he was so much more relaxed was probably the greatest change. But his awareness of his attacker's ki had also developed noticeably. This meant that instead of trying to catch up with the attack, more often than not his timing was now such that he was leading the attack.

"Good, good Sam. You are progressing well. Keep it up," said Kensho, as he observed Sam practising.

When Saturday finally arrived Kensho busied himself in his office and left Sam and the girls to talk. Kensho knew that this was such precious time for the three of them to reconnect, so he always made sure to give them time alone. At first Sam asked the girls about their news, but it wasn't long before Zoe asked the inevitable question.

"Well, come on, Sam! Tell us all about your adventure!"

"Well.....it was awesome."

"We know that Sam! Tell us in detail. What did you do? Where did you go?"

"Well....eerrr.....well...." said Sam, trying to figure out what to say without revealing too much and without resorting to lying.

Suddenly Sophie burst out laughing.

"Well...eeeerrrr...eeeerrr....well...!" she mimicked. "Come on Sam! Just tell us that you can't tell us! We know that something unusual happened. I felt you going a great distance, so I know you didn't simply go into the mountains here with Kensho. So shall we leave it that you just had an awesome time, somewhere, doing something, with someone?"

Sam laughed and put his right arm around Sophie to pull her close. "Yeah, Soph. It was amazing. I hope one day I can tell you all about it, but right now I just can't. I wish I could, I really do, but I just can't."

Then Kensho called them up to the kitchen, and they all talked and laughed while making lunch together. Kensho was enjoying chatting just as much as Sam and the girls were. His life had been dedicated to aikido and to the responsibilities of being a Guardian. He had never been able to marry and have a family of his own. So Saturdays were opportunities for him to enjoy at least part of what he had foregone.

The first indication of trouble was the hawk's arrival at the kitchen window. The window was slightly ajar, and the hawk swooped down and landed on the windowsill outside. It began flapping its wings frantically and tapping hard on the window with its beak.

At the same moment, Sophie, who had been laughing hard, suddenly stopped and gasped. Sam turned from the window and looked at her.

"Soph? Are you okay?"

"Kensho! I'm frightened!" said Sophie, turning to Kensho.

Kensho's energy had also shifted completely.

"Girls, stay here. Sam, follow me!" he said sternly.

He quickly left the kitchen and headed for the stairs. Sam was right behind him, and he too was now feeling a sense of dread. It was a feeling he recognised from his encounter that night at Hiroshi's when something was outside the house and the doors had begun to shake.

As they headed downstairs, they were greeted by a terrible sight. The dojo was in flames. All the walls were ablaze, and as they stood near the bottom of the stairs, the flames suddenly shot out into the middle of the mat and over towards the entrance to the dojo. The fire looked very odd to Sam.

"These are no ordinary flames. This is evil at work. It is cutting off our escape route," said Kensho. "Upstairs! Quickly, Sam! We will not be able to escape this way."

Sam turned, ready to make his way back up the stairs, when he heard what sounded like a shopping trolley rattling loudly as it was pushed fast along the alley and the shouts of "Fire! Fire!"

He paused, looking at the entrance to the dojo and in moments the scruffy and heavily bearded face of a homeless man appeared, peering round the edge of the doorway.

The flames were just beginning to arch around the door frame, and the mats were also now well ablaze.

"Fire! Fire! Is anyone in here?! Fire!" yelled the man.

"We are in here, but we will escape through the upstairs! Get out and protect yourself!" shouted back Kensho.

"Are you sure? I can help!" replied the man, raising his voice above the growing roar of the flames.

Sam was still standing on the stairs. As he listened to the man shouting to Kensho he thought how familiar the voice sounded. Perhaps it was the obvious English accent.

"No!" said Kensho. "It is too dangerous down here. We will be fine! We will escape through a different exit. Go!"

"Will do! I'll call the fire brigade!" called out the man.

When Sam heard the man shout "Will do!" his heart leapt. He had heard that phrase, called out in exactly that way, so many times in his childhood.

"Dad?!" yelled Sam. But the man was already gone.

"Sam, go!" said Kensho.

The girls were standing in the kitchen. Zoe was holding Sophie.

"There is something really nasty here, Zo. I hope Sam and Kensho will be okay," yelled Sophie.

Suddenly Zoe screamed and pulled Sophie away from the kitchen door, holding her even tighter. There, in the entrance to the kitchen, stood a very old, little Japanese man with a sword by his side.

Sam was still climbing the stairs slowly when he heard Zoe's scream. Upon hearing her he began sprinting the last few steps and nearly hurtled straight into Hiroshi.

"Take the girls up to the hidden room. Go!" said Hiroshi, taking Sam by the shoulders.

Then he stepped past Sam and went downstairs. The stairs were acting like a chimney, and Sam could feel the tremendous heat rising up. The smoke was beginning to build too.

"Quickly! Come with me!" he called to Zoe and Sophie and lead the way down the hall to Kensho's office. Hiroshi had left the secret panel open, and Sam guided first Sophie and then Zoe up the steep steps.

"Mind your head up there. Stay on your hands and knees and head to the far end," he said.

Hiroshi found Kensho standing halfway down the stairs.

"Kensho, we must leave," said Hiroshi firmly.

Kensho looked at Hiroshi and then looked back at the dojo in flames. The heat was fierce, and the smoke was getting thick.

"Kensho! We must leave NOW!" shouted Hiroshi as he grabbed Kensho and turned him to face up the stairs.

"I am with you, Sensei," said Kensho.

Zoe was sitting with Sophie and Sam by the altar. She looked around and presumed that they were going to break out through the skylight. Then Hiroshi emerged into the room, and he quickly went over to the wooden cabinet. He gathered all the swords that were in the drawers and came over to the altar, handing Sam his sword. Shortly after, Kensho appeared. He closed the trap door behind him and then joined them. Hiroshi handed Kensho his Divine Sword.

Sam turned to the girls and looked at them.

"Do you trust me?" he asked, calmly.

The girls immediately nodded.

"Okay. Now I know this is going to seem very strange, but I need you to kneel on either side of me now."

The girls shuffled around so Zoe was to Sam's left, Sophie to his right. Then Kensho knelt beside Zoe, and Hiroshi beside Sophie. Sam took the girls' hands and looked first at Zoe and then at Sophie.

"Okay. Now close your eyes. We are going to go on a journey together, and we will be quite safe," said Sam.

Outside, the distant sound of sirens drew closer. From downstairs, Sam could also hear the sound of smashing glass and the roar of the flames. Then he became aware of the growing hum before he felt like he was falling through blackness once more.

Almost immediately, the masked face of Tatsuya appeared out of the blackness in front of Sam. It began small and distant but quickly advanced towards him, engulfing Sam with malice. He wanted to flee, but there was nowhere to go. Sam felt dark forms beginning to sweep around him as if they were trying to trap him in darkness.

Sophie saw Sam in the blackness. He was quite a long way away, and she could see the strangely dressed man moving towards him. She could feel the evil energy, and she could feel Sam's fear. She also saw the dark forms encircling Sam. Then she saw Sam beginning to diminish, his form becoming smaller and less well defined. She sensed Sam was in trouble and instinctively she called his name. As she did so, ripples began to emanate from her and rush toward Sam.

Sam's form seemed to rise up and down on the ripples, and he began to grow again. But when the ripples reached Tatsuya and the dark forms they were struck as if by a mighty blow. Unable to resist the impact, Tatsuya quickly began to shrink and recede back into the darkness, taking the dark forms with him.

CHAPTER 43

An Adventure Together

So it was that Zoe and Sophie quite unexpectedly arrived at Hiroshi's home. As the girls became aware of their new surroundings, Sam put his arms around their shoulders and pulled them in to give them a hug.

"Are you okay?" asked Sam.

They both nodded. Zoe began to look around, her eyes darting this way and that.

"Where are we?" she asked, panic in her voice.

"This is going to take some explaining," said Sam gently, "but the most important thing is that you are safe. We're at Hiroshi's house now. Hiroshi is Kensho's master. We went on a very, very long journey. We are in Japan now."

The girls looked at Sam with incredulity.

"That's not all. We are in Japan in 1537. We just travelled back nearly 500 years."

The girls' eyes widened in amazement, as they tried to make sense of what they had just heard, just as Sam had done only days before.

Two figures were also in the room standing over them.

"Hello, Zoe and Sophie," said Hiroshi. "My name is Hiroshi and you're very welcome in my humble home. Sam, please would you take the girls and show them around outside? Do not venture too near the forest but explore the garden and show them the dojo and the bath house."

"Yes, Nagato Sensei," said Sam, standing up and bowing to Hiroshi.

"Come on you two, let me show you where we are." He lead them out of the house and into the garden.

Once the girls had left with Sam, a worried Hiroshi turned to

Kensho. "This is a quite unexpected and very serious turn of events, Kensho."

"I had no sense that such danger was so close at hand," replied Kensho. "I am disturbed that I had no forewarning. My first sense of Darkness being close was as the flames broke out in the dojo. Prior to that moment, everything had seemed quite normal."

"I too had no forewarning," said Hiroshi. "That such a thing should take place so far away from here is of great concern. Come, let us make some tea. I always find more clarity with a cup of tea in my hand."

It was a lovely spring day in the mountains of central Japan. The sun was warming the garden, which was now alive with insects and birds. Sam showed the girls the dojo and the bath house. Then, he took them part way up the garden so they could get a good view of the valley and lake spread out below them.

As Sam showed the girls around, they plied him with questions. They wanted to know who Hiroshi was, whether Sam had been here before, how they got here and so on. Sam did his best to answer all their questions while trying to conceal the truth about the Divine Swords. Of course, Sophie saw straight through him.

"I see. It's just like your weekend training trip with Kensho isn't it? You're not going to tell us everything, are you?" she said, poking Sam in the ribs with her finger.

Sam smiled and nodded."You two have to know everything, don't you!" he said, laughing. "Well I am sworn to secrecy so you'll just have to be patient!"

He went on to tell them of his training here with Hiroshi. He told them that Hiroshi was Kensho's teacher and that somehow they could move between here and Kensho's dojo.

"But that's all I can tell you for now!"

"What happened at Kensho's dojo?" asked Zoe. "How did it catch fire and why did we feel so scared even before we knew of the fire?"

"I don't know. I know some things, but I just can't tell you them right now, okay? I just know that we are quite safe with Kensho and Hiroshi."

Kensho slid the shoji open and called out to Sam to return to the house with the girls. Sam instructed the girls to take their shoes off and leave them by the door, and then they went in.

Hiroshi walked up to the girls, bowed deeply and said,

"I am sorry I wasn't more prepared for your arrival, but I will do my best to make you feel at home. I am the teacher of Kensho and Sam, so they call me Sensei or Nagato Sensei. But you are my guests, so you must call me Hiroshi, which is my first name. Please come and sit here by the fire."

"That was quite a traumatic experience for you, Zoe and Sophie," said Hiroshi once they were all seated. "You have been very brave. I am sure that you have many, many questions, so I will try to answer as many as I can. Let me begin by reassuring you that you are safe here. This house is a very safe place, and you are protected by Kensho, Sam and me. So you have absolutely no need to be concerned at all, okay?"

The girls nodded and Hiroshi continued: "Now, you have travelled a very long way and you find yourselves in a very strange place. But I want you to feel quite at home and tell me, Kensho or Sam if you need anything at all. You arrived here because Kensho and I have special swords. Magical swords, you might even say. These swords allow us to do many special things, one of which is to travel between Kensho's dojo and my home here.

"Unfortunately, there are some unpleasant people who wish to take these swords for themselves. So, we are the Guardians of the swords, and we have to protect the swords from them. Sam is also going to become a Guardian one day. That is why he came here to train with me and why he will continue to train with me and with Kensho."

Zoe put her hand up, and Hiroshi smiled and said, "Yes, Zoe."

"How long are we going to stay here for?" she asked.

"That is a very good question. I do not know. The fire at Kensho's dojo was very serious, and we need to decide on the best way to proceed. You will certainly spend the night here with Sam and Kensho. Are you happy to do so?"

Zoe and Sophie nodded, and Sam rubbed Sophie's shoulders. Sophie was actually very excited just to be spending time with Sam.

"Won't our foster parents and friends be terribly worried about us?" asked Zoe. "They will think we have died in the fire, won't they?"

"Yes Zoe, they may do," replied Kensho. "We cannot do anything about that at the moment. It is important for you to know that another strange effect of the Divine Swords is that time travels at a different speed here compared to at home. So, even if you are here for eight days, it will only seem more like one day at home."

"Who was attacking Sam on our journey here?" asked Sophie. "I saw a terrible masked face and other things that were around Sam."

Hiroshi turned to Sam, and Sam related his experience including the departure of Tatsuya when he was hit by the ripples.

"That is most odd. I've never heard nor seen such ripples," said Hiroshi, rubbing his beard.

"Oh, that was me," said Sophie, nonchalantly, not looking up as she played with her shoe laces.

For a moment Hiroshi and Kensho stared at Sophie in astonishment.

"You did it?" asked Hiroshi.

"Yes," Sophie replied, still looking down and calmly twisting her shoe laces around her fingers. Then, as she became aware of the amazement Hiroshi and Kensho were feeling, she looked up and saw them staring at her.

"Wasn't I supposed to?" she asked, sounding concerned.

Hiroshi laughed. He had a twinkle in his eye."My dear Sophie, what you did is quite the best thing I have heard in a very long time. How did you do that?"

"I don't know really," she said. "I just called out Sam's name."

"Well, Sophie, that was all that you needed to do," said Hiroshi, smiling at her. "We are living in interesting times. The currents are strong, and it would be easy to get caught in them and lose one's centre. As the Tao Te Ching reminds us:

> The Master observes the turmoil,
> but accepts things as they are,
> He lets things come and go without interference,
> and always remains centred.

"We must stay centred and flexible as events unfold. For now, Kensho and I shall go up to the waterfall and meditate. The right action will arise in time. Sam, I think you should explain all that you know to the girls. It will help."

When Hiroshi and Kensho left, Sam took the girls back outside into the sunshine. Already Sam noticed that the garden was unusually busy with wildlife, especially birds.

"Well Zo," he said, chuckling, "it seems the Japanese animals love you just as much as the Canadian ones!"

They found a nice sunny spot in the garden with a lovely view over the valley. They sat together on the warm grass and Sam told them everything he knew about Master Osawa, Tatsuya, the Divine Swords, the Guardians, tengu, oni, yokai and that he was now part of the long line of Guardians.

"It all makes sense now," said Zoe. "I knew that you would have to face great danger, but I didn't know what that danger was. Now, I do. I also knew that I would stand by your side as you faced this danger, and I will, Sam."

"So will I!" piped up Sophie.

"I think that you already did," said Sam to Sophie. "I have never seen Hiroshi even the slightest bit surprised by anything. But he was amazed when you told him you created those ripples. He doesn't know my little sister the way Zo and I do. He also doesn't know just how ticklish she is!" With that Sam dived in and began to tickle Sophie's sides, just below her ribs. Sophie screamed and rolled away from him laughing.

"I bet Hiroshi doesn't know how ticklish you are either!" said Zoe as she began to tickle Sam under his armpits.

Now Sophie joined in, and Sam, laughing hard, shouted, "Stop it! Stop it! I surrender! I surrender!"

After they had all eaten dinner, Hiroshi and Kensho set up mats for the girls to sleep on beside the fire, alongside Sam. Then, they went off to continue their discussions and left the three of them to go to sleep.

Zoe looked at the flames of the fire gently licking up the side of the logs, and it stirred a memory for her.

"Do you remember camping with mum and dad when we first got to Vancouver?" she said. "We went up to Porteau Cove with the new tents we had bought and made a camp fire by the sea."

"Yes, I do," replied Sam. "We tried to be like Canadians and roast marshmallows over the fire, but I burnt most of mine."

"I remember getting scared that a bear would come and eat me," said Sophie, "so dad came and lay in the tent beside me until I went to sleep. I miss mum and dad so much."

Sophie was lying beside Sam. He took his arm out from under his blanket and pulled Sophie close to him.

"Well, now you have your big brother to look after you. Don't forget, he has had a bear cub lick his face, and he has met the mother bear. And you have a big sister who could probably talk to the bear and tell it to go somewhere else for its dinner."

"I wish dad hadn't done what he did," said Zoe.

"I know, Zo," said Sam, stretching his other arm over to rub her shoulder. "I wish that too. I know he tried. I know that he missed mum terribly, and he felt so bad for what had happened. He kept saying that if he hadn't been drinking before he drove, he might have been able to avoid the car that was on the wrong side of the road. He blamed himself even though it was the other driver's fault. It wasn't dad's fault. He had only had a couple of drinks, and the police said he wasn't over the limit. But he still blamed himself, and that was what he couldn't deal with in the end. I know he loved us very much. You know that, don't you, Zo?"

Zoe was quiet for a while.

"I guess so," she said finally. "But why did he leave us all alone?"

It was Sam's turn to be quiet. Eventually he said, "I don't know, Zo. I just don't know."

Sam lay awake listening to his sisters' soft breathing as they slept. He thought back to the fire in the dojo and the voice of that man he had heard. His voice had sounded so much like his dad's, but it was the way he said "will do" that really struck Sam. That was exactly what his dad would say, and it was said in exactly the same way his dad said it. But how could it be his dad? His dad was dead, though his body had never been found to absolutely confirm it. Anyway, if it was his dad, why had he not come to find him and the girls? It couldn't have been his dad. But when he fell asleep, Sam's dreams were filled with his father.

CHAPTER 44

The Companions Depart

As the children settled down to sleep, Hiroshi and Kensho talked quietly at the other end of the large room.

"So, our meditation showed that we are now unable to return to the dojo," said Kensho gravely.

"Yes, Kensho. But that does not mean it will not change. Alternatively a new location might be revealed to us that we can return to. For now we cannot get the children home. As always, we must trust. Everything is unfolding just as it should."

"I am deeply concerned that I failed to sense the presence of the evil that was at the dojo," said Kensho. "It is very powerful, Sensei. I do not understand how I failed."

"You did not fail, Kensho. Darkness is changing. Its power is growing stronger as is its ability to deceive us. We must be cautious not to rush into action. But it seems action may soon be called for."

The following morning, after waking up at 4.30, Hiroshi and Kensho meditated as usual. After the meditation, they entered the main room to find Sophie and Zoe snuggled in tightly to Sam. The two masters left them all to sleep and went to the dojo to practice.

When they returned from the dojo, Sam and the girls were up and preparing breakfast. The fire had been tended, and the kettle was boiling. Sophie bounced over to Hiroshi and Kensho.

"Good morning, gentlemen. Your breakfast awaits!" she said cheerily, and grabbed them both by the hand to lead them over.

"Well," said Hiroshi, laughing. "I think we should have you and Zoe come and visit me more often. This is the kind of life an old man like me could get used to."

"For now, we are not able to return to Kensho's dojo," said Hiroshi as they settled down to eat breakfast. "We have never encountered anything quite like this before. We have also never seen anything quite like Sam's encounters with Tatsuya. Nor anything like Sophie's ability to affect Tatsuya during the journey here from Kensho's dojo.

"These are all unprecedented events and ones that must be treated very seriously. As I said yesterday, there are powerful currents below the surface of what we see. So, for now, it is clear that you are safest here."

"Why don't we return to a place other than Kensho's dojo?" asked Sam.

"I wish that the Divine Swords had such limitless powers," said Kensho. Unfortunately it is not so. Where we are able to journey to is revealed to us in our meditations. We do not control such things."

"The time for waiting is coming to an end," said Hiroshi. "The signs are clear that Darkness is growing and moving rapidly. It is time we began to move too. Kensho and I have agreed that we will travel to the Tokin-ji temple at Mount Tokin. If Darkness is going to seek us out, then let it seek us out there. We will leave in three days. It will be a long journey on foot heading west through the mountains. It will take a few weeks, so we need to be well prepared. But the weather is good, and though we must not delay unnecessarily, we do not need to rush. The most important thing is that we travel unnoticed as far as possible. We will travel from temple to temple. Taka has reassured me that the temples remain safe. There will still be many nights between temples when we will be sleeping outside though."

"I know that this is quite unexpected," said Kensho, "and must be very unsettling for you."

"This is brilliant!" said Zoe, happily. "The three of us get to go on an adventure with you and Hiroshi. Our foster parents are always taking us on hikes in the mountains, so Sophie and I are used to it. When mum and dad were alive we were always going on adventures into the mountains. We love it!"

Sophie nodded enthusiastically in agreement.

"Well, then," said Hiroshi, "it seems we have willing travel companions, Kensho. What about you, Sam?"

"We will be fine, Nagato Sensei."

"Then let us begin preparations," said Hiroshi.

But they did not have three days to prepare. On the morning of the second day, Zoe was out in the garden when she looked down into the valley. There, she saw a large column of men coming along the road. They were still a long way off, but it was obvious they were heading either to the village or towards Hiroshi's house. Although Zoe had only been in 16th-century Japan a day or so she could still sense that there was something unusual about the column, so she went to tell Hiroshi.

Hiroshi and Kensho stood together and watched the column make its way along the road.

"Hirohito," said Hiroshi.

"Do you think he is coming here?" asked Kensho.

Hiroshi nodded. "We have no time to delay," he said. "We must leave immediately. Gather what we have prepared and let us leave now. And keep out of sight of the valley. I don't want us to be spotted by Hirohito."

They had already prepared clothing and some provisions. They gathered what they could and put everything into bags they would carry on their backs. Hiroshi and Kensho also carried a number of swords over their backs as well as the Divine Swords by their sides. Fortunately, Sam and the girls had been wearing shoes that would be suitable for hiking when they left Vancouver. Sam was now dressed in the traditional clothes that Hiroshi had given him on his last visit. Hiroshi had been down to the village and Aiko had given him some old kimonos, the traditional Japanese dress. Kensho had adjusted them to fit the girls, and they wore them over some of their own clothes. Zoe's kimono was brown and had patterns of bamboo covering it. Sophie's kimono was russet, decorated with white swallows. As the girls looked at each other in their kimonos they giggled. Both of them loved how they looked, and the previous day they had danced and swirled around outside in the sunshine.

After about 15 minutes of preparation they were ready to go. Most of Hirohito's column had turned off the road and was beginning to head along the path that would lead them up to Hiroshi's house, while a smaller group headed into the village. Hiroshi guessed they had perhaps a 45-minute head start on Hirohito's group. He thought that would be sufficient time for them to be safe from any scouts Hirohito might send out in search of them, but they would still need to move fast today. The path they would travel on would not be suitable for horses, so any pursuers would have to be on foot.

"Follow me and stay close," said Hiroshi. "Sophie, walk behind me; Zoe behind her. Sam and Kensho will be at the rear. We must move quickly to begin with in order to put some distance between us and Hirohito."

So, they set off up the mountain. Hiroshi walked at a good pace but not so fast that Sophie couldn't keep up. At first, they headed up the path past the waterfall, but shortly after, Hiroshi turned off onto a trail that was barely noticeable. It wasn't as steep as the path up to the temple, but it was still steadily climbing as it weaved through the forest. The trees were developing ever more foliage, but the forest was still quite light in the spring sunshine. The available shade helped to keep the companions cool as they worked hard to climb the mountainside.

Sam kept his eyes peeled for any tengu or oni as they walked. He felt sure that Hiroshi or Kensho would sense the danger long before he saw anything, but he kept scanning the woods all the same. As he walked, he marvelled at how his life kept taking twists and turns that he could never have begun to imagine. He had tried for so long to figure out a way to get the three of them together, and here they were all going on an adventure! He knew that this wasn't just some fun hike in the mountains. But he still felt very safe accompanied by not only Hiroshi but Kensho too. He was also reassured to have his samurai sword at his side.

Up front, Zoe was feeling happy and contented. Her favourite activity back home was roaming the forests in the mountains of British Columbia. To be in this new forest – with her little sister and big brother – was doubly delightful. She could feel the vibrant energy of the forest. Somehow, she connected to this energy in an extraordinary way. The flora and fauna felt this connection which was why the animals were all so drawn to her. The bamboo gently swayed and the leaves of the trees rustled a little as she passed by. Birds flew from tree to tree, as squirrels leapt from branch to branch, each of them wishing to be close to Zoe as she walked. In her thoughts, she spoke reassuringly to the animals and the trees and asked them to protect her travelling companions from any danger that might be lurking in the forest.

Sophie was happily bouncing along too. She didn't have the same direct connection to the animals and trees that Zoe did. However she saw the energy that flowed through the forest. Different creatures and plants had different coloured energy fields. Some fields were strong and clear, while others were subtle. Even the rocks, the water, and the mountains had energy fields.

All this energy flowed together in the forest, creating an ever-changing magical vision for Sophie to enjoy. She could see Hiroshi's pure white energy shining vividly in front of her as she walked. She could even see how the energy of the forest harmonised with Hiroshi's energy. Distantly she was aware of Hirohito's anger and hatred that swirled somewhere behind them. She also felt the malevolent energy that lay hidden in the forest. But for now, it was distant enough that it couldn't dampen her spirits as she skipped along behind Hiroshi.

Once they reached the peak of the mountain, they walked along its ridge for some time before dropping back down into the steep and narrow valley on the other side. The mountains were not as high as those the girls were used to hiking at home. These mountains were snow-free already and had trees all the way to their peaks. They came across a stream, and Hiroshi stopped.

"We have been making good time for a few hours now," he said. "Let us stop and have some water and a little to eat."

As they sat in the dappled sunshine on the banks of the babbling stream, it seemed to Sam that danger was far, far away. He gave Zoe a hug and asked how she was doing.

"Great," she beamed, "it is so lovely to be surrounded by such pristine nature. The forest feels very old but very happy."

A squirrel approached her, and she gave it a little miso-soaked rice.

"We will keep walking for another few hours," said Hiroshi. "I will ease the pace a little now as I don't sense any close pursuit. We will be travelling through steep terrain like this for many days and must conserve our energy as best we can. We are not yet near the first temple where we can rest. It is still a day away, so tonight we will sleep in the forest."

They hoisted their packs up onto their backs and walked on through the trees towards the valley floor before beginning their next ascent. As they walked, Hiroshi dropped back to talk quietly to Kensho.

"This was not the route I had wished to take, but Hirohito's arrival forced it upon us. We will be passing close to the ruined temple of Shomyo-ji. It has become known as a dangerous place, and evil resides there now. We will need to be on our guard tonight, Kensho."

As the afternoon drew on and evening approached, Hiroshi decided to camp sooner than he ideally wanted. He wished to put more distance between them and any possible pursuers. However, he didn't want to get too close to the ruined temple tonight. It would be safer to pass it in the light of the morning, so he kept an eye out for a suitable spot.

Eventually, they entered a somewhat flat area with a steep cliff above and many sheltering trees. Hiroshi called a halt, and they prepared camp.

Hiroshi considered lighting a fire. It would keep the morale of Sam and the girls up, but it would also make them easy to spot if they were being followed. He decided to err on the side of caution and camp without a fire.

As the light faded and night began to draw in, a wind also began to build. Sophie cuddled in close to Sam.

"I don't like how this place feels," she said. "There is something nasty out there."

Sam held her tight.

"We have two Guardians with Divine Swords with us, Soph. We're quite safe."

But the wind was making some very odd noises in the trees. It seemed as though one could almost make out the sound of distant screams.

"Do not worry about the strange sounds," said Hiroshi, reassuring them. "Kensho and I will take turns to keep guard tonight though I am not really concerned. I sense that what danger there is remains too far away to bother us. So, please, put your trust in us and settle down for some sleep. We have another long day's walk tomorrow before we reach the temple."

Sam lay on his back with Zoe snuggled up to him on one side and Sophie on the other. Both girls seemed to be asleep judging by the steady rhythm of their breathing. Beside Sophie sat Kensho silently. A little way off Sam could just see the outline of Hiroshi standing looking towards the path. Sam tried to stay awake to help keep an eye out for trouble, but soon he too fell sound asleep.

CHAPTER 45

Darkness Attacks

Sam awoke with a start. Kensho was gently nudging him. "Sam, wake up," he said in hushed tones. Sam tried to sit up, but his back was too stiff, so he had to roll over onto his side and push himself up with one arm.

"What is it?" he asked.

"Dawn is breaking, and we need to be on our way. Gently wake the girls."

Sam did as Kensho asked, and before long, they were ready to set off once again. Sam asked Kensho if there had been anything unusual in the night, but Kensho shook his head.

"Other than the noise of the wind, there was nothing that disturbed us."

They walked in the same order as they had the previous day. The sun was still some way from rising above the mountains, but the light in the forest slowly grew as the sky brightened. After a while, Sam began to notice stones with writing on them. They reminded him of the stones he had seen approaching Taka's temple, though these stones were all broken. The birds around them were beginning to make urgent warning cries.

Then Hiroshi stopped and they waited behind him.

"This path has been altered," he said. "It is leading us astray. The original path forked with one path leading down to the valley and another up to the temple. The fork has been hidden, and we have passed it and are now being lead straight towards the ruined temple. This is not the way we should be going. Let us head back the way we came, and I will try to locate the other path that takes us down to the valley."

Suddenly, Hiroshi and Kensho drew their swords. Sophie grabbed Sam's arm.

"Something horrible is coming!" she said.

"Stay close to me...You too, Zo'," said Sam, drawing his sword.

"Quick! Back the way we came!" yelled Hiroshi.

Kensho set off running, and Sam let Sophie and Zoe go in front of him as he followed them with Hiroshi at the rear. There was a steep bank rising up above them to their left, and Sam realised they were vulnerable to attack from above. They ran for maybe a minute before the path veered away from the edge of the bank. They found themselves back on more level ground in a large glade they had walked through only a few minutes earlier.

Kensho stopped, and the girls stood just behind him. Sam stood to the right of the girls and Hiroshi remained in front of them all. Sam looked back the way they had come, and he began to make out tengu darting between the trunks of the large trees, coming towards them. Then he heard the familiar thud of oni, except this time he was sure there was more than one.

"Stay here and protect the girls," said Hiroshi to Kensho before walking out to meet their attackers.

"Should I go with Hiroshi?" Sam asked Kensho.

Kensho shook his head. "No, Sam, stay here with me. Hiroshi will be fine."

Sam and the girls stood watching as the little old Japanese man walked towards perhaps 15 tengu, some of whom were armed with spears. The tengu all stopped. Sam wasn't sure if they were waiting for something or if they were hesitating at the confident advance of Hiroshi. Hiroshi continued to approach until he was maybe ten metres away from the tengu and then stopped. He raised his Divine Sword above his head. As he did so, Sam saw diffuse light draw in toward the tip of the blade, and then the blade shone a bright white. Hiroshi swept the blade down and then cut it sideways towards the tengu. White light poured from the tip of the blade and struck them. All of the tengu collapsed to the ground motionless.

Zoe gasped and asked Kensho, "Are they dead?"

"No," said Kensho, "Hiroshi has driven Darkness from them. They will recover shortly, but they will no longer be in the hold of evil."

Then the oni appeared. There were three of them. They were all the same huge size as the one that had previously attacked Hiroshi and Sam. Each was armed with a club, and their golden eyes burned brightly. One of them looked down and grunted at the sight of the stunned tengu lying still on the floor. It walked up to one and kicked it so hard that it flew towards Hiroshi before tumbling on the ground in front of him, its body shattered. Zoe and Sophie gasped.

Zoe closed her eyes and silently called for the light of the forest to help. Almost immediately, they all heard a terrific cracking sound, and a huge limb snapped off a very large beech tree under which the oni stood. It came crashing down on top of the oni and hit one of them directly on the head, felling it instantly. Zoe stood wide-mouthed in shock.

The remaining two oni smashed their way out of the branches with their clubs and began to advance on Hiroshi, clubs held high. Holding his sword in his left hand, Hiroshi extended his right arm, palm facing the oni, and let out a piercing kiai. The clubs both shattered in the oni's hands, and they staggered back as if they had been hit by something solid. Sam noticed black blood oozing from their mouths and noses.

They shook their heads, and then both made a mad charge at Hiroshi. He stood motionless and seemingly relaxed. When the two oni were nearly upon him, he stepped to his left and cut through the belly of the one closest to him. It fell to the ground, and in a flash Hiroshi drove his sword deep into its side killing it. The second oni had turned and slowly advanced on Hiroshi once again. It wildly swung its right arm trying to smash the side of Hiroshi's head. But Hiroshi effortlessly evaded the attack and thrust his sword deep into the oni's chest before quickly extracting the sword blade and stepping away. The oni grabbed the wound with its left hand and bellowed. It took a few faltering steps and then fell backwards dead.

The tengu were now beginning to recover and stand up. As they did so, they surveyed the scene and then began to turn and run back into the forest. Hiroshi went over to the oni that had been hit by the falling limb of the beech tree and checked that it was dead. Then he returned to where his companions were standing.

"I think we should leave this place as quickly as possible," he said. "Stay close together and follow me. I will look for the now hidden fork in the path."

Zoe and Sophie were still in shock. Sophie in particular was shaking very badly. But she managed to keep up with the fast-striding Hiroshi, who quite quickly found the fork that had been hidden and lead them down towards the valley floor. After half an hour or so, they entered another small glade, and Hiroshi stopped and turned. He looked at Sophie and knelt before her, his arms spread wide. Sophie burst into tears and fell into Hiroshi's embrace.

"It is okay. You have done wonderfully, wonderfully well, and you are incredibly brave."

Sam hugged Zoe too. Though she was shaking, she did not cry. They all sat down beside the path. Kensho got some food and water out of his pack. Sophie found it hard to eat at first, but her appetite quickly returned. Judging by the sun's position in the sky, Sam guessed it was coming up to mid-morning.

"How are you doing, Zo?" he asked Zoe, who was sat beside him.

She turned and looked at him, pushing her long blonde hair away from her face.

"I'm doing okay. That was pretty frightening though. I'm just wondering how that huge branch fell off the tree like that."

"It is as you suspect, Zoe," said Kensho. "Your request was answered."

Sam and Sophie looked quizzically at Zoe

"What does Kensho mean?" asked Sophie.

"Well," said Zoe, looking down, "I asked the forest to help protect us. As I thought that, the branch fell off the tree and hit that thing."

"Wow," said Sam quietly. "That's pretty awesome, Zo."

Zoe looked over at Kensho and asked, "Are we going to be attacked by many more of those things on this journey?"

Kensho looked out into the forest in the direction they were heading and said, "I think it is possible, yes."

"We must expect to have more encounters," said Hiroshi. "The mountains are getting much more dangerous. For that reason, we must reach the temple before nightfall. Let us set off again."

As Hiroshi stood up, Zoe remained sitting. "I want a sword," she said, firmly.

Hiroshi stopped and turned to her. "You have not been trained how to handle one," he said firmly.

Zoe now also stood up, placing her hands on her hips. "I don't care. I do not want to be left standing with no protection. If we are likely to get attacked again, then I want to be able to defend myself."

Zoe's eyes were burning bright, and Sam was surprised at the fierceness that his sister displayed.

"I would like a sword too," said Sophie. "I think it will help me to feel more confident."

Hiroshi looked at Zoe and Sophie. After a few moments he said, "Very well. I will give you both a short sword."

Hiroshi and Kensho were each carrying a short sword on their backs. They took the swords off and adjusted the straps so the swords would fit well on the backs of the girls. Then Kensho showed Sophie, and Hiroshi showed Zoe, how to reach up to the hilt with their right hand and draw the sword.

Then they set off along the path once more, with Hiroshi leading and setting a goodly pace. The setting sun's last rays were just beginning to filter through the trees atop a far off mountain as they approached the temple. Once again, Sam knew they were getting close when they began to pass the outlying stones with writing engraved on them. This time the stones were standing straight and undamaged. The path was very narrow and looked seldom used, but nonetheless Hiroshi told them to be ready to hide. He didn't want them to be seen by anyone other than the monks in the temple.

They still could not see the temple itself when Hiroshi stopped. "Kensho, head off the path so that you cannot be seen. I will go on ahead and ensure all is well and return for you all."

As Hiroshi walked on, Kensho lead the rest of the companions away from the path. He found a very large ginkgo tree with a broad trunk, and they sat in silence leaning their backs against it, hidden from the path.

After a few minutes, Sophie whispered loudly, "Someone's approaching."

Kensho nodded and said, "I feel it too."

Sam held his breath and listened. He thought perhaps he could hear some noises coming from the direction they had just travelled. Kensho motioned for them to stay still and quiet. He then got up and moved so he could see the path. As Kensho watched, into view came a band of samurai warriors walking swiftly along the path with Hirohito at the front. Kensho watched them carry on past, heading up to the temple. He then turned to Sam and the girls and whispered. "It is Hirohito and 12 of his men. They have been following us after all. I suspect they found the bodies of the oni and so picked up their pace knowing that they were on the right trail."

"What about Hiroshi? How do we warn him?" asked Sam.

"It is okay. Hiroshi will sense Hirohito's approach. Let us wait here for his return."

The companions settled down again, making sure that they were well hidden from the path.

"How does Hiroshi know Hirohito?" Zoe asked Kensho.

"Sensei was Hirohito's teacher," replied Kensho. "Hirohito grew up in the village and was the son of a fisherman. He was fascinated by the samurai. As a very young boy, he would sneak up and watch Sensei teaching iaido. Hiroshi would catch him, of course, and take him back to his father who would scold him.

"Eventually, his father gave in and asked Sensei if he would become the boy's master. Sensei agreed, and when Hirohito was 12, he became Sensei's student. He trained diligently for many years and became a very gifted swordsman. When he was 18, he left the village and went to serve as a lowly foot soldier with the daimyo. He was hard working, highly skilled, intelligent and loyal, and he made swift progress through the ranks. He also mastered the politics and aligned himself with those who could help him advance.

Kensho paused, looking to the path and listening. Once he was satisfied all was well he continued. "He would occasionally return to the village and would visit Sensei and regale him with his great deeds and growing power. But Sensei saw that as his power grew so too did Darkness grow within him. Sensei tried to warn him, but Hirohito's ambition was too strong, and he dismissed Sensei's concerns as the worries of an old man.

"Finally about seven years ago, he and his political allies overthrew the then daimyo, and Hirohito became daimyo himself. With his new found power, Hirohito became ever more ruthless. Now it seems he is seeking revenge on Sensei for the dishonour he believes Sensei has brought upon him."

"Why does Hirohito feel dishonoured?" asked Sam, shifting to sit more comfortably.

"Because Sensei kept refusing to teach his samurai. That was why Hirohito was coming to see Sensei. He was either going to force Sensei to agree to teach or he was going to kill him. Sensei's refusal to teach was a blatant challenge to Hirohito's authority and brought dishonour on him. Sensei knows that if he faces Hirohito, he will have to fight him. He also knows that if that happens, he will have to kill Hirohito. Despite the mistakes that Hirohito has made, Sensei still cares for him and so he seeks to avoid the confrontation."

Then Kensho stood up, and Sam saw that Hiroshi was approaching through the forest well away from the path.

"Hirohito is at the temple," Hiroshi said hurriedly. "This is making things much more difficult. He will know we have come this way as he will no doubt have seen the evidence of our battle with the oni and tengu. He will not give up now. I know Hirohito.

"We cannot stay at the temple tonight - this much is clear. We are fortunate that the weather has been so favourable to us, but I think we can expect that to change soon. Of greater concern, however, is how we evade this pursuit. An encounter with Hirohito and his men will inevitably lead to bloodshed and so must be avoided at almost all costs. But we need to reach safety as quickly as possible."

Hiroshi fell silent. He wasn't saying so, but he was becoming increasingly concerned at the rising power of the malevolence that was around them. The tengu were clearly now completely in its control. The hidden fork in the path suggested that their journey had been anticipated. Rather than facing an enemy that was disjointed and almost random in its attacks, they now seemed to be facing an enemy that was becoming organised. All this was taking place while they were exposed in the mountains.

Hiroshi was also deeply concerned about Hirohito. Fleeing from his home he knew would be viewed by Hirohito as another slight against his honour. For this reason, Hirohito would pursue him relentlessly. While he knew he must avoid an encounter with Hirohito, Hiroshi also knew that in order to protect Sam and the girls such an encounter might be inevitable.

"Are we going to sleep here tonight?" asked Sophie, breaking the silence.

"No," said Hiroshi. "We must put more distance between us and the path. We shouldn't get any closer to the temple, so let us go this way."

Hiroshi pointed deeper into the forest, and they all got up and followed him through the trees in the twilight.

CHAPTER 46

Forgive Me

It was a colder night than the previous one. Sam and the girls huddled together under their blankets to keep warm. A fire would have been very welcome but was far too dangerous now that they knew they were being pursued. Through the canopy of the trees, the stars were bright. Sam could see the Milky Way more clearly than he ever remembered seeing it. The moon was just beginning to wax, and there was no artificial light to dim the stars.

A little way away, Kensho and Hiroshi were quietly talking. Both sat with blankets wrapped around their shoulders.

"I am growing increasingly uneasy, Kensho," said Hiroshi. "We find ourselves far from safety while all around us the storm seems to be gathering strength. Now, not only do we face the growing Darkness, but we also have Hirohito and his men pursuing us. He is convinced that I have dishonoured him. He will never give up now until he has taken my life or he himself is dead."

"We could try to evade him by making our way through the mountains, avoiding paths," said Kensho. "But that will take us a very long time and would also mean we cannot seek safety and warmth in any temples along our way. You and I have endured far worse, but it is too much to ask of Zoe and Sophie. It will also leave us exposed for even longer, and events are gathering pace, as you say. Every day the likelihood of attack grows, and with it also grows the likely strength of those attacks. The sooner we are out of the mountains and in the safety of the temple, the better."

Hiroshi pulled his blanket tighter around his shoulders. "It seems we have little choice. We cannot go back. We must go forward. We cannot delay, and we cannot avoid the paths or the temples. I will have to face Hirohito. He will not back down, Kensho." Hiroshi paused before going on. "Though it seems unimaginable to me, I can only foresee a duel with Hirohito, and that will inevitably lead to his death. I see no other choice."

"Sensei, you are right. There is no other choice. If you do not face him, then we risk the lives of Sam and the girls. We also risk the greatest danger of all - the Divine swords falling into Darkness. However, he was your friend, Sensei. The bond between the two of you is strong. Perhaps it is I who should face him?"

Hiroshi reached out and grasped Kensho's shoulder. "You are a faithful student and a good friend, Kensho. That you would take on such a terrible burden for me does not surprise me. But…no…this is my task to undertake, and it will be my burden to carry until I can let it go. Now, let us get some sleep. Tomorrow will be a very difficult day."

Dawn was slow to break the following morning. The star-lit sky was now hidden behind a thick blanket of low cloud. The forest was damp, and the smell of decaying leaf litter was strong. Sam was stirring because he was so cold even before Kensho came over to wake him and the girls. It was still close to full darkness as Sam, Zoe and Sophie got up and fumbled to pack their blankets before having a little to eat. Because they had not been able to stay at the temple, Hiroshi told them to take smaller rations of food. He did not know when they would next be able to restock their supplies.

Before they set off again, Hiroshi gave his instructions. "We must expect to encounter Hirohito today. I will stay at the rear, and Kensho will lead. When Hirohito catches up with us, please stay close to Kensho. I will deal with Hirohito alone. For now, let us travel quickly but quietly."

Kensho lead the way back through the woods towards the path. Every now and then Sam or one of the girls would stand on a dry twig or branch and it would crack loudly. It sounded like a gunshot in the silence of the forest and the companions would all halt and listen for any sounds of approaching danger. But they reached the path without incident and Kensho lead them on at a rapid pace. If nothing else, the exertion helped warm up Sam and the girls.

They passed within sight of the temple. It loomed in the darkness, higher up the mountainside above them with wide stone steps leading up to it. There was no sign of life as they passed quickly by and continued along the path. Once they were well past, Kensho slowed the pace a little.

The day grew slowly lighter though the clouds were thick and heavy with rain. It was a dreary day, and the heaviness of the cloud seemed also to be weighing on them all. Sophie was feeling very tired, and what had seemed at first to be a fun adventure was now quickly becoming an ordeal. Zoe felt much the same. She was a little happier than Sophie since she loved to be amongst the trees and the wildlife. But she was also feeling very tired, and the dampness made her clothes feel cold and clammy. Sam was concerned about the girls and the predicament he had drawn them into. Staying at the temple would have been a huge boost. But sleeping through a cold and damp night in the forest had sapped his energy too.

To make matters worse, the clouds made good with their threat and a steady drizzle began to fall. At first, the forest canopy gave a little protection. But it wasn't long before large drips were tumbling down from the leaves where the drizzle had collected. Sam snorted and scrunched his shoulders as a huge drip managed to fall precisely down between his collar and his neck, running down his back.

The path lead into a more open area, almost like a little meadow, beside a stream. Hiroshi called Kensho to halt.

"Take shelter beneath that large beech tree," said Hiroshi. "I will wait here for Hirohito's arrival."

As they gathered in the relative dry beneath the broad branches of the beech, Hiroshi turned and sat facing the way they had come. He did not have to wait long for Hirohito's arrival. Sam heard the thudding of heavy feet, and into view someway back along the path came the band of samurai walking quickly. The man in front, who

Sam guessed must be Hirohito, held up his right arm. The band of men stopped.

"What will happen? Are we going to have to fight all those men?" Zoe asked Kensho.

"I think not," replied Kensho, shaking his head.

Hirohito strode up to Hiroshi, who was still sitting in seiza. Hirohito was wearing samurai armour that was very finely decorated with a thick gold cord lacing the steel and leather plates together. He wore a helmet with two thin gold pieces of metal sticking up on either side like horns. It was hard to guess his age, but Sam thought perhaps he was in his forties. He stopped a few yards away from Hiroshi.

"Hiroshi, you have brought dishonour upon me. I have tolerated you for many years, and this is how you repay me. Stand and face me now and allow me to regain my honour."

"Hirohito, I did not wish to dishonour you," replied Hiroshi, still in seiza. "I had no choice but to leave. What you would have asked of me, I could not have done. You know that. I do not wish to fight you. You are a great daimyo, and you have the power to forgive. I beg you to forgive me and let me continue on my way."

Hirohito answered Hiroshi's request clearly by stepping back and drawing his sword. "I will not forgive you, Hiroshi. I will regain my honour when I hold your head in my hand. Stand and fight, or I will behead you as you kneel."

"Hirohito, I was your teacher, and I am still your friend. Do you not see the path into Darkness upon which you walk? Search your heart. If you kill me, you will have only fallen further into Darkness. Your honour will be restored through forgiveness, and you will also step back from Darkness. I beg you Hirohito, please forgive me."

Hirohito seemed to waver. Sam thought that perhaps Hiroshi's words were going to prevent the duel. Then, with the speed of a striking snake, Hirohito brought the sword down to behead Hiroshi. But Hiroshi was already inside Hirohito's swinging arms, having risen up on one knee. With his right arm, he pushed up into Hirohito's chin, breaking his balance and throwing him spiralling down to the ground. Sophie gasped and drew closer to Sam, holding onto his arm.

Hirohito hit the ground hard, his heavy armour adding weight to his fall. But he was soon up and approaching Hiroshi once again. Hiroshi, who had still not unsheathed his sword and was once again in seiza, shouted: "Please forgive me, Hirohito!"

But Hirohito again brought the sword slicing down towards Hiroshi, who quickly evaded it and now, at last, drew his sword.

As Hirohito's samurai watched from the other side of the little meadow, the pair stood motionless facing each other. Hirohito had his sword raised above his head. The rain slowly dripped off the rim of his helmet. Hiroshi's white hair was matted to his head, making him look even smaller as he stood with his sword at waist height pointing toward Hirohito. His white kimono looked grey and hung limply over his thin frame.

Suddenly, Hirohito let out a great yell and swung his sword to behead Hiroshi. Hiroshi stepped to his right and thrust his sword into Hirohito's chest beneath his armpit. Hirohito gasped and fell forward onto his knees, his sword spearing the ground in front of him. Then the sword slipped from his hands, and he fell to his right with his face half looking up into the grey sky.

Hiroshi knelt beside his former student and looked into Hirohito's now lifeless eyes.

"Please forgive me, Hirohito," he whispered.

Sam couldn't tell if he saw tears running down Hiroshi's wrinkled cheeks or if it was the rain. But he could see dreadful pain in Hiroshi's expression as he picked up the hand of his now dead student and friend and held it between his. Sophie turned her head into Sam's chest and began sobbing. Sam put his left arm out and pulled Zoe in close, feeling her body shake as she too began to cry. Sam tried but failed to stop the tears that began to well up in his eyes.

Hirohito's samurai didn't know what to do. One of them began to advance on Hiroshi with his right hand going to the hilt of his sword.

Kensho immediately rose up from seiza and let out a loud kiai as he held his right hand up to halt the advancing samurai. The samurai paused and then turned and headed back to the group.

Then Kensho walked over to Hiroshi and sat beside him. Kensho did not say a word, and for a few minutes they sat there, side by side, as Hiroshi held Hirohito's hand. Then Hiroshi gently laid Hirohito's arm down, slowly got up and walked towards the samurai. They began to shuffle back a little, placing their hands on the hilts of the swords, not knowing what to expect. But Hiroshi stopped a short distance away. "Collect your daimyo's body and return him to his castle. He died an honourable death."

Then Hiroshi bowed to them and walked back to Sam and the girls. "We must continue. There is another temple that we may reach by nightfall if we make swift progress."

With that, Hiroshi strode out across the meadow and onto the path, not once turning back.

Ambrose Merrell

CHAPTER 47

An Old Friend Returns

Hiroshi set a great pace. Sophie was practically jogging to keep up. They were climbing a mountainside once again, and before long, they found themselves in the low cloud. The forest was silent. There wasn't a breath of wind to stir the leaves. Zoe noticed that even the birds and squirrels seemed to be forlorn as they followed the companions along the path.

They walked for hours until finally Sophie stumbled and fell crying out in pain as her knee hit a sharp stone on the path. Hiroshi stopped and turned as Sam and Zoe helped Sophie back onto her feet.

"Sensei, I think we had best stop and let the girls have a rest," said Kensho.

"I am sorry Sophie," said Hiroshi. "I have allowed my awareness to slip. Yes, let us rest and eat. I think we should be able to make a temple by nightfall still. Let us head away from the path a little though."

They settled down beneath a large tree just out of sight of the path. Kensho reached into his pack and drew out a little jar. He opened it and asked Sophie to lift her trouser leg up past her knee. There was a little graze, and a bruise was just beginning to appear. Kensho dipped his finger into the jar and rubbed the ointment onto the cut and bruise. Sophie sucked her breath in sharply.

"I'm sorry if this hurts," said Kensho. "But it will help you heal quickly."

"It's okay. Thank you, Kensho," said Sophie, bravely.

"I wish this cloud would go," said Sam. "I feel closed in. Sounds are deadened, and I keep thinking I see figures in the mist."

"Yes," said Zoe, "it would be lovely to see sun and blue sky and feel some warmth again. I don't know if it is just because of the mist, but the animals feel on edge. They seem nervous somehow."

Sophie pulled her trouser leg carefully back down over her knee. "There is something out there, something terrible," she said, looking around the forest. "I can feel it. It doesn't feel like those ugly monsters. They felt horrible. But this feels different. Much darker. It feels...it feels...it feels like pure evil."

Sam shuddered involuntarily. Partly, it was the cold, but partly it was hearing what Sophie said.

"I feel it too, Sophie," said Kensho. "That is why we must move on quickly. How are you feeling?"

"I'm feeling fine, thank you, Kensho," replied Sophie, smiling. "If I could just have something to eat, then I will be okay to keep going."

They ate quickly and were just gathering themselves ready to head back to the path when Hiroshi said, "Quiet!"

Everyone froze. Hiroshi had sensed someone approaching. As they stood listening, they began to hear the dull sound of rapid foot falls coming from the path in the direction from which they had come.

But before the source of the footfalls was even in sight, Hiroshi called out joyfully, "Daichi!" and began to run to the path.

They followed Hiroshi and reached the path just as Daichi emerged from the mist. Daichi looked dreadful. His left arm was tucked into his kimono, and the sleeve from high up the arm was blood soaked. His face was gaunt and grey, and his legs seemed unsteady beneath him.

"Sensei! I have found you," he gasped, as he reached Hiroshi. Then he fell to his knees and began sobbing.

Hiroshi immediately crouched down and pulled his friend up from the muddy path.

"Daichi!" he said, "what has happened to you?"

Kensho helped Hiroshi guide Daichi off the path and into a little shelter from the rain beside the large tree trunk. They sat him down, and Kensho got some water and food out. Daichi drank a little water.

"Thank you, Kensho," he said, before turning to Hiroshi. "I am so glad I found you alive, Sensei. I feared that I had lost you as well."

Then tears welled up again in his eyes, but he fought them back and continued. "I tried to catch up to you as quickly as I could. I was waylaid by some of Hirohito's men. I had to fight them, Sensei. I had no choice. That was when I sustained this injury."

"Let me take a look at that, Daichi," said Kensho.

As Kensho began to carefully help him take his arm out of the kimono, Daichi continued talking. "I was far behind Hirohito, but I tried to catch up and pass him to warn you. I saw his men carrying his body, Sensei. I am so sorry that it finally came to that."

"Hai," said Hiroshi and knelt beside Daichi. He took his right hand and looked into his eyes: "What has happened, Daichi, my friend?"

Daichi started to sob but swallowed hard before replying: "Sensei, they killed Aiko."

Then Daichi could hold back his grief no more, and the tears came uncontrollably. Hiroshi knelt and held his old friend in his arms as Daichi's body shook violently and the crying turned into a wail of anguish unlike anything Sam had ever heard.

Sam took the girls a little way away, and they sat beneath a nearby tree. Zoe and Sophie were crying too, and Sam tried to comfort them. But he had little comfort to give. This was a dreadful day full of death and pain. Sam felt like they were sinking into a black mire. Listening to the heart-wrenching sounds of Daichi's agony, Sam felt that they all would soon be overwhelmed by Darkness. What could so few do against such evil?

When Daichi recovered, he told Hiroshi what had happened. He had been out in the fields and had seen Hirohito's men approaching. He had seen a group of samurai break off from the main column and head into the village. He tried to get back to the village before them, but he was too far away and arrived too late. He saw them drag Aiko from the house and kill her.

"I am so sorry, Daichi, my friend," said Hiroshi. "It is my responsibility. Had you not been a friend to me, then this would never have happened."

"No, Sensei!" replied Daichi, with surprising vehemence. "This is not your responsibility. You are a light that shines brightly. Aiko loved you, and she would have done anything to help you in this battle. She would have gladly given her life. Her death is not your responsibility. Nor is Hirohito's, Sensei. It is the work of Darkness. It is because of the light that fills you that so many lives are saved."

"You are right of course, Daichi," said Hiroshi. "I apologise. I am allowing my own feelings of inadequacy and guilt to mislead me. What has happened must toughen our resolve. This is but a tiny glimpse of the violence and suffering that would be unleashed if Darkness prevails. Let us not lose ourselves and allow our spirits to be broken. Can you walk with us, Daichi?"

Daichi slowly stood up. "I will walk with you always, Sensei."

Hiroshi beckoned Sam and the girls to come over. "Diachi I would like you to meet Sam Stone, Kensho's disciple." Sam and Daichi bowed to each other.

"And these are Sam's sisters, Zoe and Sophie." Daichi bowed to the girls and they bowed back.

Hiroshi looked at the faces of the companions. "Let us let go of today's events. Let us focus on the task at hand, which is simple. We have a good few hours of walking before we reach a temple. Our company has grown stronger with Daichi's arrival. We are no longer being pursued by Hirohito. Let us take heart."

Then Kensho drew his sword and held it straight above him. As with Hiroshi's sword, it drew a diffuse light to its tip and began to shine brightly.

"This is the light that surrounds us and fills us," said Kensho. "Take courage that it shines brightly still."

So it was that the company resumed its journey. But now, Sam, Zoe and Sophie were all feeling much encouraged. As they walked into the afternoon, the light grew. Patches of blue began to appear in the clouds, and the rain eased and then stopped.

They reached the tell-tale stone markers of the temple sooner than Hiroshi had thought. He left the group hidden off the path and went on to the temple. Not long after, he returned saying all was well and that they would be able to sleep in the temple that night.

The monks welcomed them wonderfully. They fed them and gave them fresh clothes, taking their wet and dirty clothes to be washed. They prepared baths and Sam and the girls were able to wash and then soak in the hot water. After bathing, they gathered around a large fire with the head priest, who knew both Hiroshi and Taka. He suggested the best route to take to avoid the most dangerous areas. He also confirmed that the temples along their route were still safe.

Then Hiroshi, Kensho and Daichi went off to bathe while Sam and the girls finally curled up to sleep in the warmth and dry of a little room, knowing that Hiroshi, Kensho and Daichi would be sleeping close by. They felt safe, and their stomachs were full. They slept a long and peaceful sleep.

CHAPTER 48

The Transmission

Hiroshi didn't wake Sam and the girls too early. While he was keen to get going, he also knew that he must allow them to rest and recover. So, they did not set off until around eight o'clock that morning. The air was still damp from the previous day's rain, but the sky was clear again, and the sun soon warmed them. Steam rose from the path as they made their way in the sunshine.

The forest seemed more alive with wildlife than ever before. It seemed to Zoe that the creatures were responding to their new-found courage and resolve. For the first time, she saw wolves tracking alongside them some way off in the woods. At one of their rest breaks, she also saw a bear come lumbering by. It didn't approach them, but that afternoon, as they walked, she kept catching sight of it off to her right. At first she thought it was a male cub, since it was small compared to the black bears that lived in British Columbia. However, as she connected to him, she realised he was older. So, she guessed that bears in Japan must be a little smaller than at home.

Their journey for the next few days was uneventful. They had to spend many nights out in the forest, but the weather was growing ever warmer, and the rain held off. They had restocked their provisions at the temple, and so they were able to eat quite well. Most importantly, now that Hiroshi did not fear pursuit, he allowed them to have camp fires. This made the nights far more pleasant for Sam and the girls if for no other reason than it reminded them of camping at home. Sophie's only complaint was that they didn't have any marshmallows to roast.

Daichi's arm was healing fast, thanks to the care Kensho was giving it. Daichi also looked much better. His journey to catch up with them had been without any food, so perhaps his improvement was partly due to eating again. But Sam thought most of the reason

Daichi looked happier was because he was with Hiroshi and Kensho. He was fulfilling his purpose, and this gave him great strength.

Daichi was teaching the girls how to handle their swords with Sam's help. Zoe had an uncanny gift with the sword and seemed to pick it up almost instantly. Sophie wasn't quite so at one with the blade, but she learnt pretty quickly too. Daichi was keen to impress upon both of them that they were only learning the very basics. He didn't want them to become overly confident in their abilities.

"Always stay close to Nagato Sensei, Iwata Sensei and to me," he said to them. "If you find yourself in real trouble, try to escape and hide. These swords are only for you to use in the direst of circumstances."

Those direst of circumstances were closer than the girls knew. Hiroshi and Kensho were very aware of the growing menace that for now stayed on the periphery of their journey.

In the early evening of the eighth day, they took themselves a little distance away from the others.

"We are walking into a storm," said Hiroshi. "Tatsuya knows where we are making for. Of that I am certain. His control of the creatures of Darkness continues to grow. We must expect to be confronted by a large and determined enemy before we reach Tokin-ji temple. Tatsuya will do all he can to prevent us arriving there."

"Sensei," said Kensho, "has the time come to consider giving Sam the Transmission? I know that this is many years too soon. However, we must weigh the danger of receiving the Transmission too soon against this present danger. Tatsuya's attention seems focused on Sam. It seems clear he sees Sam as a threat that he wishes to eliminate. Any coming battles will see the enemy continue to try to destroy Sam."

Hiroshi looked over at Sam, sitting with the girls and tending to the fire. "Yes, Kensho, it is something that I too have been considering. If we give him the Transmission before he is ready, we know the consequences. But without it, he may not live through the coming days. He is an exceptional young man. He has a spirit unlike any I have encountered before. Had he not, I would not consider this course."

Hiroshi continued to look at Sam as he struggled to decide the correct course of action. "We must discuss this with Sam. It is he who bears the risk."

Hiroshi and Kensho walked back to the others and sat down. Sam was helping Zoe sort and repack her stuff while Sophie was watching a flock of little birds that were flitting between the trees around them. They all turned towards Hiroshi and Kensho as they approached.

"Kensho and I sense that we are approaching great danger," said Hiroshi. "We must reach Tokin-ji temple. It was where Master Osawa once sought refuge, and it is where we too might find safety, for a while at least. However, our enemy will seek to do all it can to prevent our arrival. I sense that its forces are gathering ahead of us.

Sam put down Zoe's bag and turned his full attention to Hiroshi.

"Sam, you have only just begun your training with Kensho and me. Many years of dedicated training lie before you. It is that hard training that polishes and purifies your spirit. There are no shortcuts in this process. Traditionally, the final step in one's martial art training is called the Transmission. When your teacher believes you are ready, he will give you a transmission of the final secrets of the art. As a Guardian of the Divine Swords, you too will receive a transmission from Kensho. The Transmission for a Guardian is different from traditional martial arts though. This transmission brings with it great powers, far beyond the transmission of a martial artist.

Kensho sat in seiza beside the girls. Sophie stopped looking at the birds and focused on Hiroshi.

"The danger we face is dire. Our lives are all at risk. We must not underestimate the determination or the guile of our enemy. For this reason, Kensho and I have been discussing whether, in these exceptional circumstances, you receive the Transmission now. Sam,

I want you to understand the danger in this. Acquiring the powers of a Guardian when one is not ready carries enormous danger in itself.

"If the spirit is not strong, then the power that one wields will draw one inevitably towards Darkness. That is why in normal circumstances, we would not consider it for many years. But, as I say, these are far from normal circumstances. Never before have the Guardians faced such grave danger. For reasons that are not clear to Kensho and me, Tatsuya is focusing the powers of Darkness upon you, Sam. It is to protect you from this that we are considering giving you the Transmission.

"Sam, if Kensho and I did not have confidence that you were able to receive this transmission, we would not now be discussing this with you. Nonetheless, our confidence may be misplaced. It is you that will suffer the consequences. It is your life that is at stake here. On the one hand, you must be aware of the possibility of your death in the coming days. On the other hand, you must understand the danger of your descent into Darkness if your spirit is not ready for this great power."

Sam had been listening intently. He now sat quietly and considered what to do. Rather than just think, he also looked inside himself at the feelings that manifested themselves. Part of him that so craved the power. He craved to be the hero, to be famous as the saviour, to be known as the great Guardian that defeated Darkness, to be both adored and feared by all who met him. However, he had already become wise enough to know that this ambition was precisely the danger that Hiroshi spoke of. It was this craving that would destroy him. He had seen that destruction in Hirohito. He had felt it that day in the school dining hall. He knew it was very powerful, very seductive and very real.

He could feel the fear: fear that Tatsuya sought to kill him and fear that he would slide into Darkness with this power of which Hiroshi spoke. But Sam also had the wisdom to know that being driven by fear would not lead him to the right decision.

So, Sam sought to see through the craving and the fear and to find that quiet voice inside that would tell him the answer. He sat quietly, his eyes cast down, looking at the leaves that littered the ground. He heard the breeze stirring the branches high above him. He heard the rustle of the squirrels and the songs of the birds. Then, as he breathed deeply and slowly, he heard the words,

"Trust in yourself. You are ready."

He looked up at Hiroshi and Kensho, sitting quietly before him. He turned to Daichi and then to Zoe and Sophie. Sophie was smiling broadly, and it made Sam smile broadly back at her.

"Trust in yourself. You are ready," she said.

The smile faded from Sam's face, and he drew in a long, deep breath. Then he nodded and turned to Kensho. "Sensei, I am ready."

Kensho smiled and nodded. "I know that you are, Sam. Then let us prepare."

They had passed a small waterfall shortly before making camp. So, they all returned to it and watched as Sam made his way to stand under the icy water and purify his spirit. The girls asked Hiroshi what he was doing, and Hiroshi explained to them what misogi was.

Sam stood still as the water turned his shoulders numb and the shivering began to overwhelm him. He breathed deeply, and as he did, so he began to focus on each breath in and each breath out. His shivering eased, and his mind settled on this simple act. He focused purely on following his breath in and following his breath out.

The pain of the freezing water left him. The shivering ceased. Time itself seemed to shift. He lived in the moment, and so the moment never moved. With this shift, suddenly Sam got a glimpse of reality as it was. No longer did he feel insignificant and lost in a universe of unimaginable size. He felt like he was the universe and the universe was him. He felt a great sense of ease fill him. Kensho shouted "Hai!" and Sam steadily lifted his arms above his head and lowered them down to his side. Then he slowly but deliberately stepped out from beneath the waterfall and back onto the bank.

After he had dried off, they returned to the camp. It was beginning to get dark, so Kensho collected some more wood and stoked the fire. Then, Kensho and Sam sat down facing each other and began to meditate. The Divine Swords of Kensho and Hiroshi lay unsheathed between them. The light of the flames danced on the faces of Kensho and Sam.

The familiar low hum began to become audible. Steadily, it became louder and louder, and then suddenly it stopped. Everyone sat still in anticipation. Then slowly, Sam began to slump to his left side. Kensho leapt up and caught him. He laid Sam gently back on the ground.

"Is he alright?" asked Zoe, looking concerned.

"He will return to us shortly. He will be very tired, but he will be okay," said Hiroshi. Then he began to boil some water on the fire.

With Kensho kneeling beside him, Sam began to stir. His head moved from side to side, and he appeared to be trying to say something. Then his eyes slowly flickered open, and he tried to sit up, looking around in confusion.

"It is okay, Sam. You are quite safe. Lay back and rest for a while."

Sam did as Kensho said and lowered himself back to lie on the ground.

After a few minutes, Hiroshi came over with a cup of tea. Kensho helped Sam sit up and then Sam began to sip on the tea.

"How are you feeling?" asked Zoe.

Sam paused for a few moments. "Exhausted...but also very different, it's hard to explain."

"It will take a while for your mind and body to integrate the Transmission," said Kensho. "Over the coming hours and even days, you will begin to notice changes. Your perception of ki will become greatly heightened. You will see the flow of energy in and around people and all living things. You will sense things from a great distance. These changes will seem overwhelming at first. I am sorry that we have not been better able to prepare you, Sam.

"Your skills with the sword will be equal to those of Nagato

Sensei. You have not experienced the hard work and struggle that is normally required to develop such skills. It may seem a gift to be simply endowed with these skills, but the truth is you have suffered a great loss. It is the result of the circumstances in which we find ourselves."

Sam looked around at his companions, the forest and the animals that were around them. He was beginning to see the light that was within them and around them just as Kensho had said. He could see the ki of the animals move just before they physically moved. Then Sam began to become aware of things beyond sight. His dim awareness of the threat that lay around them suddenly grew unimaginably strong. He jumped up spilling his tea on the forest floor as he looked around in terror, feeling as if Darkness was upon them.

Kensho stood up and held Sam by the shoulders, catching his gaze. "Look at me, Sam. Look at me, Sam! You are safe. The danger is yet still far away. You are safe."

Sam looked into Kensho's eyes, and the terror eased. Kensho guided him to sit back down, and Hiroshi passed him another cup of tea.

"Drink it," said Hiroshi. "It has some herbs that will help you."

Sam's awareness and perception continued to grow, while Kensho sat taking care of him. Far into the night, eventually exhaustion overtook Sam and he fell into a fitful sleep disturbed by many nightmares of the malice that surrounded them.

The following morning Zoe awoke first. She rolled to her side and saw a hawk sitting on the branch of a nearby tree. It didn't seem possible, yet she knew she was the same hawk that watched over her at home. She smiled at her and whispered, "How did you get here?"

The hawk swooped off the branch and came down right beside Zoe. She cocked her head and looked into Zoe's eyes. Zoe felt an incredible connection, far beyond what she felt with other animals.

"Who are you?" asked Zoe quietly. "Where do I know you from?"

But the hawk just perched there looking at her. Then, she took off, and as Zoe turned to watch her fly, she saw on the edge of their camp a huge black bear.

Zoe slowly sat up. She felt no danger from the bear. In fact, she felt quite the opposite. It seemed intrigued, but also protective of them. Zoe reached into her bag and pulled out a little miso rice. Then she slowly got up and walked over to the bear. It lifted its head up to smell as she approached. Zoe knelt down in front of it, and the size and power of the bear filled her senses. Its head was high above her, and the bear lowered it to look at her. She noticed it had grey hairs on its snout and chest.

"Are you an old man?" she whispered, as she held out her hand with the miso rice resting in her palm.

The bear gently licked the rice from her hand with its rough tongue. Then it lifted its head and sniffed the air before slowly turning and lumbering off back into the woods.

Zoe turned to find Hiroshi standing behind her smiling.

"You have made a new friend I see, Zoe."

Zoe smiled back and nodded. Then Hiroshi knelt down beside her. "Zoe, you have a most unusual connection to the animals and plants. Do you know why?"

Zoe shook her head. "No, Hiroshi. It has just been this way ever since I can remember."

"They feel your heart, Zoe. They know that you love them. They know that you are their protector. They sense all our hearts, Zoe. They are drawn to you because of your deep love for them. Because you seek to protect them, they will seek to protect you. Remember that."

Zoe looked at Hiroshi's bright and compassionate brown eyes. She had begun to think of him as the grandfather she had never had. She nodded. "I will remember, Hiroshi."

Sam was still sleeping, but he began to move around and mumble.

"He's having a nightmare," said Zoe and went over to comfort him.

But Sophie, who was sleeping beside him, rolled over and placed her hand on his head. Sam immediately began to settle again. Sophie curled up beside Sam and held her hand on his head. She stayed that way for an hour or so as the others stoked the fire and prepared a small breakfast. Then Sophie gently spoke to Sam and drew him out of his sleep.

"How are you feeling Sam?" asked Hiroshi.

"Tired, Sensei. Very tired."

"We will walk slowly today. You need time to recover. I have prepared a special breakfast that will help you."

After Sam had eaten, they set off once again. Still the weather held, and their spirits were high. The mountains looked beautiful, bathed in the rays of the rising sun. Spring was marching on, and the trees were becoming ever more abundantly clothed in new leaves.

Over the next few days, they continued to make good progress. Sam's strength returned, and he began to explore his new found skills with the sword. The biggest change he noticed was in how much more centred and grounded he had become: That and how relaxed he was. He practised with Daichi, and now that he could perceive the movement of ki, it became so easy to anticipate and evade his attacks.

However, Sam did feel a little odd. He felt as though he had cheated. He began to understand just what Kensho had meant when he had said that Sam had "suffered a great loss". Even with his previous relatively limited experience of aikido and iaido training, Sam had realised how rewarding it was to feel one's progress through hard work. Now, he had these great skills, but none of the satisfaction of knowing he had worked hard to earn them. This was the great loss of which Kensho spoke.

CHAPTER 49

The Bandits

It was in the afternoon of the 11th day that they drew near to a village Hiroshi had visited on past journeys. The path that they followed was not the main route to the village. So it was rarely travelled. As a result, they had encountered no one on their journey to this point. The village was still some way away and out of sight when Hiroshi called a halt.

"We have a difficult choice now," he said. "Our supplies are falling very low. We are still some days away from Mount Tokin. So, it would seem prudent for one or two of us to go into the village to purchase some more supplies. However, to do so exposes us to danger. Questions will be asked and suspicions raised. If Darkness holds any sway here, then we could find ourselves split up and in grave danger."

"My counsel would be for Daichi and me to enter the village unseen," said Kensho. "We can then see how strong the grip of Darkness is upon the villagers."

Daichi nodded in agreement.

"Very well," said Hiroshi. "I will take Sam and the girls off the path, and we will await your return."

It didn't take Kensho and Daichi long to reach the edge of the village. The fields were strangely empty. It was the end of the day, but they still expected to see villagers hard at work. When they reached the first houses, Kensho turned to Daichi and said, "Wait here. I will go in alone and call for you, should I need your help."

Daichi nodded and Kensho proceeded.

He found himself walking straight into a drama unfolding in the centre of the small village. A group of bandits had gathered together some of the village elders and were holding them in a small group. The rest of the villagers were standing close by. As Kensho watched, it became obvious that the bandits were also seeking supplies. But they were choosing not to pay for them. Instead, they were threatening to kill the elders if the villagers did not arrange for the supplies they wished to be brought out to them immediately.

Kensho found himself in a dilemma. He could not stand by as these bandits threatened or even killed someone, but he also knew that to engage them would quite possibly lead to bloodshed. Ultimately, he had no choice. He had to protect the villagers and accept the consequences. He stepped out of the shadows and walked straight up to the bandits.

There were five of them, all armed with swords. At first they did not notice his approach, so intent were they upon threatening the elders. Suddenly, one of them spotted Kensho and shouted a warning. All five turned. The leader pushed the elders away and walked towards Kensho.

"Who are you?" he shouted.

"I am a traveller passing through," replied Kensho, calmly. "Who are you?"

"None of your business: If you are a traveller passing through, then you'll keep going if you know what is good for you."

"I wish to buy some supplies from the villagers. I shall need to speak to the elders. Please put your swords down."

The bandits laughed.

"You have money then?" said the leader. "Well, why don't you give us your money, and we will see if we can spare some supplies!"

Again the bandits laughed.

"Please put down your swords and leave," said Kensho.

Now the leader became angry and began to advance on Kensho.

"You don't give me orders, you fool! Give me your sword and your money, and maybe I will spare your miserable life!"

Kensho calmly walked towards him. The leader hesitated, realising that Kensho wasn't reacting as he had expected him to. He knew he was in trouble, but he also knew his men were watching and that he couldn't back down now. So he gripped his sword tightly in his hands and attacked.

The bandits were not trained swordsmen. They relied on intimidating poor farmers to secure their ill-gotten gains. Kensho's aikido made a mockery of the leader's attack. Kensho effortlessly disarmed him and used a pressure point to render him unconscious. The rest of the bandits tried to rush him, but one by one he disarmed them and rendered them unconscious.

In barely a minute, all five bandits were passed out on the ground. The village elders rushed over to Kensho, bowing and expressing their deep gratitude. Kensho told them to securely tie the bandits hands and feet and then to alert their daimyo. Dusk was now falling, so the villagers locked the bandits up in a barn for the night and placed guards to watch them. They would send someone to the daimyo in the morning.

The elders wished to repay Kensho for his help and told him that he must stay with them for the night. They would prepare a feast the likes of which he had never before seen. Kensho thanked them but explained he simply needed to buy some supplies. The elders flatly refused to accept his payment and gave him the rice and other supplies he requested, as well as other fine foods, by way of thanks for saving them. Kensho called to Daichi to join him. He explained to the villagers that they were on a pilgrimage from temple to temple together. Then the two men thanked the villagers for their wonderful generosity and made their way back to join their companions.

Darkness was fast approaching as they walked back through the forest. The moon was close to being full, and it was high and bright in the sky, lighting their path through the trees. After a little while, they entered a small glade, where Kensho stopped to question Daichi.

"Would you be able to carry all the supplies up to the camp?"

"Of course," replied Daichi. "I heard him too."

Kensho passed his supplies to Daichi, and Daichi strode on through the forest.

"I know that you are following us," said Kensho in the direction they had just come.

A lone figure stepped out from behind a tree a little way off. "I saw what you did! You dishonoured my family!" the figure said.

"So, you are a family of bandits then?" said Kensho. "I see no honour in stealing from those who are weaker than you. You brought dishonour upon yourselves. See the error of your ways and put down your sword. If it is truly honour you seek, then find it by helping others, not harming them."

The figure came closer, and Kensho could see that this was a young man, perhaps 17 or 18-years-old. Moonlight glinted off the sword that the young man had already drawn, ready to attack.

"I am Kenichi Uchiyama! You have brought dishonour to my family. I will reclaim our honour by taking your life!"

Then Uchiyama screamed and attacked Kensho. But Kensho stepped to the side, and the attack passed him by. Kensho could feel the anger, hatred and confusion in this young man. He knew that Uchiyama believed in honour. He also knew that the hatred and anger that filled Uchiyama was hatred and anger at himself. There was a light to his ki that ran completely contrary to his life as a bandit.

Nonetheless Uchiyama was relentless in his attacks. Over and over again he charged at Kensho, swinging his sword wildly. Each time Kensho would easily evade the attack as he repeated over and over again that he wished Uchiyama no harm and that he would not fight him. But rather than calming Uchiyama down, Kensho's refusal to fight seemed only to enrage him still further.

"Fight me, you coward!" screamed Uchiyama as he lunged to drive his sword deep into the Kensho's chest. Kensho easily anticipated the attack and no sooner had it begun than he was standing behind Uchiyama, his posture relaxed, his expression grave. Uchiyama whirled, his muscles taut, his breathing increasingly laboured.

"As I have told you many times, Uchiyama, I will not fight you," said the older man. "I wish you no harm."

Uchiyama's grip tightened on the sword handle as his face darkened with fury. "Wish me no harm? You brought dishonour to my family. There is no greater harm. Tell me your name so I might know whose life I shall end. Or shall you forever be known simply as the 'Coward'?"

As he spat out the last word, Uchiyama brought the sword in an arcing cut from high on his right down to his left, aiming to slice the older man in half. Once again Kensho moved quickly and easily so that Uchiyama's sword cut nothing but air. Uchiyama's exhaustion was now complete and he stumbled and fell. As he hit the ground, his grip on the sword failed, and it rolled across the forest floor.

Moonlight glinted off the curved blade once more, as Kensho picked it up and came to stand over Uchiyama, who lay on his back gasping for air. Fear filled Uchiyama's face as he awaited the final cut. Instead Kensho smiled warmly and said, "I wish you no harm, Uchiyama."

Then, after carefully laying the sword down on the ground beside Uchiyama, he vanished into the forest making no sound as he left.

Uchiyama lay exhausted on the ground. He was too tired to move and too tired to think. He simply lay there listening to his breathing. His gaze fell upon the moon high above him. For the first time in his life he noticed how incredibly beautiful it was, and tears welled up in his eyes.

Daichi returned shortly before Kensho. Hiroshi looked in amazement not only at the quantity of the supplies but also at the incredible range of delicious foods he was carrying.

"Daichi! How did you afford such wonderful things? And how did you persuade the villagers to part with them?" asked Hiroshi.

Daichi told the story of the bandits and of Kensho's actions. "Kensho will be along shortly. One of the bandits must have been outside the village, and he then followed us. Kensho stayed back to deal with him."

Just as he finished saying that, Kensho appeared.

"Are you okay, Kensho?" asked Sophie.

"Hai," said Kensho as he came and sat down.

"Did you kill the bandit?" asked Zoe.

"No, Zoe," said Kensho, shaking his head. "I would do everything in my power to avoid that. He was not a bad young man. He was not much older than Sam. He had just been lead astray by his elders. I could sense the unhappiness in him. I simply let him defeat himself."

"Won't he come and attack us here?" asked Sophie, looking concerned.

"He will not. He is on a different path now," replied Kensho.

"Where is he going?" asked Sophie.

"No, I mean he is on a different path in his life now, Sophie," said Kensho, laughing. "He will make better decisions, I believe, from now on."

"Ah, I see," said Sophie feeling a little foolish.

Zoe, Sophie and Sam sat together after they had eaten.

"Do you see a sort of light around people and things, Soph? Even trees and birds?" asked Sam.

"Yes, it is like a haze. Sometimes it is very bright, and sometimes quite dull. Though the dull ones are only ever around people. Not people like Hiroshi and Daichi, but people back home. They look very dull, and the colours are often darker and, well, less vibrant, I guess. But animals and plants are always bright and shiny! Unless they're sick or dying. Do you see that too, Sam?" Sophie asked excitedly.

"Yes," he said. "When I look at Iwata Sensei, for example, I see this incredibly bright white light around him and flowing through him. Same with Nagato Sensei and Daichi. In fact, you two are also pretty similar though you're more violet, and, Zoe, you're more golden. I seem to be pretty white, but there is a tinge of golden perhaps? What do you see, Soph?"

"Well, for a start you are shining so much more brightly than you did before you met Kensho. There were lots of darker colours flowing around and through you. They have almost all gone, and yes, there is a golden tinge too. You're vibrating with energy now, Sam. Do you also see people's intentions through the energy, I mean, their ki moving?"

As she said that, Sophie went to reach out for her bag, but Sam grabbed it before she had even moved.

"What do you think?" he said, grinning broadly.

"Get off!" said Sophie, giggling.

"I can see the dim outlines of the energy or ki around people," said Zoe. "But I don't see much more than that. What about the animals and trees, Sam? Do you feel them?"

"Well, I see the ki flowing through them, and I see their fields around them. I see their ki move before they actually move. But I don't really feel them any more than I did. I think that is still your unique gift, Zo!"

Zoe smiled. She did find it a little hard being unable to see what Sophie and Sam saw, but it made her feel a little better that she could feel what they could not.

"We will be okay, won't we Sam?" asked Sophie. "I'm scared. Darkness is angry and full of hate. It's getting stronger and stronger. There are so few of us. Can we really get to the temple okay?"

Sam looked at Sophie, and he felt very protective of her. He couldn't bear the thought of her being harmed in any way. But he knew he had to be honest. "I am scared too, Soph. I feel what you feel now, and it is horrible. But I trust Hiroshi, Kensho and Daichi. They believe we will be alright. You feel that too, don't you?"

Sophie nodded, and Sam continued, "Well, then we must trust."

Sophie nodded again. Sam looked at Zoe and asked, "Do you trust, Zo?"

Zoe nodded too. "My trust is that what we are doing must be done. I trust that whatever happens happens just as it should. I don't know why we are here or why we have to face this horrible Darkness. But we do. So, I will do whatever I can, and if I die, then I die. I am not going to run away scared."

Kensho had just walked over to join them.

"Very wise words, Zoe," he said. "You could almost be quoting from the Tao Te Ching. It says:

> All things change and to die is everyone's fate.
> When you fully accept you will die, you have no fear.
> When you have no fear your actions are powerful.

"No one knows how their life will unfold. Events unfold, and we must respond to them. Zoe spoke with great courage. She spoke as a true samurai warrior would speak. That is the spirit with which we must live our lives, always.

"But please, do trust Hiroshi. He is a great warrior and wise beyond compare. He will lead us to safety. Now let us get some rest."

Ambrose Merrell

The Temple at Mount Tokin

The morning of the 12th day dawned cold and grey. The companions shivered as they gathered their things together. As she packed her bag, Sophie said to no one in particular, "We will be attacked today."

"Yes, Soph. I feel it too," said Sam.

Hiroshi was standing, waiting for them to finish packing.

"Yes," he said. "I too feel Darkness is poised. But we have no choice but to continue to head for Mount Tokin. Everyone, be on your guard. I think we are perhaps a day away now, unless we are waylaid."

As they set off, Hiroshi walked beside Daichi, out of earshot of the girls.

"Daichi," said Hiroshi, "come what may, I want you to stand by Zoe and Sophie and protect them, no matter what happens."

"Hai, Sensei. I will give my life to protect them."

"I know you will, my friend."

The clouds remained heavy and low, but the rain held off. Sam walked beside Zoe.

"Your friend the bear walks on one side of us and the wolves on the other," he said to her. "Do you remember when I was crouching, hiding in your garden, being licked by a bear cub? That seems a lifetime ago now. It almost seems to have happened to another person."

Zoe smiled at the memory of Sam and the bears. "I know. It does seem forever ago, doesn't it? A world away too. Take care today, Sam. I know you have been given great skills with the sword, but don't take any silly risks, okay?"

"I won't, Zo. I just want to make sure that you and Soph are safe.

That's all I care about."

By mid-afternoon, they found themselves walking along a wide path near the bottom of the valley. The mountains rose high on either side of them, thick with trees and bamboo groves, their peaks lost in the low cloud. The woods thinned out somewhat as the path lead the companions alongside a fast-flowing and wide mountain river.

Suddenly, the hawk came flying out of the woods to their right screeching and circled above Zoe and the companions. Hiroshi stopped.

"It is a warning!" he said. "The danger is so strong now, they must be nearly upon us." Then he looked to his left: "They hope to trap us with the river behind us. We must ford it! Let us get into the open space on the other side!"

Daichi grabbed Sophie under one arm and strode through the freezing rapids. Sam got Zoe to clamber on his back over his rucksack and carried her over too. Then, Kensho and Hiroshi followed.

"Stay close together!" called Hiroshi. "The attack is nearly upon us!"

Daichi stood in front of the girls, Kensho behind. To the right stood Sam, and to the left and slightly in front stood Hiroshi. They didn't have to wait long for the attack to begin. The trees on the mountainside before them began to shake and crash down as huge boulders came tumbling down the slope. The boulders rolled across the path upon which they had, only moments ago, been walking before crashing through the river, raising great waves of water as they came. The companions leapt from side to side dodging each boulder as they rolled on past them. Had we been caught on the path, thought Sam, we would never have had a chance to escape being crushed. The hawk saved us.

The boulders were only the beginning of the danger. For behind the boulders came dozens of huge oni, running down through the trees. They were much bigger than those the companions had previously encountered. These oni still had the golden eyes, but they were black-skinned and had two huge pointed horns on their heads.

Zoe snapped out of the fear that had overcome her and began once again to call for the trees and the animals to help them. This time, many branches came crashing down upon the oni. Some were also tripped by roots and tumbled down the slope bellowing in pain. The momentum of the attack was broken, and some oni didn't get back up after being hit by the falling branches. But many still made it through.

The leading oni were now approaching the far side of the river when a great howling broke out in the woods to the onis' left. The oni stopped and turned to see a huge pack of wolves descending upon them. The wolves were small, but they were nimble, and though the oni swung their clubs in panic, they failed to hit the wolves. Instead, in the chaos, they managed to hit each other while the wolves bit and tore at their legs. Some of the oni now fled across the river towards the companions. Kensho stepped forward as the first oni tried to make its way out of the river. First, Kensho cut its leg, and then, as it fell, he beheaded it.

More oni were now coming over, and, as Hiroshi advanced to meet one, Sam took a deep breath and went to face another. The oni saw Sam and bellowed before raising its club to strike. But as it did so, two things happened. First, dozens of small birds dived at its face, distracting the raging creature. Simultaneously, Sophie unsheathed her sword, and, quite by instinct to protect her brother, drew the white light surging through her sending it out through the tip of the sword, blinding the oni.

Sam seized his opportunity and, darting to the right side of the oni, he brought the sword slicing through the back of its knee just as he had seen Hiroshi do. The oni bellowed mightily and fell forward, and Sam instantly took its head off. He paused for a moment in shock at what he had just done. Then he heard Zoe scream, "Tengu!" and looked back across the river to see many dozens of tengu rushing towards them.

The wolves now broke away from the remaining oni and ran howling at the tengu. A few of the tengu immediately turned and fled back into the woods but most continued, ferociously swinging their swords. Unfortunately, the tengu were more agile and accurate than the oni, and the wolves began to be cut and killed. Nonetheless, they slowed the tengu's assault, which allowed Hiroshi, Kensho and Sam to deal with the remaining oni.

Daichi stood close to the girls, doing just what Hiroshi had instructed. He was also keeping an eye on the forest to their rear in case of a sneak attack. Sophie continued to blind the oni as best she could, and the birds that Zoe had called kept distracting the oni, helping the fight.

As the last oni fell, the remaining tengu swarmed across the river. There were so many of them and they had spread out so widely that it was impossible for Hiroshi, Kensho and Sam to fell them all. Hiroshi and Kensho used their kiai to batter the tengu, but these were hardy tengu, and though they staggered, they still came on. Hiroshi tried to drive Darkness from them with a sweep of white light from his sword, but to no avail. The grip of Darkness upon them was too strong, and still they came.

Daichi realised that they were going to be outflanked, and called Kensho back to help. The tengu charged at them, and Zoe drew her sword. Sam and the men cut through the charging tengu with amazing speed. Zoe and Sophie were well protected, and for a little while they thought that they were getting the upper hand.

But the real danger was only now beginning to approach.

On the mountainside in front, dark shadows could be seen weaving through the trees.

"Yokai!" cried Daichi.

Then behind the yokai, came still more oni and tengu.

"Kensho and I will hold off this assault!" said Hiroshi. "Daichi, take Sam and the girls and make for Tokin-ji temple. We will join you when we can. Quickly!"

"Hai, Sensei!" said Daichi, before calling to Sam and the girls, "Follow me!" They all began to run along the side of the river, with Daichi leading the girls and Sam at the rear.

Just before they disappeared into the forest, Sam glanced back. There stood Hiroshi and Kensho side by side as the dark shadows neared the river. Tears began to well up in his eyes as he looked at the two old friends standing together, full of courage and light, knowing that he may never see them again.

"Sam! Come quickly!" said Daichi.

Sam turned, and began running through the forest.

The bellows of oni and the piercing screams of yokai echoed through the valley as they ran. They were not on a path, and so their progress was often slowed by steep gullies or thick patches of undergrowth. After they had been running for about half an hour, Sophie cried out, "Stop!" and she fell to the ground exhausted.

Daichi turned and ran back as Sam bent down to help her.

"Are you alright, Soph?" Sam asked.

"I'm ok. I'm just too tired to run anymore."

Daichi dug through his pack and retrieved water and some food.

They all drank and ate a little in silence.

"I am sorry, Sophie," said Daichi, "but we must keep moving. We have to try to reach the temple before nightfall. Can you manage to walk at least?"

Sophie nodded and slowly stood up stretching her legs as she did so.

"Will we ever see Kensho and Hiroshi again?" she asked.

"Without a doubt, Sophie," said Daichi, confidently. "They will join us soon. Now, let us be on our way."

Sophie knew that Daichi believed what he said and she nodded before getting to her feet and setting off once more.

Though Daichi was confident they would see Hiroshi and Kensho again he was still very concerned about the plight he and the children found themselves in. He feared dusk would come early due to the low and heavy cloud that hung just above them. But as the afternoon wore on, the cloud thinned and broke. Perhaps it was good fortune, or perhaps it was Zoe's call for help. As the cloud broke, they began to catch glimpses of the top of the mountain toward which they climbed.

They were heading north up a valley, which Daichi knew reasonably well. He had been to the temple with Hiroshi a number of times before. However, he realised the temple would be hard to find and the journey would be that much more tiring if they stayed off the path. But he also knew that the path was likely to be watched and that the likelihood of attack was that much greater. In the end, as they scrabbled through yet another deep and dangerous gully, he decided the risk of attack on the path was better than becoming lost in the forest and enduring a night exposed on the mountainside.

So, Daichi led them back down to the river, which was already noticeably narrower now that they were higher up the mountain, and it was fed by less tributaries. They forded it once more and rejoined the path that still ran close to the river's edge. Immediately, they began to make much quicker and easier progress.

The path grew steadily steeper, and the river beside it became ever louder as its waters crashed over rocks and down small waterfalls. The sun was descending in the sky, and soon it would dip below the ridge to the west. But for now, it was warming their faces and lifting their spirits.

Sam kept looking behind, hoping to see Hiroshi and Kensho coming to join them. He sensed that they were still alive. He also sensed that Darkness was not yet done with them and that it would make a last attempt to prevent them from reaching Tokin-ji temple. He just hoped that the companions would be reunited before that attack came. He was still developing his new found perceptions, but he thought he felt another presence behind them. One that was unfamiliar to him.

"Stop!" called Sophie, suddenly.

This time it was not because she was exhausted. "I am certain that we'll be attacked just up ahead. I can feel it."

Sam tried to feel ahead to where Sophie sensed the danger, but he couldn't bring focus in the same way she could. All he could feel was the all-pervasive malevolence that surrounded them constantly now.

Daichi looked up the path. "I do not doubt your words, Sophie," he said. "But we must reach the temple before nightfall. There is no other path for us to follow. If we go off the path into the woods, we still risk attack, and we also risk getting lost or taking too long and dusk is already upon us."

"Should we wait here for Nagato and Iwata Sensei, Daichi?" asked Sam.

"While I am certain they will come," replied Daichi, "I do not know for how long they will be delayed. We have no time to spare. We must go forward. I know that this is the right thing to do, and I have to trust that I am guided well. Whatever we encounter, we will overcome. I ask you all to put your trust in me."

They all nodded, and Daichi lead them on, up the path.

The sun finally dipped below the ridge, and as it did, so the air grew noticeably colder, chilled by the icy cold waters running alongside them. Their senses were all heightened as they made their way up the steep, rocky path. As Daichi climbed up and around a little cliff he met the danger Sophie had sensed.

"Yokai!" he called out, and his heart sank.

Perhaps 20 or so dark, shadowy forms stood menacingly amongst the trees some way off on either side of the path. They made no move as Daichi and the others edged forward. Daichi stood to the left side, Sam to the right, with the girls in the middle.

"I think these things are too much for even the trees and animals to help protect us from," said Zoe, her voice shaking with fear.

No birds, squirrels, wolves or any animals were in sight. There was just the sound of the rushing water.

Step by slow step, they inched their way along the path. Sam looked at the malevolent figures and wondered why they didn't attack. But the yokai were waiting until the companions were in their midst before they began their slow, terrible advance.

"Oh, where are Hiroshi and Kensho? We need them now!" cried out Sophie.

But Hiroshi and Kensho did not come. Slowly, the shadowy forms surrounded them and began to close in.

"We can strike them with our swords! It will drive them back!" said Daichi. Though as he said it, he knew that their swords were too weak and the yokai too large in number. Great as their swords were, they were not Divine Swords. Despairing thoughts began to rise in Daichi's mind, but then he heard Hiroshi's words, "Trust, Daichi. Trust."

"I trust," said Daichi.

Then something wholly unexpected happened. Sophie began to sing. At first her voice was quiet and faltering, and the song was lost beneath the sound of the rushing stream. But as she sang, her voice grew stronger. Still, the yokai closed in on them. Steadily, Sophie's voice grew ever louder. Then, Zoe joined in the signing. She too started quietly and falteringly, but as she sang, courage began to fill her, raising her voice too.

The yokai slowed and then stopped. Now Sam began to sing with the girls, their three voices filling the air. The yokai began to withdraw. As they did so, Sam thought he noticed their pitch blackness almost beginning to fade. It was as if they were becoming translucent. All three of them were now singing loudly and joyfully, and the yokai continued to retreat until their dark shapes dissolved into the shadows of the woods completely.

Daichi stood in amazement as Sam, Zoe and Sophie continued to sing. He did not know the song they were singing, nor did he understand what had just happened, but he knew now was their opportunity. "Let us walk as we sing!" he said.

So, the companions continued once more to make their way along the now clear path with Daichi leading. As they walked, they sang, partly to keep the yokai away and partly because the singing gave them courage. Daichi joined in the best he could, following the melody and repeating the words of the song without understanding them.

After they'd had been walking only a short distance, Daichi called out, "Look!" As they looked up the mountain to where he pointed, they saw walls and rooftops. "It is Tokin-ji temple!"

They all stopped singing.

"How long 'til we get there do you think, Daichi?" asked Sam.

"It is deceptively close. As the crow flies we would be there in no time. But our path is steep and winding. I think we should arrive in an hour or so. Just before dark if we are fortunate."

Their pace picked up markedly now. They had their journey's end in sight, and all were keen to reach its safety as soon as possible. The path parted company with the stream and began to wind its way up the steep slope to the temple. Their progress was aided by the stone steps that now formed the path. Stone lanterns began to appear at intervals alongside the steps.

Eventually, the path flattened out as they reached the top of the mountain. It was still quite wooded, but in the dying light they could make out the temple some way off through the trees. The path was now made of smooth stone slabs that lead right to the main gate.

"I see the temple!" cried Sophie in delight. "We did it!"

But even as safety seemed within their grasp, Darkness sought to thwart them, and once more it launched an attack. This time, it was not yokai but many tengu that descended upon them, screaming. Most of the tengu had clubs and spears, but a few had swords. They were attacking from the left. Sam and Daichi stood side by side, their swords at the ready. Zoe and Sophie stood behind them with their swords also drawn.

When the first tengu reached them, Sam and Daichi easily cut them down. But there were so many tengu that it was difficult for them to protect the girls. One tengu half-slipped through. Sam caught it with a cut of his sword, but it managed to continue advancing and raised its club to strike Sophie. Before it could, Zoe thrust her sword deep into its chest and killed it instantly.

"There are too many of them!" said Sam to Daichi as he swung his sword. "I can't keep them all from getting to the girls."

"We must try Sam!" said Daichi. "Careful! They are outflanking us!"

At that moment there came a cry from behind them. Daichi turned to see a young man, whom he did not recognise, charging at the tengu swinging his sword wildly. He clearly wasn't a trained swordsman, but his courage and determination were something to behold. He hacked his way through the tengu that attacked him until he was by the companions' side. As the stranger fought, he shouted, "I am Kenichi Uchiyama. I fight beside you for my honour!"

Now with three swordsmen they were able to surround the girls and protect them. With the initial shock of the attack gone, Sophie began filling the wood with the light from her sword. She was becoming very adept at blinding and repelling the tengu. Zoe also began her silent call for help. Immediately tree roots began tripping the tengu, and branches ensnared them, or crushed them.

Then, with a mighty roar, the huge bear that had licked the miso-rice from Zoe's hand a few days before, charged into the battle. It overwhelmed the tengu who, despite their weapons, could not manage to strike the bear before, one after another, they were felled by a blow from its enormous paw. Zoe and Sophie cheered!

"Let us use this opportunity to move towards the temple as we fight!" called out Daichi.

So the companions steadily fought their way in the direction of the temple, as the bear continued to draw most of the tengu away.

Once again, just when it looked as though they may reach safety, Darkness hit back. They heard a bellow, and three of the huge, black-skinned oni lumbered into view. These had their horns painted red. Or perhaps they are red with blood, thought Sam. These oni were quickly joined by a further five that came from the other side of the mountain.

Sam, Daichi and Kenichi were all beginning to tire. Daichi thought that to try to fight these terrible creatures would surely prove too much.

"Let us run for the temple!" he shouted.

Then he mustered the last of his strength and fought to clear a path through the tengu that stood in their way, opening a gap.

"Run for the gate!" Daichi said to them.

Zoe and Sophie immediately sprinted as fast as they could. They had perhaps a hundred metres to cover, and they could see the gate. But they had their rucksacks on the backs and they were exhausted.

Two of the oni saw the girls running, and the oni also began to move quickly in order to cut off Zoe and Sophie's escape. The ground shook with the thumping foot falls of the oni, as they took huge strides and moved with terrifying speed. Sam realised the girls were going to be caught, and he cut through two tengu that blocked his way before dashing after the girls.

Zoe and Sophie halted behind the trunk of a large fir tree. The gate was only 30 metres away now. They were so tantalisingly close. But between the girls and the gate stood two oni, and they were advancing on them.

Sam ran past the girls and stood before the two huge creatures. He could smell their stench as they cautiously approached him. These two seemed more intelligent than the others they had fought. They were separating and trying to outflank Sam.

Sam chose the one he thought presented the greatest danger and attacked it. He dodged its swinging club and managed to cut its leg but not enough to fell it. The other oni now closed in on him from behind.

"Watch behind you, Sam!" cried Zoe.

The oni swung its club, and Sam only just managed to leap out of the way. This time, he managed to cut well with his sword, and that oni fell to its knees howling with pain. But before he could finish it off, the other oni was upon him. He ducked behind a tree, and the club the oni swung smashed into its trunk splitting it. The tree began to fall. Sam tried to escape, but he did not get far before he was hit by its branches and knocked to the ground.

Fear filled Sam as he realised he was pinned beneath the tree. He tried to wriggle out, but it was difficult to free himself. The oni was advancing on him with its club raised and ready to strike. Just as the oni was about to crush Sam with a mighty blow Sam heard a kiai. Then he saw a sword, white with light. It flew through the air and pierced the oni's chest from behind. The oni fell dead to the floor and crashed down right beside Sam. Sam looked over and saw it was Hiroshi who had saved him.

But to Sam's horror, just as Hiroshi had thrown his sword, so the injured oni had managed to raise itself and swing its club. Hiroshi tried to spring out of the way, but it was too late. The end of the club smashed into his side and sent him flying through the air. He hit the trunk of a tree and crumpled to the ground.

"Sensei!" screamed Sam, tearing himself from beneath the branches.

Kensho now rushed into view and beheaded the oni as he ran past it to reach Hiroshi. At the same time the gates of the temple opened and out poured dozens of monks, all armed with long sticks that had curved blades at the top. Some of the monks went to rescue the girls, gathering them up in their arms and racing back to the temple. The rest of the monks went to fight the remaining tengu and oni.

Daichi and Kenichi were exhausted and close to being overwhelmed by the tengu when the monks arrived to save them. The monks told them to make for the temple as they began to beat back the tengu.

Sam watched as Daichi and Kenichi ran through the trees, relieved

Ambrose Merrell

to see that they were uninjured. He then turned back to Kensho and Hiroshi. Kensho had Hiroshi in his arms and was making for the temple.

"Sam! Bring Hiroshi's sword!" said Kensho.

Sam looked over and saw Hiroshi's sword still in the back of the dead oni. He rushed over, jumped onto the creature's back and pulled the sword out. Then he began to run back to the temple. An oni thundered towards Sam, determined to kill him before he reached safety.

Sam had two swords in his hands now, the Divine Sword in his right and his own in his left. He let out a mighty kiai and cut the oni with both and it fell. Then he turned and ran for the gate, his lungs burning and his legs feeling so heavy he could barely lift them. He dived through the gateway, collapsing in a heap on some beautifully raked gravel, scattering the little stones across the garden. Behind him followed the monks who had come out to help them. Then the gates were slammed shut. The companions had, at last, made it to the Tokin-ji temple. But they had paid dearly for their sanctuary.

CHAPTER 51

A Terrible Price

Sam rolled over, gasping for air. Slowly he picked himself up and, still clutching the swords, went over to his companions, who were all kneeling beside Hiroshi. Many monks were also gathered around. The flames from torches they held were lighting the garden. Sam knelt beside Kensho and saw that he was holding Hiroshi's hand. Sam was shocked to see how old and frail Hiroshi suddenly looked. Hiroshi's eyes were open and, despite his frail physical form, they shone as bright as ever. When he saw Sam, he smiled.

"Sam, I see you have my sword," he said.

Sam looked at the Divine Sword he was holding. "Yes, Nagato Sensei. I brought it back for you."

But Hiroshi shook his head.

"No, Sam," he said with a smile. "You have my sword now. It has passed to you. You are now its Guardian, Sam. You are now a Guardian of the Osawa Scrolls. Your courage and light are beyond doubt. You are a very worthy Guardian and one who I have been deeply honoured to teach."

Sam could feel the tears beginning to roll down his cheeks.

"Sensei, you are strong," he said. "You will get better. Kensho will help. We are safe now. You will get better."

But Hiroshi shook his head. "No, Sam. It is my time to return to the source. It is where we all came from and it is where we all return. I am ready."

Hiroshi looked up at Kensho and squeezed his hand. "Kensho, my friend. You are ready for this. I know that you are."

Then Hiroshi turned to Daichi. "Thank you Daichi for everything that you have done for me. You have been a great friend to me. Please, do one more thing for your old sensei. Teach Kensho the song you taught me. Kensho will know."

Then he looked at Zoe and Sophie. "You two are the most courageous people I have ever met. More than that, your spirits are beyond compare. Remember that the Light has given you both great gifts. You are of great importance in the defeat of Darkness."

Finally Hiroshi looked around at all of them and smiled. "Remember, my dear friends - trust! All is well. Trust!"

With that, Hiroshi slowly closed his eyes, and his breathing steadily became shallower until he breathed no more.

"Sensei, you loved me as you would have loved your own son," said Kensho, still holding Hiroshi's hand. "You cared for me and guided me to the Light. I loved you as a father. My gratitude to you is eternal, just as our love for one another is eternal."

Then Kensho looked around at the faces of his weeping companions. "Heed these words from the Tao:

My mind is empty,
I am centred in stillness.

All things arise,
but I watch their return to the source.
Like trees that grow tall,
but return to the soil.
To return to the source is serenity.

Not knowing the source,
you will be full of confusion and sorrow.
Knowing the source you are naturally tolerant, impartial,
open-minded and kind-hearted.
Being in accord with nature, you are one with the Tao.
Being one with the Tao is eternity. Though your body dies, the Tao
never ends.

"Nagato Sensei has returned to the source, to serenity. Please do not be sad, for this is the great gift we will all one day receive. To honour Nagato Sensei, let us immerse ourselves in the Tao, just as he did. "

The companions would, in time, understand the truth in the words that Kensho spoke. But for now they were overcome with grief at their loss. Sam got up, went over to kneel between his sisters and held one in each arm, pulling them tightly into his chest. As they cried uncontrollably, rocking backwards and forwards, Sam found himself tapping their backs and saying,

"There, there. There, there."

Though Sam was not aware, it was just as their mother had done when she had comforted them as young children.

"Why are they all taken away from us, Sam? Why?" said Zoe, between sobs.

Sam squeezed her even tighter, his body shaking as he too cried.

"I don't know, Zo. I don't know," he finally replied.

The head priest began chanting a mantra for Hiroshi's spirit, and all the monks of the temple joined him in the chant. The head priest guided Kensho and some of the monks to carry Hiroshi's body inside. Then Kensho returned to the companions.

"Let us gather ourselves together," he said. "We need to eat and to rest. It has been a long and hard journey."

Then Kensho turned to Kenichi. How mysterious are the workings of the Tao, thought Kensho. Just a day before, this young man had been trying to take Kensho's life, and now here he stood side by side with him in the battle against Darkness.

"Last night you asked me for my name," said Kensho. "It is my great honour to now tell you. My name is Kensho Iwata. I am deeply honoured to meet you Kenichi Uchiyama." Kensho then bowed to Kenichi.

"The honour is mine," said Kenichi, and he bowed to Kensho.

Daichi, Sam, Zoe and Sophie also bowed and one by one introduced themselves to Kenichi.

"Thank you for your courage and bravery," said Daichi. "Without you, we would have been lost."

The monks prepared baths for the companions. After they had bathed, they were given a feast of a meal in a large hall.

"Sophie, what was that song that you sang?," asked Daichi. "I have never heard it before, but its power over the yokai was quite incredible and quite unheard of in my experience."

"It was something our mother used to sing to us when we were little," said Sophie. "If we had a nightmare or we woke up at night or if we were unwell, she would come in and sing it to us. She said it was a mantra."

"Our mother was a yoga teacher," said Zoe. "Every day she would sing mantras. She would wake up very early in the morning and practise while we were still asleep. I can remember lying awake, listening to her and feeling so safe. I miss her so very, very much now." Then Zoe started to cry.

Kensho stood up and came over to console her.

"Zoe, your mother is with you," he said. "Just as Hiroshi is with us now. The Tao flows through everything. The Tao is us, and we are the Tao. When we die, the ki that is in us doesn't die; it just returns to where it came from. I know this is hard to understand. Don't try to understand. Just feel. If you feel, you will know that Hiroshi's ki surrounds us just as that of your mother and father does. Each of us always were and always will be. The manifestations change, but the ki stays the same."

After listening closely Zoe nodded and stopped crying.

"I feel my mother and father," said Sophie, "though I feel my father differently. I don't know why. I feel Hiroshi too. I don't understand what you mean by words like manifestations, but I know that you're right, Kensho."

"I knew that you would feel them, Sophie," said Kensho.

"Why are we safe in here?" asked Zoe. "Why don't they just smash through the gate and come and attack us?"

"Because there is too much light and strength in the temple for Darkness to overcome," replied Kensho. "It is not the physical walls that protect us, but the strength of the Light. This is a sacred space into which Darkness cannot enter. Also, I sense that the malevolence is receding somewhat. It has failed to prevent us from reaching here, and it has withdrawn for now, I think."

Then Kensho turned to Kenichi: "And what of your story, Kenichi?"

Kenichi looked down at his soup. "I heard your words, Kensho. I realised I was in error and that I must change. I followed you because I thought that you might teach me. But when I saw what was attacking you, I fled in fear. I ran through the woods, and I was filled with shame. I knew I should have helped you, but I was too frightened. I didn't know where I was going. I just felt drawn through the forest up the mountain. So it was that I came across the tengu attacking Sam and Daichi, and I saw Zoe and Sophie. I have younger sisters. I could not just stand by and watch. I knew if I was to ever regain my honour, then I must find courage. I don't know why I ran up the mountain. It makes no sense. If I had thought, then I would have run down the valley to escape."

"It makes perfect sense, Kenichi," said Kensho. "This is where you were meant to be. You followed the Way though you did not know it. You stepped out of Darkness, and you have joined us in the Light. For that, I am grateful."

"No, it is I who will be eternally grateful to you Kensho," said Kenichi. "You spared my life when you could so easily have taken it. You helped me to find the Way."

"Sam," said Kensho, "you too have acted with great courage and strength. The challenges that you have faced over the past few days, and even weeks, have been exceptional. No disciple has ever been through what you have been through. Never before, have we faced such concerted and large attacks."

"I have done my best, Sensei. I wish that I had done better. It was because I was trapped beneath the tree that Hiroshi died."

"No, Sam!" said Kensho sternly. "That is not true. Hiroshi gave his life in the protection of Light. It was Darkness that took his life. Hiroshi was ready. Remember what he said, 'Trust. All is well. Trust.' Everything unfolded just as it should Sam. If you carry guilt, then it will dim your light, and this is exactly what Darkness wants. Do you understand?"

"Hai, Sensei."

"Are we going to stay here forever, Kensho?" asked Sophie. "Or will we leave this temple? And what about going back home? I don't really want to go back, but I was just wondering."

"I don't know, Sophie. The next steps are not yet clear to me. I trust that in time they will be revealed. For now, we will rest and recover our strength in the safety of this temple. It concerns me that you three have been away from home for as long as you have. It will seem like nearly four days in Vancouver since the fire. But there is nothing that we can do about that for now."

As they had all finished eating, the monks came in and showed them to their quarters. They were the same simple little rooms that they had become familiar with from the previous temples.

Sam and the girls were in one room together. Sam waited until Zoe and Sophie were asleep, and then he took out Hiroshi's Divine sword. He knew that it was now his, but he would never think of it as anyone's but Hiroshi's. He thought about Hiroshi, and all that his master had taught him. As he did so, the blade began to softly glow white. Sam thought, "I know that you are with me still, Sensei."

Then Sam put the sword back in its sheath and laid it beside his bed mat. He lay on his back in the quiet of the temple and wondered what the future held.

As sleep began to take him, Sam heard Hiroshi's words: "Trust. All is well. Trust."

Outside the temple, the forest was still and silent. The darkness was held at bay by the fine silver light of a near full moon. Through the trees, moved a shape blacker than darkness. An observer might have mistaken it for a yokai. But beneath the feet of this black shape, the dry leaf litter crunched and twigs snapped.

The figure approached the gate through which the companions had escaped. It lifted its right hand and brought it up to touch the wood of the gate. The moon's light was lost in the black stone of the ring upon one finger. As the hand moved against the wood, a dark flame began to burn. Then, the figure withdrew its hand and disappeared back into the darkness.

Burnt deep into the wood of the gate was a symbol. It was the Japanese kanji for death.

THE END

What it means to be a martial artist

Author Ambrose Merrell gives some background to the writing of The Sword That Saves and advice if you have been inspired to find out more about the martial arts and the history of the Samurai.

Reverend Kensho Furuya was my friend and my teacher. He dedicated his entire life to teaching the martial arts, was a world expert on samurai swords and was also a Zen priest. He lived in his dojo, a replica of a 16th century samurai's home, in Little Tokyo, Los Angeles. His great teaching was influenced by how he lived his life, a life in service to others.

Our friendship began after I read *Kodo: Ancient Ways*, a collection of essays that he had written for various martial arts magazines over the years. I found the website for his dojo, the Aikido Center of Los Angeles, and we began to communicate by email. Some years later I moved from England to British Columbia, Canada. At last I was close enough to visit him and finally meet in person. But shortly after I arrived in Canada, on March 6th 2007, I awoke to discover that Kensho had passed away.

I was living on Bowen Island, just outside Vancouver. It was a miserable morning, low cloud and drizzling rain, which was forecast to stay all day. Nonetheless I knew that I had to hike to the top of the mountain on the island. I took my jo and began the hike. The forest was dark, damp and silent. But the higher I climbed the brighter it became. By the time I reached the summit there was not a cloud in the sky.

As I stood in the sunshine looking east I saw an eagle gliding towards me from the north. It circled twice, just in front of me, and then flew south. I knew, without a shadow of doubt, that it was

Kensho saying goodbye. I practised with the jo for a while and then hiked back down. By the time I reached the foot of the mountain it was thick cloud and drizzling once more.

If you are interested in learning a martial art, or understanding more about the samurai, then the very first thing I recommend is to obtain a copy of *Kodo: Ancient Ways* by Reverend Kensho Furuya. Sadly, these days, it seems to be out of print, but you can still obtain used copies. There is no finer book for truly understanding what it means to be a martial artist.

I also highly recommend visiting Furuya Sensei's dojo website http://www.aikidocenterla.com where you will find an archive of his newsletters which always offer interesting insights into various aspects of martial arts. Somewhere in one or two of those newsletters are even some emails from me to Furuya Sensei.

In the June 2003 newsletter Furuya Sensei wrote:

A samurai is a warrior of feudal Japan which began in the early 11th century and ended in 1868 with the restoration of Emperor Meiji to the throne and Japan once again became a monarchy.

During this feudal period, Japan was under feudal warlords occupying their territories and who employed warriors to serve them. These warriors were called 'samurai', which comes from the Japanese word, 'samurau' meaning 'to serve.' The noun form of this word is 'samurai' meaning 'one who serves (a feudal lord)' or 'warrior'.

Another indispensable aikido resource is www.aikidojournal. com which is run by Sensei Stanley Pranin, who has been practising aikido for well over 50 years. He has done an enormous amount of research into O'Sensei's life. Since O'Sensei's death aikido has, sadly, fragmented. Pranin Sensei has tirelessly sought to uncover O'Sensei's aikido.

Whatever martial art you study, the two keys to your progress will be the quality of your teacher and your own attitude. A great teacher has no interest in becoming wealthy by teaching their martial art.

He or she has no interest in guarantees of a black belt in x number of months or years. They simply want to teach their martial art to the best of their ability. They will recognise and communicate the martial art's limitations. No martial art is perfect. Most of all they will demand total commitment from you. That is the attitude that you must bring. Total and utter dedication to the martial art and a never ending humility.

O'Sensei said, shortly before his death, "I am still a beginner in aikido".

Finally, if you would like to read the Tao Te Ching then there are many different translations to choose from. A good version to begin with is the translation by Stephen Mitchell. However, it is a very loose translation so it is worth reading other versions to get a good feel of the Tao. But if you really want to feel the Tao, look inside yourself.

The Author

Photo: Kiku Hawkes

Ambrose Merrell grew up exploring the fields and woods around Cambridge, England, before going to boarding school in Canterbury, Kent. After completing a degree in economics he established a web development business in Cambridge in 1995. In 1999 he discovered aikido and began practising at the Cambridge Aikido Club. In 2005 his business failed and in 2006 he emigrated to Vancouver, Canada, with his wife and three children. Nervous breakdowns, depression, the demise of his marriage, separation from his children, all brought him to the black pits of despair. But after many years in the darkness he found a new light. In 2012 he wrote *The Sword That Saves*. Today he lives in Vancouver with his partner and their daughter, and practices aikido at Vancouver Isshinkan Aikido.